The Lives of Women

Christine Dwyer Hickey

THE LIVES OF WOMEN

DALKEY ARCHIVE PRESS

Originally published by Atlantic Books in 2014.

Copyright © 2014 by Christine Dwyer Hickey
First Dalkey Archive edition, 2018.

Library of Congress Cataloging-in-Publication Data
Identifiers: ISBN 978-1-62897-256-6
LC record available at https://catalog.loc.gov/

www.dalkeyarchive.com
Victoria, TX / McLean, IL / Dublin

Dalkey Archive Press publications are, in part, made possible through
the support of the University of Houston-Victoria and its programs in
creative writing, publishing, and translation.

Printed on permanent/durable acid-free paper

1
Winter Present
November

HAD I NOT GONE SEARCHING for the number of some dead roofer called Fenton and found the attic room in need of an airing, I may not have heard a thing. Or had it been summer and the trees in the back yard stuffed with leaves, I'd hardly have noticed. It's years since I've ventured that far into the cul-de-sac anyhow, and since my return I'm rarely even out on the road – well, not without the hard shell of a car around me. And so, unless one of the neighbours managed to nab me at the gate – say on bin day, or just as I was taking the dog back in from his walk – weeks may well have passed before the news finally wound its way to me. By then, who knows – this business with my father could well have been over, and I might even have gone back to New York. By the time my next visit came round – if it ever came around – the house backing on to ours would no longer matter.

The rooms would be scrubbed clean of all the old stains, the dust and damp of the vacant years cleared away. While this new family – the now owners – would have had time to peel off the skins of paper and carpet and paint, and to smear all the rooms with its own ethological scent. And I wouldn't have to keep thinking about something that happened more than thirty years ago, and the old ghosts would not now be whimpering at the far side of my back wall.

As it stands, I did open the attic window into the gaudy light of a winter sun, and the view over the bare trees and across the back lawns could not have been clearer. And so that's how I know, and can't pretend not to know, that the Shillman house has been sold; that the Shillman house can finally be called something else.

The patio doors have been pinned back, the side entrance gate removed. The upstairs windows, stripped bare of curtains, are wide-open gills sucking on air. From the interior some sort of a machine is screeching. And men in overalls are coming and going, turning the house inside out, streeling its guts all over the lawn.

All day I've been returning to the window – even the dog is beginning to wonder, shadowing me upstairs to the landing then cowering at the bottom of the spiral stairwell that leads to the attic room. 'What are you doing up there?' his whine seems to say. 'What the hell are you *doing*?'

I'm drinking my mid-morning coffee while two men do a Laurel and Hardy routine down the patio steps, the Shillmans' grey leather sofa like a dead hippo between them.

I'm back with my lunchtime sandwich, watching a young hay-haired man, stretched out on the same sofa, spouting cigarette smoke overhead like he's some sort of fountain.

I'm licking the yoghurt off the back of my spoon as, one by one, a whole family of mattresses is flung against the back garage wall and the bones of old beds, cots and bunk frames are stacked up alongside them.

More than once I return to the young man on the sofa and wonder when young men started looking this good.

By twilight I'm polishing the dust off my father's old binoculars.

I see it all now: the four-sided bookcase they had shipped from India; the pony-skin rug that used to hang on the dining-room wall. The contents of the Shillman kitchen, the contents of the Shillman living-room, always referred to as a lounge.

I am struck by the amount of belongings: boxes and boxes of belongings, many of which have already been emptied, contents arranged into heaps on the lawn. Books, toys, coats, boots, riding helmets. Shoes. Tennis rackets. Skateboards. Schoolbags. It's as if the Shillmans closed the door behind them with little more than the clothes on their backs.

Hay-head slips into view then, soft mouth and strong hands filling the lens. I watch as he hoists Mr Shillman's golf bag onto his shoulder, then picks his way round the boxes and piles to the end of the boundary wall. He lifts the bag and lowers it into the gap between the Shillman house and the Caudwells'. (Jesus – that gap! I'd forgotten all about it). And I watch, again, the innocent, easy-hipped saunter of him as he makes his way back up the garden path and disappears via the side entrance around to the front of the house.

By now the bare windows on the Shillmans' house are stark yellow squares on an inky dusk. Other houses around show a flimsier light through curtains and blinds. Everything braced against darkness: pegs clenched on clothes lines, garbage bins backed to the wall, witchy long fingers clawing out from emaciated trees. The rusty old swing in Jacksons' garden is sturdy as a hangman's gallows. In the Caudwells', a rolled up patio umbrella has turned into a tall, thin hooded monk.

It occurs to me, then, that I may not be the only one looking down from a window, that the Shillman house is visible from at least four other houses – or at least it used to be when I was the local babysitter. The thoughts of sharing this moment with one of the old neighbours: Anne Jackson or Bill Tansey or – God forbid – Miriam Caudwell.

I move from the window, lay the binoculars down, my wrists aching from the old-fashioned weight of them.

I know I should leave well enough alone now: go back downstairs, do what I am supposed to do, which is to feed and medicate both father and dog. From the landing, a long drop of leftover rain flops tiredly into the bucket, reminding me that the reason I came up here in the first place was to find the number of a roofer my father is convinced is still alive – a man I recall as already quite old when I was a child. All afternoon he's been patiently waiting, hand by the phone, to make his first call in weeks. I could, at least, make an effort.

I stand rubbing my wrists for another while then step back up to the window. Not a sound nor a movement indoors or out. There is only the stir of old turf club badges when I lift the binoculars back up to my face.

Whatever I see now reminds me of something: an occasion, a moment, a feeling. Rachel's old-fashioned boarding school trunk. Michael's orange Colnago racer. Danny's yellow tricycle. There's the hats Mr Shillman brought back from Texas. The Russian candelabra he told Agatha that story about and made her cry.

There's the black rag-rug that their 'girl from the country' made, and the glass cocktail cabinet with the crack up the middle. Mrs Shillman's desk where she wrote her letters; and the painting Serena gave to her, and later regretted, one afternoon of heavy drinking.

I see the green roll of an army sleeping bag and my heart begins to tighten. I see Karl's haversack and my blood turns cold.

*

Next day I take the dog walking on what was once Arlows' land – the last place I should be, considering the night I've just put in: scattergun dreams and rooms filled with lost faces. A dozen jittery trips to the bathroom in between. I was late up and late bringing breakfast to my father. He didn't complain – he never would; at times I think he'd as soon have me starve him to death.

Over the years Arlows' place has been sold off in parcels and patches, 'so houses like yours could crawl like reptiles all over my land', as Maggie Arlow, rosy with gin, once said to me.

On a few acres of land the Arlows had probably forgotten they even owned, Mr Jackson built our little estate more than fifty years ago, holding one house back for himself – two rows of good-sized no-nonsense family homes with a cul-de-sac looping off the middle – and for a long time it was the only housing estate around here.

All that is left of the Arlows now, their house and its grounds, orchard and stableyard, is the rear view they once enjoyed over the valley and the random stone wall to the front. The wrought-iron gates have been removed but the pillars remain and now serve as an entrance to the final housing estate to be built around here, maybe fifteen years ago, or at some stage, anyhow, during my long absence. And if Maggie thought our reptiles were bad, I don't know what she'd make of these dormer bungalows with their Tudor notions, plonked all over what was once her driveway and front lawns.

The valley itself, now a council-owned park, is still good and rough round the edges. Pathways and cycle tracks are etched into the slopes. Where the paddocks once were, there are mown grass patches. A proper car park sits near the entrance along with a map indicating where the wildlife can be found. At the squat stone bridge where the river splits, the ruins of Hoxtons' house still stand, not looking any worse for wear than it did when I was a child. Over a ditch in a nearby field, there is a tree railed in by four brass bed-ends: here lies the shrine to the dead tinker-man.

Fat Carmel has her own take on the wildlife down here and frequently sings it for me in that sugary Welsh accent of hers whenever I drop by her shop to pick up my father's newspaper. Campfires are her speciality – Rizla papers and scraps of tin foil mean the fire has been made by junkies. Broken glass and burnt beer cans indicate the ordinary everyday drunks. She tells me all this as if I couldn't have figured it out for myself.

To listen to her, you'd think she was down here every night of the week with her torch, instead of sitting alone in her flat above the shop, munching unsold cakes and sausage rolls for dinner.

It could be a blow-in's interest, of course – she has, after all, only lived here for ten years – or it could be a simple need to belong, but Carmel seems to have this need to be at the centre of things, even from a distance, and even in retrospect: the who-lives-where-for-how-long-and-who-with of it all. She will find out about the Shillman house and much more besides – of that, I am certain.

When I was a kid, I practically lived in Arlows' valley. But since my return at the end of August, it's been an occasional spur-of-the-moment visit. Not because of the obvious dangers – junkies and drinkers at their little campfires don't bother me in the least. People do walk their dogs – you might even see the occasional morning jogger. But the unspoken rule of the neighbourhood is: come mid-afternoon, leave the park to those who belong in the shadows.

Even my father – a man of few words that grow fewer each day – has been moved to open his cake-hole on the subject.

'Don't go down there, it's dangerous,' was about the extent of this once-off warning. I didn't like to ask if he meant dangerous in general, or dangerous for me.

For me the only danger down here is memory.

I remember the way blackberry picking left the tips of my fingers flayed, and sitting in the grass trying to work out which was the blackberry's blood, which was my own. I remember pinkeen fishing, the twist and turn of the net in water that was green and luscious with river dirt. And the shock of that cold-rotating slap after slap on my face when rolling down a hill packed with snow. And later, of course, much, much later, the spot where we used to stash the flagons of cider in the afternoon before returning that evening to drink them.

I remember the drunken paddling in the river. The boys daring each other to climb up and dive off the rusty old cattle bridge, and the bruise under Karl Donegan's ribs that was shaped like a map of Australia. I remember the smell of horse shit on the air when I lay in the long grass beside him. Patty's American voice in the dark. The tight glow of a cigarette tip; the loose red bud of a joint and the slight crackle as it took light and began to burn. The trees growing dense with menace at nightfall. And most of all, I remember the night before they sent me away, hunkering behind the wall of Hoxtons' bridge, as I looked up at dozens of flashlights wobbling all over the bowl of the valley, and thinking, I'm drowning now, I'm at the bottom of the ocean; in a moment I'll be dead, and here is the last thing that I'll ever see: this shoal of electric jellyfish floating over my head.

I come down here to cure or maybe kill something, in a hair of a dog sort of a way, but all I ever do is remember. Days of brooding then follow. Brooding on the past, on the horror of being young: on all the stupidity and ignorance and misplaced loyalty that goes with the territory. Then I start with the thinking. I think about what it was like to be living here at that time. I think about Karl and Paul, about Patty and Serena. About Jonathan. I think about all the others. About my mother and the other mothers. About my father and the other fathers and non-fathers alike. About the unimportance of children and the importance of men. I think about the lives of women.

And so that's why I tend to avoid it, not because my father thinks it's dangerous or because Carmel's junkies are going to skin me up and smoke me. I avoid it because I never come away from here feeling any less than sick in heart, stomach and of course mind. And yet, every once in a while, this is exactly where I find myself.

I whistle for the dog, whistle again, then turn on the pathway leading down to the stone bridge. I pass last night's campfires and a few medallions of melted green plastic from the bins the kids have stolen and burned out to get stoned on the fumes. I see the rags of small plastic bags caught on the hedgerows, bearing supermarket logos of what Carmel calls 'those German *baaaastard* dives, intent on killing our youth with their mind-twisting, liver-corroding, cheap liquor'.

And I see, lying naked on the grass, two large bars of chocolate bought solely for their heroin-friendly foil which, unless I am very much mistaken, have come from her 'bargain basket' of out-of-date, or very nearly out-of-date, sweets.

I look back up to see the dog appear on the crest of the hill, blond and black and frisky-looking, and then kick the chocolate away in case he is tempted.

I whistle again. And he comes in a canter down the hill, for that moment or two joyful and so much younger than his years.

He arrives to heel, an old dog again, half-blind and utterly exhausted, then he folds himself down on the ground and looks at me sideways, as if ashamed of his own frailty. I find myself wondering which I will be left with in the end, the dog or my father, and then try not to think which one I'd prefer.

When the dog has recovered, we continue downwards, taking our time, him cocking his leg every few seconds along the way, me trying to keep my thoughts vague and away from the reach of the past. On a ditch, a pair of knickers, slight and tangerine coloured, lie like a delicate and wounded bloom. And on the far side of the trees, I can hear the river breathing. A few seconds later there is a sound of rowers returning upriver, back towards the city: the coxman's call, long and short, long and short. Nearer and louder. Come on boys – let's push. Now let's *puuuushhhh*.

I imagine the determined young profiles grimacing with each jagged movement and the muscles of their arms puffing up to the task. Bare legs splayed with first hair, folding and unfolding from the knee. Skin damp with winter sweat. I feel a vague pity then that I don't quite understand: maybe for the girl who wore

the tangerine underwear and whatever disappointment she may
have felt after the event. Or maybe for the middle-aged woman
who is standing here in my shoes.

A long blade of sound swishes by. I close my eyes to look at
it. And there is the boat, honed and completely mastered, as it
cuts up river, like a tailor's scissors cuts through a bolt of new
cloth

We come to the ditch at the tinker's shrine and I decide to cross
over and take a proper look at it. Clipping the lead onto the
collar, heaving the poor dog over and up, we both stand there
and stare in, one of us panting slightly more than the other.

It is obviously an ongoing work of art, this shrine: some
trinkets are weather-beaten, others appear to be recent additions.
Blue is the colour – all shades of blue. From a high, thick
branch, a huge set of wooden rosary beads hangs, and from
lesser branches, other more delicate sets dangle like Christmas
tree decorations. Along with pieces of threaded glass and wind-
chimes, they tinkle and whisper. Blue and white ribbons are
spiralled round the bedposts. Inside the rails, in the centre of
the plot, there is a small statue of a piebald pony and, behind
it, a framed photograph of the dead man. He has a look about
him of Burt Reynolds in his heyday. I'm guessing he either died
here or was injured here and later died. I guess, too, that this
shrine is dedicated to his spirit and that his body lies in another
place – a plot in a formal cemetery or in an urn on a shelf in
a tinker's caravan. The small carved cross stuck into the earth
gives the year but, for some reason, not the month of his death.
Long after I left anyhow. Long before I came back.

Whoever he was, and however he died, great lengths have
been taken to ensure that he is never lonely. Plastic see-through
Holy Marys filled to the chin with holy water are posted around
the tree. Little toy angels guard his picture. In a blue heart-
shaped frame, a small girl, a daughter – or by now, more likely,

a granddaughter – is frilled to the brim in a white first holy communion dress. A glass jar, etched into the clay, is stuffed with what appear to be small folded notes which I take to be messages for Burt. In another jam jar, a single tight-headed rose reminds me: November has arrived, month of the dead.

I am moved by the love that's expressed at this shrine and continues to be expressed, fourteen years after the tinker has died. And I am moved, too, by the lack of shame in his death. Even a death that may well have been by murder, or as a result of some sort of violence anyhow, deserves to be both cherished and mourned.

Apart from two weddings in upstate New York, I haven't stepped inside a church since I left here and, if I can help it, never will. Nor can I say I believe in, or even approve of, prayer. But I say a prayer here for Karl. I say a prayer for Rachel. I even say one for Paul and Jonathan. And Agatha, of course – I say a special prayer for her.

*

In my half-sleep, I sometimes see myself walking. A long, narrow path that veers into the distance. The ground is uneven, gnarled by the reaches of old tree roots and ancient worn-down stones. On one side of me, a high grey wall shawled with ivy. On the other, a stand of oak trees.

I stop and turn to look back along the considerable way I've already come. There's a figure in the distance that has also stopped to turn and look at me. She is young, but not a child.

Or again, just as I'm about to doze off – on a crowded city street at rush hour: hundreds of faces coming towards me, each, in its own way, distinctive. Yet only one stands out. There is something about her, a certain expression – what it is, I couldn't say.

I have this overwhelming need to understand her anyhow; to know who she is or why she is here. To know her story. To forgive it, even, if that's what it should come to.

But how do you tell the story of yourself as you were more than thirty years ago? How do you know what you were like then? The workings of your troubled mind and heart – how do you begin to resolve all that?

I have looked at a photograph – the only photograph I could find in all the rooms of my parents' house. She has the same eyes as mine. The same blood and bones. Her name is my name. I know she's supposed to be me. But no matter how many times I pick up the photograph and no matter how long I stare into that bleak, adolescent face – all I can see is a stranger.

2
Summer Past
May

HER NAME IS ELAINE. She writes it on top of a page in one of the journals she keeps under her bed. *My name is Elaine Nichols.*

It physically hurts her to write these few words, but seeing them crawl out from under her twisted fingers brings its own pleasure too.

The doctor said writing will help her hands come back to full use, and so her father brought up to the hospital a block of unused legal journals, parcelled in smooth brown paper.

Each morning, as soon as she wakes, she reaches for the rubber ball on her bedside locker. Her hands will have clawed overnight and be stubborn as steel; the ball will help coax them to life.

The first words of the day are always the toughest. As the day moves on and her hands start to loosen, the words will become easier to release, less measured. No matter which journal she happens to be on, no matter how many pages she uses in one day, she always starts with the same thing. *My name is Elaine Nichols.*

Whatever else she may forget in her life, she knows it won't be that name.

She has been sick for months. At the end of January she went down with a virus and now it is almost summer. One Saturday morning she'd felt a bit off. By afternoon, she'd had to cancel a babysitting job for the Jacksons – something she hated to do, knowing full well that Junie Caudwell would be in like a light, making the Jackson twins love her more with her bag of sweeties, her big blonde curls and crolly-dolly eyes. For a while she had tortured herself with images of Junie up in the bathroom sniffing Mr Jackson's aftershave, or twirling around in his big leather chair, or even kissing the photograph of him on the mantelpiece with his tanned face and rolled up shirtsleeves, taken in some far away place like Saudia Arabia.

By Sunday morning she'd forgotten all about the Jacksons and June Caudwell. By Sunday morning she'd hardly known her own name. She'd woken to find a three-headed version of her mother at the end of the bed, asking if she fancied scrambled eggs for breakfast.

It seemed only a few seconds later when she'd opened her eyes to a different light. Thick grey dust at the window, a globe of red from the silk lightshade above, and her mother, back to the one-headed version, standing by the bed holding a plate, in a voice, slightly hurt, asking why – *why* had she eaten nothing all day?

'Even the eggs, you haven't touched. And just how? *How* do you expect to get well if you won't even make the smallest of efforts?'

And then her mother, scooping cold eggs onto cold toast, had begun eating them herself.

At some stage an ambulance was called. Later she would remember being wheeled out to it; night sky above and the voices of strangers.

She would remember, too, Doctor Townsend coming from across the road and climbing into the ambulance ahead of her, a hem of pyjama leg showing under the end of his trousers along with a hard knob of ankle. After that she had gone down a hole and disappeared into a delirium.

She was gone for a long time. She crossed a desert and was almost drowned in a crimson sandstorm. It filled her eyes, nose and throat.

A man pulled her out of the storm. He wore a large scarlet turban and had a big silver moustache. When he spoke, it was through a hole in his neck. When he smiled, there was an arc of gold-speckled teeth instead of an Adam's apple.

There were goats on the journey. Sometimes in a herd, but mostly alone. She hated the goats. The way they shot out of nowhere, nudged her nightdress back with a cold, damp snout, gave a few bleats, before biting down on her buttock and disappearing again.

She liked the man, though, and his safe brown arms with their mane of fine silver hair.

The man whispered words into her ear – right down into it. The words were small, warm shapes made of air. She could feel them entering her head, winding their way round and nesting in her brain. She knew they would always live there, that they would grow strong and never leave. They would become part of her. She also knew she would never quite hear them, never mind understand their meaning.

When she came through to the other side, there wasn't much flesh left under her skin, her hands were crippled and her legs were two hockey sticks that showed no interest in walking. She was in quarantine, in a small square room with a glass wall on either side. There had been a baby in the room to her right. Beyond it, similar rooms that seemed to go on forever: layers of glass and the movement of nurses. Hers was the second-last room on the row. On her left, in the last room, was a man in paisley-print pyjamas.

Three months later the doctor said she was in recovery.

She had wanted to ask what that meant exactly, but the doctor's back was turned to her, and he hadn't been speaking to her anyway, he'd been speaking to her mother. Over his shoulder she could see her mother nodding away, touching her hair and looking up at him sideways as if she'd been expecting him to ask her to dance.

In his opinion the girl was greatly improved but by no
means completely recovered. Nonetheless he would consider
discharging her, depending on the results of a few last minute
tests.

'Well, of course, Doctor,' her mother was saying. 'If you
think that best, of *course* . . .'

For a young girl to be stuck so long on her own . . . The
loneliness – you see? It gets to them. 'She is what now?' he asked
then, reaching for the chart at the end of the bed.

'Seventeen in December,' her mother said.

He lifted the chart and squinted into it. 'Sixteen,' he
corrected, 'and a young sixteen at that – would I be right?'

'Well, yes, Doctor, indeed. Like myself, she's an only child
and, well, we are inclined to be a bit reserved.'

The previous few months had been the loneliest of her life. Days
had gone by without a single visitor and only the baby seemed
to make sense to her – the two of them lying on their sides and
gazing at each other through the glass wall. Different sized nurses had passed through her illness, night into day and back again,
but there'd been no conversation beyond a few generalities that
only seemed to concern the weather or her bowels. There had
been little or no interest shown in her at all, except by the man
in the paisley pyjamas who had made her skin crawl, the way he
sometimes stared in at her.

For all that she had grown used to the hospital. She liked
being on her own. She liked, too, not having to put up with
her mother's habit of asking endless questions about everything
and anything that happened to wander into her head. Or being
nagged into constantly eating just to keep her company. She
liked the small portions they served here. The little silver bowl
of jelly and ice-cream for dessert every day, and the way she was
given her own little pot of tea. She liked that she didn't have
to share. She had her radio and her two pillars of books – one

short, the other tall – and knew she could rely on Mrs Hanley to keep them coming.

Her mother, for all her suffocating ways, had only come to see her twice a week: once when her father drove her after church on Sunday, and for an hour or so every Wednesday afternoon when she came by herself. For the week-day visit she took a taxi and it had been clear from her jigging about that she couldn't wait to get back to her housework. On Sundays, she put in more of an effort, bringing a bag of homemade buns along with a compendium of games. Elaine always looked forward to these visits, but no sooner had they started when she wished they were over. Her father in the corner of the little room, plucking cake flesh out of the buns and reading the Sunday newspapers. Elaine and her mother by the bed, half-heartedly rattling dice in a plastic cup and pushing coloured buttons up ladders and down snakes.

The doctor brought the good news in person. Her tests had come back. She was to be discharged this very afternoon.

She'd been reading one of Mrs Hanley's novels at the time and her heart had been thumping on some faraway beach in the South of France.

His sudden appearance gave her a fright. For some reason, she felt ashamed of the book, turning it over and covering it with her hand. She'd had trouble understanding him or even why he should be addressing her in the first place. She kept looking around, expecting her mother to be standing there behind her in the doorway.

The doctor sat side-saddle on the end of the bed and called her 'young lady'. He tapped his thigh as he spoke. There would be certain conditions, of course: a weekly check-up in the outpatient department. Bed rest and quarantine for a further two weeks. After that, afternoon naps and early to bed to allow her immune system to build itself up. 'In short, young lady, you will be a hot-house plant, but at least you'll be a hot-house plant in the loving comfort of your own home where your own people can take good care of you.'

Then he wished her good luck and sauntered off down the corridor, leaving her bereft.

She had thought about getting up and shouting down the corridor after him. She thought of all the things she might say: 'But I don't feel better, Doctor. I don't feel ready.'

Or, 'Please, can't I just stay for another week, a few days even? Oh, *please?*'

Or, 'I'm not going! Do you hear me? I'm just NOT!'

But she stayed as she was, clutching her book in her old lady's hands and staring down at a photo of F. Scott Fitzgerald, who stared blandly back with his girlish eyes and thin sardonic smile.

It had been strange to find herself standing in clothes again. It had been strange to be standing at all. Her yellow jumper poured off her like thick custard, her jeans barely stayed up on her hips. Even her shoes seemed too big. Next door, a nurse had lifted the baby, making his little hand wave at her through the glass. And she felt this warm, sharp gush come into her chest as if she might be going to cry, although she couldn't see why – because how could she love him when she'd never even touched him and probably wouldn't recognise him again, should their paths ever cross in the outside world?

Her mother piled books into a cardboard box and praised Mrs Hanley's good taste. She said she hoped there'd been no spillages – jam or tea stains or such like – because the books, of course, would have to be returned.

'But Mrs Hanley said . . .'

'Oh now, I'm sure she didn't mean–'

'No, no, she said, she said . . .'

'Now really, we can't expect. At least not forever.'

'They're mine! I'm telling you, she said they were *mine*.'

'All right, all right. Calm down. Surely you're not going to start crying over a few old books! Tell you what, I'll pop over, offer them back and see what she says.'

As her mother began rolling clothes into the hold-all, Elaine felt a chill in her stomach. She remembered, then, the way her mother would sometimes come back from the shops pinkened by the news of some medical woe: this man's cancer, that woman's pleurisy, the butcher who had a daughter who had a friend who had a neighbour who had a baby who'd just died.

Now, bustling around the hospital bed, the little grin on her face said it all – there would be weeks of playing nursies ahead. Her daughter would become her project. Her something to talk about. Her something to *do*.

She'd felt so old then; old and cornered, the way she imagined old people must feel when they find themselves trapped by the mercy of others. A few months ago she'd been a chubby adolescent, and now here she was, a skin-and-bone adult, watching her mother stuff toiletries into a washbag, squeezing and plumping the sides with the palms of her hands, drawing the edges of the zip together: tug, tug, tugging until it finally closed over and everything had been forced to stay jammed inside.

*

There would be changes. New chair in her bedroom; new set of towels waiting on the bedside table; new rug on the floor. The garden puffed up with early summer. The shed painted a thin shade of green. In the garage, a chest freezer that growled like a peevish beast.

The two biggest changes concerned her mother.

For one she'd started to smoke again. In her youth she'd been an occasional smoker but had always assured Elaine this had only been to give herself something to do while waiting by the wallflower wall at tennis club dances. And it helped show off her hands, which she considered to be her best feature. It had been an excellent means, too, of striking up a conversation – a man might offer a cigarette, one would accept and then naturally a conversation would follow. Elaine had always imagined these conversations taking place against black-and-white settings and conducted in fruity uppercrust accents – 'Care for a cigarette?' 'How kind, don't mind if I do.' 'I say, what perfectly lovely hands you have!'

Now it seems her mother was back on the cigarettes, only this time she meant it.

While they were waiting for the nurse to complete the paper-work, her mother broke the news about her new smoking life. It had started as a way to calm her nerves while Elaine had been at the height of her illness. When she was taken off the critical list and declared out of danger, she had decided to stick with it be-cause Martha Shillman told her it was a great way of keeping the weight down. Instead of the afternoon bun, she'd been reaching for the packet of fags. Two cigarettes in and all thought of the bun would go flying out the window. Already she could feel her skirts beginning to loosen their grip. Martha Shillman had been right all along. Martha Shillman was no fool in such matters.

Martha Shillman's name, Elaine had already begun to notice, was cropping up quite a bit in recent conversations.

She'd been expecting to see her father's car on the hospital fore-court. At the same time, she hadn't been all that surprised to find, instead, Martha Shillman in her husband's car, grinning out over the steering wheel. Even so, Elaine had decided she should probably ask.

'Your father? Oh – who knows? Off racing, I suppose. Anyway, thank goodness for Martha Shillman, says you.'

On the way home they went in for a drink. Really it was just to

have a fag in comfort, Martha explained. 'Shillman goes mad if
you smoke in the car. I wouldn't mind, but he thinks nothing
of stinking us out of house and home with those bloody awful
cigars of his.'

She had forgotten that Mrs Shillman called her husband
by his surname. She had forgotten too about the amount of
make-up she wore and the fug of her perfume. Her mother, she
noticed, was wearing more make-up than usual and had also
doused herself in perfume, and it not even Sunday.

Elaine opened the back window of the car and half-listened
to the conversation up front. Mrs Shillman was explaining
something to her mother about China, using a story heard in
diplomatic circles to illustrate the point. Mrs Shillman, Elaine
knew, was an intelligent woman. She spoke fluent French. She
knew about politics. She had once taken a correspondence
course in psychology and often wrote letters to the letter
page in newspapers; some of them had even been published.
Even the men listened to her in mixed conversation. While
she spoke about China, her mother made muttery, agreeable
sounds. Elaine felt a pang under her ribs. Her mother wasn't an
intelligent woman – in fact she could be quite stupid. That was
something else she had almost forgotten.

The pub – a dirty dive: damp, clumpy sawdust over a black-speck-
led floor. An ungentlemanly stink from the gentlemen's toilets.
A man on his own, throwing rings at a board. Further away,
another lone man, using both hands to forklift his glass from
the table to his face.

The barman told them it was too early to open the lounge: if
they wanted a drink, they'd just have to put up with it – counter
service only. Oh, but Mrs Shillman *much* preferred these old
fashioned bars, so full of charm and character – wouldn't he
agree?

He looked at her with a blank, pasty face and waited for

her order. Elaine followed her mother to a table. Mrs Shillman began seeing to the drinks. A large gin and tonic for herself, a large vodka and lime for her friend and 'What about you, Elaine dear, what would you like?'

Elaine would like nothing. Elaine would like to go home, get into bed, put her head under the covers. But she didn't want to spoil things and so ordered a Coke. But no, her mother said, a Coke was out of the question; a soda water was the only thing for an invalid's delicate stomach. Then she lit up a cigarette and sent a good thick whack of it across the table.

Elaine turned her face to the window. In the hospital she had forgotten about seasons; now she saw it was summer outside. People passing by, coatless and sleeveless. Girls in sunglasses. Children in shorts and sandals. Inside, the barman swiped a tea towel over his sweaty face. A man in shirtsleeves pushed through the door and shouted for a chilled pint of lager. Her mother fanned her throat with a beer mat; Mrs Shillman drew the side of her glass along her forehead. Elaine pulled her big winter coat about her and blew into the cold cup of her hands.

She followed the minutes on the clock behind the bar until ten of them had edged by. Mrs Shillman wondered, then, if they wouldn't be better off having one for the road to allow the traffic a chance to clear? The traffic at this hour can be simply horr-*endous*, she said. Her mother considered this for about a half a second before heartily agreeing, her face dropping then at the realisation that, this time, she would be the one to go up to the counter.

Her mother was unused to pubs, to walking across bar-room floors and standing at a bar counter, waiting on a strange, sweaty man to notice her there, before ordering a round of drinks in broad daylight. There would be the worry of fumbling through her money – her housekeeping money at that. The worry of how to get the drinks safely back to the table. And the worry too that somehow she was being watched – by her husband, the neighbours, Mr Hanley even, who had once told her she was his idea of 'the perfect lady'.

For a moment Elaine considered offering to go up to the bar on her behalf. But she felt exhausted suddenly and more than a little bewildered. The room was too big and too brown. There were too many red stools bleeding into her vision. And everywhere she looked she saw dirt: cigarette stubs on the floor, beer splashes on the wall, a bluebottle sniffing a crusted blob of mustard on the floor. And as for the noise! The rubber rings banging off the ring board. The woman on the television screaming out the news. Martha Shillman yelling a story about her husband called Shillman and a funny incident that had occurred on a golf course in a city she'd never even heard of.

From the corner of her eye, she kept a nervous watch while her mother's shape moved gingerly across the floor, the trembling tray of drinks in her hands. She was back then, lowering the tray, shaken but safe and far from defeated.

Elaine pulled her eyes away from the room, up, up towards the yellowing ceiling. Four round vent holes cut into the uppermost corner of the wall; four long fingers of sunlight poking through, lifting and trickling through the afternoon dust. She stared into it until the room had dessicated into a soft glittery spin

Far below, the sound of the two women sucking and blowing; their conversation compact and happy, like two little girls, she thought, who had learned how to smoke. Neighbours' names strayed out from their chat – familiar names in unfamiliar circumstances.

And here she realised the second big change: for the first time in her married life, or at least for as far back as Elaine could recall, her mother had started to make friends.

*

She smells the cigarettes on the breath of the house the minute she walks through the door, and finds in every room long forgotten ashtrays. A cut-glass square in the hall, a marble slab on the kitchen windowsill and, in the sitting-room, a chrome bowl perched on one leg. By her mother's bed there is a souvenir from Paris and on the bathroom ledge another from London: mementoes from two 'glorious' holidays in the years before she married, when glorious holidays would become a thing of the past. The Parisian ashtray had a picture on the base of a slinky black cat smoking from a holder; Elaine can vaguely recall eating jelly babies out of it when she was very small.

She walks through the house, remembering the rooms. Her mother is never far behind with offers of tea, toast and ice-cream. In between, she chatters about all her new friends.

They had stopped her out on the road. They had sidled up to her when she'd been paying the grocery bill in McKenna's. They had paused at the garden wall while she was clipping the hedge. The more confident ones had marched straight up the driveway and rang the doorbell, often bringing a little gift in their hand – Mrs Hanley with her books, Mrs Tansey with her talc and bath-cube set and Mrs Townsend, who, as the doctor's wife, presumably carried enough authority as it was, came with one arm as long as the other.

Other women soon followed – most of whom her mother had hardly even spoken to beyond a nod and a smile delivered at a distance, a compliment on a freshly painted door maybe. At most, a goochy-goo into the pram of a new arrival.

There had been get-well cards and a holy medal; a set of hankies from Mrs Owens; a bottle of cologne from the woman with the funny teeth who lived next to the Prestons. Chats that had started at garden gates soon progressed into hallways and ended at kitchen tables. Tea cups and cake crumbs had barely been cleared away, ashtrays barely emptied, dinners just about shoved into the oven in time for a husband's return from work.

At first her mother had been a little wary of all this attention. As Elaine well knew, she had always been torn between the desire to make friends and a fear of strangers knowing too much of her business. But really it had been out of her hands – in fact there'd been no need to make any effort at all on her part: there had been none of the usual anxiety about trying too hard, or indeed not trying hard enough. Everyone had been simply marvellous – except for Mrs Ryan next door, who had consistently let herself down by sticking her head over the back garden wall like a labourer's wife each and every time her mother happened to go out to hang a few clothes on the washing line.

Martha Shillman, on the other hand, never let herself down. Martha Shillman had outdone the lot from the start, calling in one evening when Elaine's father was at an evening race meeting, with a bottle of wine in each hand. Coincidentally, it was the same night that Elaine's fever had reached its crisis point.

How her mother would have survived that awful night – those touch-and-go hours, when she could have no idea if her only child would live or die and, if she did live, if she'd be a vegetable for the rest of her days – she would never know, were it not for Martha Shillman keeping her company as she'd sat, worried out of her mind, by the telephone.

It's her first evening home. Elaine lies on the sofa. Her mother blows grey chiffons of smoke into the sitting-room and, giddy with hunger, vodka and too many fags, tells her all this.

She is on her way up to bed when her father's car pulls into the driveway, smearing the walls and floor of the hall with its grainy white light. Her mother is in the kitchen organising Elaine's pills and filling water into a hospital-style carafe, bought specially for the occasion.

The front door swings opens and there he is suddenly, a dark figure in a dark doorway.

'Oh!' he says when he sees her.

He stares at her for a second, turns to close the door and comes back. 'They discharged you, then. And when . . .?'

'This afternoon.'

'I see and how did . . .?'

'Mrs Shillman.'

'Ahh. And how are you feeling . . .? Shouldn't you . . .?'

'I'm just going up now.'

She looks for his binoculars, his donkey-brown derby hat, the coat he usually wears to the races. But he carries only the tools of his trade: a stack of ribboned papers under his arm, wig dangling from the tip of his fingers, barrister's cloth bag in the other hand. In fact, he looks as he always does when he arrives home after working on a late consultation or after spending the day in a court-house on the country circuit.

He takes a step forward. For a moment she thinks he might be going to embrace her. But then her mother comes bustling out of the kitchen and, placing one hand on Elaine's back, turns her towards the stairs. Her father steps back.

In the bedroom, her mother unpacks the bag she earlier packed, and tells her more of the neighbourhood gossip. A father and son have just moved into the house with no number on its door. The son long and streaky, the father's face a sullen sight whenever it drives by. No sign of a mother.

The Osborne house has been let at last, new people expected any day. That awful Gerry Caudwell got drunk and vomited into the Slaters' hedge and his father just been given another promotion in the police force – pity he couldn't police his own children while he was at it. June Caudwell just dropped out of her secretarial course and gone off to work as an au pair – in Brussels of all places! You wouldn't mind so much if it was Paris. Oh and Agatha's mother has bagged a part in a London play – there was a very good piece in the paper about her. The photo didn't do her any favours, though – made her look blurred instead of beautiful.

Elaine takes a pill from her mother's fingers and pushes it between her lips, then she sucks down on the side of the plastic tumbler her mother's hand is holding to her mouth. She gets under the covers. Her eyeballs feel swollen; her lids thick and dry as blotting paper.

Her mother potters about the room, putting things out on the dressing table and chipping at drawers, closing and opening the wardrobe door.

There is a question Elaine would like to ask her. She tries to arrange the question in her mind, to get the words to line up and come out of her mouth, one by one and making sense.

Her mother says, 'What dear? You're mumbling now. I can't understand what you're saying. I didn't tell what–? I didn't tell *who*?'

Elaine closes her eyes and sees her father's tired face suspended in the doorway of the hall. She sees him as one of those Roman masks the Hanleys have attached to their back wall. A mask cast in grey plaster – the shape of an 'oh' on its lips. Her mother comes over to the bed and tucks her in. The covers feel too tight around her, the bed too close to the wall.

*

The doorbell rings at intervals and all afternoon women pass through the house: footsteps from the hall to the kitchen, foot- steps on the stairs. A face looms round her bedroom door, says a few words – always the same kind of words – then slips out of sight again. Footsteps tipping back down the stairs before disappearing into the warm scent of buns and the ticking of teacups. From the kitchen, her mother's over-excited voice flutes through the ceiling.

At some point the telephone rings. She is falling asleep when this happens, her thoughts beginning to warp. She doesn't hear her mother answer the phone or know how long has passed before her voice is calling up the stairs saying something about Mrs Hanley. Elaine shakes herself awake. Is Mrs Hanley on her way up the stairs? Is that what her mother has just said?

Mrs Hanley is not beautiful like her actress sister and not pretty like her niece Agatha. She is too wide at the forehead and her mouth is too small. Her eyes are dark and stare hard at you when she talks to you and even harder when you speak back. She came to see Elaine in hospital once; it was in the early days when she had just begun her recovery. She brought her grapes and a brand new book – a special gift, she called it. 'It's about obsession, madness, love – all that jazz,' she said with a small, mysterious smile.

Mrs Hanley went out to the sink on the corridor and washed the grapes herself. Then she came back in with a small plate she had sent the cranky tea-lady to fetch. As she patted the grapes dry with a tissue and laid them gently on the plate, she told Elaine she was glad that Agatha had her as a friend. 'You're very kind,' she said, 'you and Rachel both.'

Elaine had wanted to say their friendship with Agatha had nothing to do with kindness, that they liked, no loved, Agatha as much as they liked or loved each other. But she has always found it hard to say anything to Mrs Hanley without feeling stupid.

That was when Mrs Hanley took the book out of her handbag. 'It's about how our past turns us into the people we become,' she said. 'It's about someone you already know from another book – I won't say who it is, but do let me know when you guess.'

Elaine hadn't particularly liked the sound of the book and had put it to the end of the queue and then forgotten all about it. She wonders how far down the box it is now and worries in case Mrs Hanley has come to discuss it.

But when the door opens, it's her mother standing there, leaning in, breathless and maybe annoyed at having to leave all her new laughing friends in the kitchen.

'That was . . . that was . . . Mrs . . . Mrs Hanley on the phone. Look out the . . . You're to look out. The window. *Honestly!*'

'Why?' Elaine asks, but her mother just makes a few impatient points at the window.

Elaine gets out of bed. When she goes to the window

she sees Agatha standing at the Hanleys' front step, already
waving.

'Agatha!'

'Oh yes, she's here for the summer.'

'How long has she been here?'

'I don't know. A few weeks maybe. But now, you can't see her
yet. No visitors for at least a fortnight – remember?'

'Why didn't you tell me?'

'I did. '

'No, you did not!'

'I was sure . . . Did I not?'

'You never tell me anything!'

'What are you talking about? I'm always telling you things.'

'You never tell me anything I want to know!'

Agatha is wearing a new yellow dress and, beneath her
sunglasses, there is her smile. She is holding a large sign to her
chest: 'Welcome Home Elaine!!!'

Mrs Hanley stands beside her. If Mrs Hanley wasn't there,
Elaine would open the window and hang out of it to call across
the road to her friend. She would do it even if her mother said,
'For God's sake, you're like someone out of a tenement in Naples!'

She can feel Mrs Hanley's eyes on her. Elaine lifts her hand,
shyly waves. Then waves again. The sign slips in Agatha's hand
and Mrs Hanley straightens it. Mrs Hanley leans into Agatha
and says something. Agatha gives one more wave then begins to
turn away.

Elaine stays at the window until she sees the Hanleys' front
door close and the shadows pass over the glass of the porch.

There was a sea in the title, she remembers now. A wide sea or
a wild sea, she can't remember which.

*

For days she remains on hospital time; waking not long after
dawn, reaching for the rubber ball on her bedside table, squeezing it.

Until her father's slow step begins through the house and the world beneath her window hatches out of the suburban silence.

Each day is just like the last one.

The men leave around the same time each morning, except for Mr Jackson, who is usually first out of the traps, and Mr Donegan, who plays in the orchestra and goes out as everyone else is coming back in. Front doors snap and car doors gnash and from the house next door she hears Jilly Ryan imitate each engine in long, throaty arcs.

Men, mostly in suits, some with briefcases bricked by their side. Mr Hanley in sports jacket and mouse-coloured trousers. A scarf thing – a cravat – noosing his neck. 'Because he's an architect,' her mother once told her when she was around eight and going through a stage of asking questions about Ted Hanley.

If two men appear at the same time, a few words may drift across a wall or over the road – rumours of a heatwave; something vaguely sporty; the gist of a radio news story half-heard while shaving. Abstract things that go on somewhere behind these houses, beyond these rooftops. Way out there, anyhow, in the big, broad world where the men live the hours of their day.

The men call each other by first name. Or even the short form of first name: Bill, Jeff, Terry. Lar. Bob. Bob – her father.

Doctor Townsend, they usually call 'the Doc', although her father, Shillman and Hanley – the other 'genuine' professionals (as her mother would have it) – refer to him as Gordon.

She hears everything from this front upstairs bedroom: every hall-door slam, every echo of a slam. Every gate, every footfall, every word that drifts under her window. She hears the forced jaunty notes in the early morning mouths of the men.

Once the men are out of the way, the next rank can start coming through: secondary school girls with freshly brushed hair and pleated skirts to the knee. The shuffly steps of spotty Karl Donegan, schoolbag squeezed hard to his chest. From the Townsend

house, beautiful Paul comes through the side entrance and carefully closes the tall gate behind him. And from the house with
no number on its door, the new boy, the boy with the tired eyes
cuts over the garden and vaults the wall like a colt, taking with
him her heart squeezed in his fist.

And now the small children. They come wriggling out
of their houses, flat footsteps stomping down driveways,
schoolbags banging off backs. Little birdie voices joining other
birdie voices and disappearing in a swarm towards the village
school. Byyyyeeee. Byyyyeee. A wave to a mother shadowed in
a doorway, like someone ashamed.

And, finally, Mr Slater.

Even though he's retired, he goes out every morning Monday
to Friday, walking all the way into the city in long jaunty strides,
grey coat billowing behind him. She often wonders if he has a
turning point, something to touch before allowing himself to
return – say a spear on the college railing or maybe he crosses
the bridge to the far side of town to touch the feet on one of the
statues of angels.

Because he's retired, she sees Slater more then the other men
and, for some reason, likes him a lot. She likes his gangster
hat and long coat. His garden of flowers where, from her
bathroom window, and even better with the help of her father's
binoculars, she sometimes sees him working. She likes the way
he pretends not to hear his hump-backed wife when she raps
her angry knuckles on the window at him. She likes to look out
the landing window in the dead of night and see that the lights
in his garage are on, and know that he's in there playing with his
model train sets, and to know, too, that she isn't the only one to
be awake in the neighbourhood. And mostly she likes the way
he never says hello to anyone, not even in reply.

She waits for him to lunge past her window, cross the road
in a few diagonal strides, coast the side of Townsends' house and
disappear around the corner. All gone.

A lull like a broad sigh over the estate. A window cracks open. Milk bottles jangle. A front door gives a wary creak. The squeaky sound of a baby's pram as Mrs Ryan eases it over the top step.

Other prams soon follow, nuzzling out of other front doors and lumbering down porch steps. One or two are pushed straight down to the shops, others parked in the garden while a start is made on the housework.

She opens her journal and reads over yesterday's page:

> The suburb is like a ship, a big ship permanently anchored. A different group of passengers inside each cabin. Sometimes they come out, stroll along the deck, nod to each other, maybe even stop and chat. But in the end all return to their own little cabin, to huddle and whisper with their own little group, to look out on the same stagnant ocean.

'It doesn't matter what you write,' the doctor has told her, 'it doesn't even have to make sense.'

But it has to make sense to her, and so she turns the pen in her hand and, stirring it like a spoon, buries her observation under a bed of scribbles.

> The suburb is not like a ship. It's the opposite to a ship. On a ship babies and women always come first, in the suburbs, they always, always, come last.

Her bed by the window. If she pulls herself up and looks through the slit at the side of the curtain what does she see?

She sees a fat sleeping toddler stuffed into his pram, soother dangling from the side of his mouth. She sees an old pair of tights tying the Ryan gates together for when he wakes up and starts running amok around the front garden. She sees her mother's forgotten shears under a rose bush where she left them down to gossip with Mrs Caudwell. And a child's knee sock picked up from the pavement and strewn across the – by now unruly – hedge of the Osbornes' old house.

There's the identical faces of the three houses opposite, the profiles of the house on each side. To the right, the corners that turn onto the main road; to the left, the corners leading into the cul-de-sac. And all the jigsaw pieces from that cluster of houses: a poke of chimney, a brow of dormer, an edge of window frame. White bird-shit splashes on slate.

Little to tell one house from another. At least not on the outside. Some detached, some semi-detached. Redbrick to steep roof. Some gardens bigger than others. Apron of lawn front and back; elbows of lawn at the sides of a detached house. A driveway. Square pillars, double gate. A hedge to the front: not so high that the house could hide behind it, but not so low that a child could climb over and hurt itself – or, worse, ruin the line of the hedge. The house with no number has no hedge. Almost all have a garage – although she's noticed since coming out of hospital that garage conversions are really starting to catch on. In which case the garage has been duly renamed: playroom, television room, utility room. Den.

The Hanley house, designed by Monsieur La Cravat himself, is by far the grandest. At the back of the house is a large extension made out of glass that is used for entertaining. The Hanleys call this the Garden Room. (A sign on the door, with a silhouette of a man swinging a golf club, also calls it 'Ted's Den'.)

At the bottom of the back garden is a wooden prefab shed lined with books that Mrs Hanley calls her 'little haven'. At the west side of the house is a further extension – again mostly glass – with clever curved walls and a special bathroom attached. The Hanleys call this the Guest Room. Agatha calls it the Glass Prison.

Outside each house, a patch of grass from which a caged tree grows. In the middle of the road, a pond-shaped green, trimmed with white plastic frill. Bins are left out on Tuesday morning. On Saturdays cars are given their sponge baths. Saturday nights are for occasional house parties. On Sundays, lawnmowers rumble.

3
Winter Present
November

WE ARE A HOUSE of no names – I am thinking this as I come back up from the shop with my father's newspaper, eyes to the ground so they don't feel the need to meet the eyes of a neighbour – we were always that way: a house of no names. If my father wants me he lifts his little handbell or passes a message through his day nurse, Yin-lu, who goes by the name of Lynette. Otherwise he waits for me to come into his room.

I used to think her name was Wynette. For the first couple of weeks that's what I called her. One day she took a pencil out of her pocket and wrote on a piece of paper – Lynette with a heavy double line under the Lyn part.

'Sorry,' I said, 'it sounds like Wynette.'

'You no listen, is all.'

I sometimes wonder how he refers to me when asking Lynette to give me a message. Does he say 'my daughter' or 'the woman in the kitchen' or simply 'her'. I can't imagine him using my name.

And I never use his – except in my mind where I can sometimes catch myself off guard still calling him Daddy.

I can't remember my parents addressing each other by first names either. In fact, I can barely remember them addressing each other at all. I know my mother used my father's name, but only in his absence, when on the phone maybe, or if she wanted to be part of a general husband-themed conversation – Bob says. It depends on Bob. Bob likes. Bob doesn't like. Bobbedy, Bob. Bob-bob.

They left notes for each other on the kitchen table, business-like
notes initialled at the bottom:

> If you could oblige by leaving navy pin-stripe into
> dry cleaners. B
> Please leave cheque for E's visit to dentist. S
> At Cheltenham for the next few days. B
> E needs a new coat. S

And of course, they had me to act as messenger. 'Tell your
mother I'll be away on circuit until Friday.' Or, 'Ask your father
if he's going racing this evening and if he'll be eating out.'

And one time when I was small – at a funeral I suppose it
must have been, what with everyone dressed in black – I heard
my father respond to a woman's question with, 'Oh, you'd have
to ask Sara that.'

I had looked around at all these women clumped together on
sofas and armchairs, or moving across the frame of an opened
kitchen door with plates of sandwiches and cakes in their hands
– Who's Sara, I had thought. Which one is Sara?

Sar-ah Sar-ah ah ah ah.

*

She called me about six weeks after I arrived in New York: our
first conversation since I'd left here. The last time I'd seen her
she'd been shoving me into a taxi cab in the middle of the night,
Patty beside me, her mother, Serena, up front. Patty and I bawling our brains out. My mother's face pale in the dim light of the
cab's interior, not crying – not that, but with a tear in each eye
like two silver studs. It's for your own good,' she said. 'You'll see
that in time.'

She nearly had to break my fingers to unclamp them from
her arm.

A glimpse that has stayed in my mind to this day: my
mother, head lowered, arms ledged under her weighty bosom,
crossing the road in a pair of slippers, the budge of her rounded
backside like a horse's in the tight skirt of her very best suit

which she'd worn to the meeting earlier that day and not yet taken off. And the light in the window of our sitting-room, where only a moment before my father had been standing, now switched off.

He may have been still standing there in the dark. He may have grown bored already and gone up to bed.

When I'd turned back into the car, there was Serena kneeling up on the seat, arms stretched over the back of it, holding Patty by both hands. 'Oh, sweetie, don't cry. Mom is here with you. It's all gonna be fine. Everything's gonna be . . . Oh, sweetie.'

Then she settled back down into the passenger seat, face turned to the window. 'How could it have come to this?' she asked her black glassed shadow. 'How could it have even happened?'

But my mother's first phone call – it was still a big ordeal back then, involving operators, and time checks, and worry about the second by second cost of it all. She must have said hello first. She must have at least asked how I was. But no matter how many times I went over it later – and even now when I replay it in my head – her first words remain: 'We have a dog now.'

'A what?'

'A dog. We have him nearly a month. You know, I think I'm going to have to get a kennel built out in the garden for him – he's small enough now but apparently they can grow to a size that–'

'Is that why you phoned me? To tell me about your dog?'

'No. No, of course not. I'm just saying.'

'It's weeks since I left – I haven't heard a word from you. How could you not even–'

'I knew you were all right.'

'How? *How* could you know?'

'Serena told me.'

'Serena? You spoke to Serena? When?'

'When we were making arrangements to send money.'

'Money? What money?'

'Well you don't think she's keeping you for nothing, do you? Anyway, I brought him to the vet today for his vaccination. He's a right handful, I don't mind telling you.'

'Is that all you can talk about – your bloody dog?'

'Please don't raise your voice to me.'

'Aren't you going to say anything about what happened? Aren't you going to tell me how–?'

'Everything is fine here.'

'Well, what about–?'

'That's all you need to know. There's no need to discuss anything. It's all in the past now. It's all sorted.'

'Can't you just tell me at least–?'

'I'm telling you, everything is all right. Don't ask me about anyone. I don't want to hear mention of anyone's name. And if you keep asking I'm hanging up the phone.'

'I only, I only–'

'I mean it! If you don't stop, I'm hanging *up*. Actually, I'm hanging up anyway because I've just about had enough of–'

'No, no, no, wait. Please, I didn't mean. Wait. I just want to ask. About. About the dog. I want to ask about the dog.'

'The dog?'

'Yes. What sort of a dog is it?'

'Oh. Well, it's a – what do you call it? – German shepherd. A German shepherd, that's right.'

'Do you mean like an Alsatian?'

'I suppose. A pup, you know -- into everything of course, driving me up the . . . I don't mind telling you. He's made mincemeat out of my good shoes. Worse than a– Worse than a– Well, you know.'

'Yes.'

'What? What? I can't hear you now.'

'I said yessss. *Yessss*.'

'Anyway, I suppose I better be . . . I'll give you a ring again.'

'What do you mean – *again*?'

'Another time.'

'No wait! Hold on . . .'

'What? I have to go. I really have to go now.'

'What – what did you name him?'

'Who?'

'The dog. Yes, what's his name?'

'Oh. He doesn't really have one.'

'How do you call him then?'

'I whistle. Sometimes I click my tongue.'

The dog was to replace me. Something to feed, clean up after, do duty by, *endure*. And it didn't even have a name. On the few occasions she called after that, she talked about 'the dog'. After that dog died, she talked about another nameless one. And a few years later, that time she came to meet me in Paris, she said, 'When this one dies, I don't think I'll bother with another one.' But she did get another – she must have done – because in a later conversation there was yet another Alsatian pup chewing up her shoes.

There's a photograph of a young Alsatian on my father's piano but I don't know which one it is. It was taken on the lawn out the back garden on the far side of the shed where the rose-beds begin. The dog's head is raised; it has a thick healthy coat, a waggedy tongue, hard, bright amber eyes. It looks like a poster for a Hollywood dog.

Not this dog, though, not this old soldier beside me. The markings are different for a start; so is the expression in the eyes. The present incumbent has much softer eyes: eyes like melting caramels. Or maybe that's just the cataracts.

I wonder if it's too late to give him a name. I could call him Boy. I often call him Boy anyway. 'Here, Boy' or 'Down, Boy.'

I think he deserves that much – a name, even something as stupid as Boy.

'Come on, Boy,' I say. 'Come on, you can do it.'

I can feel the weight of him on the end of the lead as I pull him along, the vibration of his legs, as if the bones inside them are beginning to dissolve. We are almost at the dip in Arlows' wall; I pull him along until we are beside it. Then I sit into it and let him rest for a while. It was here Maggie used to perch in the evening to smoke a cigarette, after she was done working in the yard, thrilling us with her outrageous talk and feeding us French fags that she bought by the carton.

'Now, girls, you should know this – a man will say anything to get his way.'

Or, 'Never mistake the pleading eye and trembling limb for love – that's just the erection talking.'

And once when Agatha was going on about older men being more romantic: 'Romance! Don't make me laugh. Take a look at the women around here – where did romance ever get them? Into a twelve-by-twenty kitchen is where, hoping for head-pats and hand-outs from their lords and masters.'

Across the road, a pair of school uniforms trundle past, two cherry noses sticking out from gabardine hoods. The afternoon must be getting on. I feel the cold air cling to my face like a cellophane wrapper.

'Poor Boy,' I say. 'Poor old Boy. Better get you home before you catch a chill.'

We leave Maggie's perch and cross over the main road, then turn the corner onto the straight. Only one house to go before home – I point this fact out to encourage him. 'Look, nearly there now. Only one house, then ours. A few more steps, that's all, that's all.'

But he's dragging his paws. Just before the gate he digs them in completely, twisting his head backwards as if he's trying to get away. I'm worried that maybe his hind legs have finally given up: it's the first question the vet always asks, and I know it will be the last one. 'How are the old hind legs doing?'

I consider attempting to lift him into the house or at least calling Lynette to help lift him in. But then I see what he has already sensed – a figure at the door.

This dog is mute. The vet has told me that some five years ago his bark completely disappeared. Apart from the occasional plaintive howl at a distant ambulance, or maybe a bit of half-hearted whimpering when his teeth are giving him pain, this dog has nothing to say for himself. He's deaf in one ear. He views the world through the holes in his cataracts. He'd prefer a bar of chocolate to a meaty bone. And now, to top it all off, he's become afraid of strangers.

'Some bloody Alsatian you are,' I say to him, and drag him whimpering through the gate.

The figure – familiar and yet not – is standing with her back to us. At first I think she's her mother – the rounded shoulders, the stiff little hairdo, even the way the coat hangs off-kilter. It's on the tip of my tongue to say, Mrs Caudwell? But of course it's not Miriam Caudwell. It's her daughter, Brenda. Jesus. A middle-aged Brendie Caudwell.

We stand looking at each other and then do that skittery laugh that people who haven't seen each other in years tend to do. We become minstrels: goggling our eyes, widening our mouths and lifting our hands in amazement.

I forget sometimes that I'm nearly fifty. I forget that while I'm trying not to look appalled at the state of Brendie Caudwell, bloodless and beige and slightly humped on my doorstep, Brenda is trying not to gawp at the state of me – bedraggled and scrawny or however the hell I must look – dragging a geriatric Alsatian behind me.

When we finish laughing, we tell each other how little each other has changed, and a few more lies besides. Then, because I feel I ought to, I ask her into the house. She looks freezing: beneath the mask of brown make-up lies a face that is brindled with cold.

'Have you been waiting long?' I ask. 'You didn't you ring the bell?'

'I gave the door a little knock but didn't like to disturb your dad – I know he's not been well . . .'

'Oh, he is well. Very well. He's in a wheelchair, that's all.'

I push a cement block out of the way with my toe and reach down for the key.

'Well, I didn't want to drag him out to the door, you know.'
39
'His nurse would have answered if you rang the bell.'

'His nurse?'

'Yes. She's with him now.'

'A full-time nurse?'

'A couple of hours a day.'

'Oh. Oh, that's great now – isn't it? And people always complaining about how dreadful the health service is.'

I recognise her mother in there, the same old begrudging glimmer in the watery eye. I stick the key in the lock and look at her.

'He pays for it himself. She's a private nurse.'

The glimmer remains – the fact that he can afford to pay for his own nurse is not helping Brendie at all.

'Oh right,' she says, 'but you know now, you could probably qualify for the carer's allowance, Elaine. It's a government thing, you see, and then you wouldn't have to–'

'I don't want the carer's allowance.'

'Yes, well, I'm just saying...'

'I'm not his carer.'

I unhook the dog and we follow him into the kitchen.

'I was so sorry about your mother,' she says, laying a hand lightly on her breast.

'Thank you.'

'And how are you now?'

'Me? Oh you know . . .'

'You need to give yourself a bit of time, Elaine. It hasn't been long.'

'No.'

'I was at the funeral . . .'

'Thank you.'

'Oh no, of course I'd be there. Of *course*. You didn't make it back yourself, Elaine?'

'No. No, unfortunately. I tried but . . . Well, the way things worked out, I just missed it.'

'That must have been terrible for you.'

'Yes.'

I pour water into the dog's bowl and lower it to him, his tongue hooking up to it even before the bowl reaches the ground.

'And how is your father taking it?' she asks. 'It must be tough losing someone after all those years.'

I can't think of anything to say and so just keep nodding my head, slowly.

'I've been meaning to call round. But I wasn't sure if – well, you know . . .?'

'And and . . . what about your lot, Brenda, how are they all doing, huh?'

'My kids you mean?'

'You have kids? Great. You married then? You always said you wouldn't.'

'Yeah, should have listened to Maggie Arlow. Anyway I bloody didn't. Sorry, we separated a while ago. I'm still a bit – you know – raw. The kids are with me. Well, me and my mother. I'm back living at home.' She rolls up her eyes and gives a bitter, flimsy laugh. 'Imagine? At my age? Jesus. And you? Did you?'

'Marry? No.'

'So are you back for good now?'

'Just till my father is sorted. What about the others, Brenda – how are they?'

'The others?'

'Your brothers and June. How's June?'

'Gerry is a policeman, a detective actually – must have inherited the genes – quite high up too, just like Daddy. Peter is a market gardener up North. He married a lovely Chinese girl, two of the most beautiful children – but he's divorced now. Daddy died a couple of years ago, you heard?'

There's a short silence and I wonder if this is where I'm supposed to say how sorry I am. I take off my coat and throw it across the back of the chair.

'And June?'

'June? Oh you know. June lives in Birmingham. Or she did, last I heard. She doesn't really keep in touch. She used to phone Peter the odd time but . . .'

'I see.'

'Yeah, well, that's June for you.'

'She was such a beautiful girl.'

'Yeah. But you know, I really, *really* don't want to talk about June.'

'Right. Would you like tea, Brenda?'

She nods, opens her coat, pulls off her scarf and stands clutching it in both hands, blinking at the table. Then she finally comes out with it: 'I see the Shillman house has been sold.'

'Has it?' I turn away and begin filling the kettle.

'You didn't notice?'

'No.'

'Well, it's been sold. At least I think it's been sold – there was no sign up or anything but the whole place is being gutted. I'm surprised you didn't hear the racket?'

'I heard something all right, but you know – people are always fixing up their houses, aren't they?'

I stick my head into the cupboard and begin fussing around with cups.

'It's been rented here and there over the years.'

'Has it?'

'Lying empty for the past while, though. God there were some right specimens went through those doors, I don't mind telling you. The United Nations building, my father used to call it.'

'Who bought it – do you know?'

'Never mind who bought it, Elaine! Who sold it? That's what I'd like to know!'

I put two mugs on the counter and go back to the fridge.

'And where did all that stuff come from?' she continues.

'What stuff?'

'Their things. The garden is full, front and back. Furniture, clothes, everything. I was in the house a few years ago. I didn't see any of it. Come on, I would have noticed.'

'I'm sure you would.'

'What's that supposed to mean?'

'Nothing. The attic. That house has a huge attic. They never converted it.'

She nods and then: 'We never heard from them after, you know. Not a word. They just upped and went and . . . Not a word.'

'No.'

'What do you call that candelabra thing? Shaped like a spade?'

'A menorah.'

'That's right. A menorah. Why would they leave that behind if it meant so much to Mr Shillman? Apart from anything else, it must be worth a packet.'

She looks at her scarf again, turns it once or twice in her hands, then blurts, 'I saw the haversack.'

I take the biscuit tin off the top shelf.

'Elaine?'

'What?'

'I'm saying, I saw the haversack.'

'A haversack,' I say, 'is a haversack. Could be anyone's from over the years. One of those tenants you mentioned.'

'I thought I saw it on the lawn and a couple of days later when I went in—'

'You went in?'

I slide a few biscuits onto the plate and then come back to her.

'Just to the garden.'

'You went in, Brenda?'

'The workmen were gone home. Nobody saw me. I found it in the shed. It wasn't as if I was breaking in – there's no lock on the door. The badges were on it. All the cities he was going to visit? Remember? It was Karl's haversack, I'm telling you.'

'You didn't take it – did you?'

'No. Of course not. I didn't touch it.'

'Did you look inside?'

'No! No, I didn't fucking look inside. I couldn't look inside. I couldn't touch it.'

'All right, Brenda, Jesus, take it easy will you?'

'Yeah, but what if there is anything inside it, Elaine? What if . . .?'

We stand staring at each other. She is waiting for me to say something, to tell her what we should do. I can think of nothing to say. I can think of nothing but the small, cold eel twisting around in my stomach.

Lynette comes to my rescue then, popping her broad brown face round the door, smiling her mile-wide smile. 'All happy now,' she says, 'concert time.'

'Oh, good. This is Brenda, by the way, a neighbour.'

'Ahhh, a neighbour. A *neighbour*. I think sometimes all houses maybe empty round here.'

She gives us one of her sideways waves, disappears back out to the hall and there is the lonely sound of the front door clicking behind her.

'See you tomorrow,' I call after her.

The first few piano notes tip into the house. We listen.

'He still plays then?' Brenda asks.

'Every evening for a couple of hours. He's no trouble really.'

'What does he play?'

'His scales for a while. Then whatever happens to be next in the pile.'

I pour the tea, pass a mug across the counter to her. Then hold the milk carton over the mug –

'Leave it now, Brenda. There's no point. It's too late.'

'I'm just saying, I saw it, that's all.'

'Fine, you saw it. But forget it now.'

She sighs. 'You wouldn't have a drink – would you? Something a bit stronger than tea?'

'We don't keep drink in the house any more, I'm afraid.'

I pour the milk into the mugs.

'No? Not even a drop of brandy or something? Not even for medicinal purposes?'

'Nothing.'

'How times change.' She gives a sad and slightly sarcastic smile then begins to put her scarf back around her neck.

She stands and goes to the window looking out towards the Shillman house as though checking out the view. But these gardens are long and heavily shrubbed and, at this level anyhow, there is nothing to see.

'Jesus, though,' she says then, 'it makes you think about it – docsn't it? It makes you–'

'Only if you allow it.'

'Oh, come on. You're not saying you don't?'

'No. Not really.'

'All right for you, I suppose. You got away. You got to go to New York while . . . I was left here, facing them all, day after–'

I open my mouth to swipe back at her, but I don't need a row with Brendie Caudwell right now.

We watch the dog waddle around the kitchen, then ease

himself down into his battered basket. My father continues to work the piano. I can usually gauge his mood by the tone of his playing. Today he's morose – even his scales have a touch of the Death March about them.

'Well, I should probably go . . .' she says.

'Mrs Hanley,' I say then. 'Sometimes I think about her. And Agatha. Of course I do. I've never stopped thinking about her.'

I follow her through the hall, open the front door and we exchange a sort of grimace, easier with each other now that we are almost done. She steps outside and turns to me.

'My youngest will be home from school soon. Fourteen. The others are seventeen, nineteen.'

'Yeah?'

'The two lads, they're great. Both in college, one doing business studies, the other . . . one of those fancy computer courses – I can't even think of the name of it. She's a bit of a handful, though. Misses her old school. Her home. We'd a lovely home, Elaine, you know, we really did. She blames me for everything. Thinks it's my fault the marriage broke up and that we lost the house. It wasn't my fault. None of it was my fault. It wasn't even his, before you ask.'

'No?'

'It was the bank's fault. And he wouldn't fight them, you see. He just wouldn't even–'

'The bank's?'

'It's always the fucking bank, Elaine. If you don't know that, you're one of the lucky ones.'

I can see she's getting a bit tetchy now.

'Okay, sure.'

'God, you sound so New Yorky,' she says, and I know this is supposed to be an insult.

'Well, I have lived there longer than I ever lived here.'

'And you know, you shouldn't really leave the front door key out here like that, just lying there under a brick. Jesus.'

'No?'

'Anyone could just walk straight in. It's not like the old days around here, you know.'

'Just as well, maybe.'

She glares at me and then turns away. 'Anyway, I better get back. If I'm not there, it'll be dump the schoolbag and off with her till God knows what hour. Walks over my mother. And she's not been well at all. Poor old Mums.'

I watch her pass through the gate, her tweed coat tightening at the hips as she closes the buttons, the sleeve of her coat on the far side of the wall, buffing the gaps in the hedge.

And, 'Fuck poor old Mums,' I think.

Back in the kitchen, I stand for a moment looking out into the darkening garden. Another day sneaked off behind my back.

I empty the tea down the sink, put the biscuits back into the tin and tidy away all traces of Brendie Caudwell. Then I open the connecting door to the garage, step down and prise open the lid of the chest freezer. For a moment I can't remember what I am doing standing here, watching gusts of icy breath whisper around my wrists. My mind is stuck in New York, in the moments following that first phone call from my mother. The way everything stopped after I'd hung up the phone. Where there had been television voices in another room – there was a silence. Where Serena had been banging around the kitchen making canapés for an event the next day – there was a deathly stillness. Even the purl of traffic coming up from West 57th ceased in that moment of absolute deafness.

And I can see myself now as I was then, standing in the hallway of Serena's apartment staring at the phone, drowning in my own snot and tears, breathless with shock, *breathless*. At the realisation that I would not be going home again. Not in my mother's lifetime anyhow.

'You should be grateful,' she'd said. 'You should realise just how lucky you are.'

'I'm begging you, *please*–'

'Oh, for goodness sake. If this is going to happen every time I telephone . . . all this emotionality. All this . . .'

'Well, can I speak to Daddy then?'

'He went out a few minutes ago.'

'But it's the middle of the night!'

'Oh dear! Don't tell me I've woken Serena and Patty?'

'*Your* night. Yours. We haven't even gone to bed here yet. Are you drunk?'

'How *dare* you?'

'How can you not know if it's the middle of the night?'

'I don't sleep any more. I don't sleep! That's how! And stop that crying. They'll hear you crying. Crying like it's somebody else's fault. Like there's always somebody else to blame . . .'

'I'm sorry, please, I'm sorry.'

'Sorry is no good to you now. Sorry is not going to make the slightest difference.'

'No, no wait. I. I just want to ask when can I come home. I want to come home. Just give me a date – I don't care if it's weeks or even months away.'

'Didn't you hear what I just said? Can't you just listen? We got you out of it, your father and I. We risked everything to get you out of it. And now we're finished with you. *Finished*.'

I go into the sitting-room and bring the horse-shoe ice bucket to the cabinet. Behind me, my father is playing 'Red Sails in the Sunset' with knobs on. I take two Waterford cut glasses and arrange the ice, two cubes to a glass. I watch his turn to amber with a measure of Scotch and mine turn to diamond-white with two measures of vodka and a tip of tonic.

I go to the piano, place his Scotch on the coaster and stand for a moment watching his fingers slither over the keyboard.

He stops playing – as he usually does whenever I linger. Then he closes the manuscript book, drops it onto the stack on the floor and picks another off the smaller pile that he keeps on the top of the piano.

'Brenda Caudwell was just here,' I say.

He settles the new music on the stand and flicks through the pages. I wait for a moment then move towards the door. Behind me the chime of ice in a glass.

'What did she want?' he asks.

'She came to tell me the Shillman house has been sold. I think she may be worried one of them is moving back – their furniture, you see, is all–'

'If she calls again, don't bring her in.'

'What? I can hardly just leave her standing on the doorstep.'

He takes another short swig from his glass and puts it back down on the coaster.

'Let me make myself clear. I don't want her or anyone belonging to her in *my* house – is that understood?'

I am cut by the tone of his voice.

'Fine,' I say, 'it's your house.'

'That's right, it is.'

He returns to his piano and glides his hands back into the music.

4
Summer Past
May

MOST OF HER LIFE is spent lying down. Lying on her bed up in her room. Lying and listening and thinking. On warm afternoons, she goes out to the back garden and lies on the patio lounger. In the evenings she lies on the sofa watching whatever television programme her mother happens to be watching, saying yes, no, I don't know, maybe, to all of her pointless questions about people named Crystal or Sue Ellen or Mavis. As if they really existed and, even if they did, as if they could possibly lead such convoluted lives. At first touch of nightfall, she goes back upstairs and lies on her bed again.

And her mother is everywhere, everywhere – following her out to the garden, popping up in a room she has just entered, yapping at her when she's trying to read, trilling up the stairs to call her for another meal, snack, pill, temperature-taking.

'Elaine. Ela-aine. *Elaaaaaine*. **Elaine!**'

Even the sound of her voice.

There are times when it physically pains her. She has to wonder if this revulsion she feels towards her own mother could be some peculiar after-effect of the virus. She remembers when she was younger, how she used to sneak into Dr Townsend's surgery with Rachel and Paul in search of disgusting things. They found a photograph in one of the medical books once – it looked like a fat scabby caterpillar resting on a rock. *Nevus Maternus* the photograph was called. Paul said it meant 'Mother's Mark' – and that it wasn't a rock, but a big bald head. What had started out as a tiny forceps scar on a baby had grown as the head had grown and then suddenly turned cancerous. Could she have something like that she wonders now – a mother's mark, but on the inside where it could be felt but not seen? A sore, swelling thing, festering away on her brain? Her heart? Or right here, then, in the middle of her gut?

Because she can't remember feeling this way before she got sick. Yes, there had been times when she'd felt like screaming; times when she'd felt if she'd a gun in her hand . . .

But nothing so ferocious, so all unforgiving, as this.

It has a life of its own. It climbs on top of her in the middle of the night and presses down on her chest; it breathes sour, hot breath on her face. It makes her cry with temper, with sadness and sometimes even with shame.

She thinks to herself – tomorrow. I will make an effort tomorrow. I will try to be nice to her. The effort I make will be strong enough to break the grip in my stomach and then I'll be able to breathe again.

In the early hours of the morning she is filled with hope for tomorrow's effort. And then the next day, the second – the very second – she sets eyes on her mother queasily coming out of the bathroom and padding down the stairs in her frilly dressing-gown, the laundry basket held high in her arms, empty bottles whispering inside it – she hates, hates, hates her, all over again.

And yet, she had loved her once – in fact, she had been almost in love with her. They had slept together until she was nine years old. Elaine had thought it quite normal then – the husband sleeping in one room at the back of the house, the mother and child in another at the front. They shared the same bed. They ate sweets together under the bedclothes. Snuggled up and told stories. Gossiped about the neighbours. Spied on them. Mummy, she called her then.

It might have gone on like that forever, only Brendie Caudwell found out about it and blabbed it all over the school.

It was around that time Elaine had gotten it into her head that

Ted Hanley could well be her father. Later she would realise that she'd simply been picking up on her mother's crush. And not just the crush she had on him, but also the admiration – if not for his wife exactly, then the impression they gave as a married couple. The Hanley couple – their clothes, their furniture, their *taste*. 'Note,' she had said more than once, 'the way *they* don't need children in order to be happy.'

When her mother spoke about Ted, her whole face lit up. If they were lying in bed she would cuddle Elaine tighter. The clothes he wore, the car he drove, what he had done to that house – such clever ideas – practically an artist, in fact. 'I mean – those *hands*,' she would say. 'Those *hands*.'

Once at the bus stop coming home from town, her mother had fallen into a conversation with another woman and started to describe the garden room Ted Hanley had built at the back of his house. Ted did this. Ted would only do that. Ted simply wouldn't have it any other way. She had become so animated that even the woman had started to look at her oddly.

For a moment Elaine had thought her mother was going to confide in this woman, to lower her voice and say, 'Between you and me – the man I live with? Well he's not actually my real husband . . .' and that she would have to listen very carefully to the whispering voice behind the hand if she wanted to learn the adult reason for living in one house with one husband, while desperately longing for another house, including the husband that was already in it.

Her parents were once invited to a party in the Hanleys'. She'd been about eight years old at the time. She watched them cross the road together. Her father holding her mother's elbow and guiding her through the gate, the way he did when they went to church on Sunday – the only other time Elaine ever saw them touching. He had a bottle wrapped in tissue in his other hand, holding it out and away from his body as if afraid that it might explode. He was wearing pale coloured trousers and a patterned shirt. There was something almost shocking about seeing him without his suit, as if he was going out in his underwear.

Her mother, in a green dress, hardly looked fat at all; her hair, all done up in a Saturday-night do, had made her seem taller. She was wearing high heels and walking in short, nervy steps.

*

Now when she spies out the window, she spies alone, and at least with some degree of shame. Agatha teases her and calls her a spy-arse, but she is spying on Agatha's behalf as well as her own. Agatha seems to forget how greedy she is for visual detail: colours, shapes, movement – the overall impression left by all that. She wants to know everything – not just what Elaine can see in the moments they spend together, but what she has seen since yesterday, last night, weeks ago even.

'Tell me about the new arrivals,' Agatha says on the end of the phone line, 'the new arrivals in the Osbornes' old house.'

'I've told you already!'

'Tell me again.'

Elaine goes into her father's room, lifts the receiver from the extension phone on his desk then returns to the hall where she hangs up the house phone. Back at his desk, she stretches out in his leather chair and tells her again:

How they arrived in the middle of the night, so nobody noticed. How, at first, everyone thought they were sisters.

'They were coming and going, in and out so quickly, but from a distance looked similar, you see.'

'And then?'

And then the delivery vans. They began to arrive the first morning and continued to arrive all week. Furniture, paintings, groceries even. Fully formed shrubs in fancy tubs that were brought round the back along with the garden furniture.

'What did your mother say? Do the voice!'

'A ready-made garden! Either they're bone idle lazy, or they don't intend staying too long.'

Agatha laughs. 'And then *you* saw them?'

The woman first. From the back of the taxi when Elaine was on the way home from her hospital check-up: the woman, leaning her backside against the ledge outside the Osbornes' front porch, smoking a fag. Her shirt tied up at the front, beneath it a block of brown belly. The shirt, pale pink. Jeans snug to the hip, cut-off to just above the knee. She wore no shoes; even her feet were tanned.

'Good figure?' Agatha asks.

'Oh, excellent.'

'And the girl?'

The girl came a minute later. She appeared out of the garage, drinking from a Coke bottle. She wore a man's shirt as if it was a dress and was shuffling along on flat, white slippers, the sort you get in hotels – like the ones the Shillmans have all over their house. It was hard to say what age – 'Our age, maybe.'

'What do you mean 'our age', Junior?'

'All right – your age then. Seventeen.'

'Give me five words to describe her,' Agatha says.

She gives her more than five – tall, tanned, tennis-player's legs; blonde fuzzy plait over one shoulder. Slow bouncy walk.

'And . . .?' Agatha says.

'And what?'

'The cigarette! The cigarette!'

The girl walked over to the woman, took the cigarette from her hand, helped herself to two short pulls, before returning it to the V between the woman's fingers. The woman looked up then, spotted her standing there and waved. Elaine pauses a moment to imagine how she must have looked to the girl then, after the taximan had pulled away, leaving her exposed on the pavement like something that had been under a rock, grey-faced and gawky, blinking into the light.

'And what did you do then?'

'I waved back, but I don't think they noticed.'

Days went by. The women talked of nothing else. Elaine heard them through the kitchen window while she was lying on the patio, reading. Their voices straying out along with the smell of cigarettes and coffee. They were German, it was decided.

Mrs Osborne was known to have German relatives – wasn't she? *Was she?* I didn't know that. *Oh yes, now that I think of it, you're right.* She's right. I heard that too. *It would certainly explain the sporty look of them.* Sporty! Is that what you call it? And now that you mention it, Mrs Townsend's cleaner thought she'd heard funny talk coming from the back garden while taking in the washing. *Funny talk?* Yes, you know, foreign. *Oh, foreign.*

'Oh God!' Agatha says. 'What next!'

Next, the double beds. Two double beds – brand new, mattresses wrapped in plastic, confirming it all: two sisters waiting to be joined by two husbands. Mrs Caudwell said, 'It wouldn't be everyone's cup of tea, of course, two couples living together in the same house, but they do things differently in these countries, I believe.'

'And the car?' Agatha urges. 'Don't forget the car.'

'Yes, the car.'

The German sisters bought a car. The younger one drove it home. She banged it off the side of the gate when she was pulling into the driveway. Then she jumped out of the car, slammed the door, screamed something through the window at the other one, before stomping up the drive and kicking the garage door. That one kick to the garage door changed everything.

'Your mother?'

'My mother. She got on the phone to Martha Shillman.'

'Don't forget her voice!'

'Not sisters at all, Martha, I'm telling you. Mother and daughter. Of course I'm sure. Good God, if I can't recognise a teen-tantrum by now!'

'A teen-tantrum – Jesus!'

The women were back, this time they took to the sitting-room. There was no smell of coffee, but the ice bucket was missing. Elaine had to earwig over the banisters.

There had been reports of the newcomers sunbathing in bikinis in the back garden.

When the sun turned in the evening, the mother – as she was now called – had been seen in the front garden reading a book, although she at least had the decency to throw on a few clothes.

'If you could call shorts and T-shirt clothes,' Agatha says, taking off Mrs Townsend's voice.

'Yes, exactly, and my mother agreed – as usual – with everything Mrs Doctor had to say.'

There was something quite common about the whole sorry scene, it was agreed, sitting by her front door on a kitchen chair. It was the sort of thing people living in terraced houses on the far side of town were rumoured to do. And all that waving at the men as they drove by on their way home from work, flashing that smile.

'And who did she wave to?'

'Only randy Caudwell and that was probably because he drove by with his tongue hanging out.'

Agatha squeals. 'Don't stop now!'

Who was she anyway? This woman who dressed like a teenager?

What was she doing going around in bare feet?

And what about that paintbrush in her hand?

Why would she be painting the house herself when she

clearly had money to burn, with her car and her ready-made garden?

And as for those teeth? Did they not look a bit too perfect now to be real?

And the hair? Was that not a bit long now for a woman her age?

And what about the way she let her daughter smoke like that in front of everyone? And get behind a wheel of a car, too – the child might have been killed!

But more to the point – much, much more to the point – where, oh where, was the *husband*?

'The husband!'

'And after all that,' Elaine says, 'they simply knocked on our door. *Our* door. They crossed the road, came through the gate and rang the door bell. You should have heard my mother with her posh accent, trying to pretend she hadn't noticed anything going on across the road – Oh yes, the Osborne's house, of course, of course. I'd forgotten it was even let. Do step in. Elaine . . . Elaaaainnne. Come here a moment would you . . .?'

'So now at last – you saw them up close. What did they look like?'

'They shook hands!'

'But what did they look like?'

'Well, like people on the television. You know, all bright and confident and expecting everyone to be happy to see them. The mother looked older up close. The daughter younger. Serena is the mother's name. Patty the other.'

'Patty Cake.'

'Patty Cake.

'They only stayed a few minutes. Refused an offer of tea. They wanted to know if we could recommend a good doctor, a dentist, a dry cleaners. Then they wanted to know about the local facilities for teenagers. Facilities for teenagers? My mother's face! "I'm not sure what you mean by facilities . . .?"

"'You know," said the mother, "where they socialise? What there is for them to do?"

"'Socialise! To do? Well. I suppose, there's the stables, if she likes that sort of thing. And the Shillmans play tennis in a club somewhere. They drive there or take the bus. When Elaine is better, I'm thinking of sending her.'"

'Really?' Agatha asks.

'First I heard of it.'

'She wants you to make new friends.'

'You could come too.'

'I don't think so.'

'Why not? Of course you could–'

'Never mind all that – get on with the story.'

'My mother thought they'd never leave so she could get on the phone to Martha.'

'Marvellous Martha!'

"'I know you're probably going out, Martha," she said . . .'

'When is Martha ever staying in?'

"'I won't keep you a minute. But guess what? You'll never guess what? They were here. Yes, yes, I'm telling you – came up the drive and knocked on the door. That's right. On the door. And, well, very nice actually. Not at all what I expected. She said, We just called to introduce ourselves. Yes, I know. It probably should have been the other way around. But well – wait till you hear this – this explains everything. They're from New York, Martha. Yes . . . yes, that's right. *Americans*. Well, that's just what I think – it all makes sense now, doesn't it.'"

Agatha sighs. 'Oh the relief!'

'You could hear it in her voice. We could all rest easy in our beds now. These new people were't going to harm us. They weren't dangerous at all – they were from America, that's all. *New Yorkers*. They simply couldn't help the way they were.'

Elaine's mother raps on the door. 'Don't waste your youth on that phone,' she says.

'I'll just be a minute.'

'We don't want you wearing yourself out – do we?'

'Oh, for God's sake, I'll be a minute, I said!'

'You know I'll be staying with the Shillmans again this weekend?' Agatha says as she brings her ear back to the phone.

'The Shillmans? No, but why?'

'A colleague of Ted's is getting married or something.'

'But you can stay here.'

'No, it's fine.'

'Really, I can ask.'

'Don't, Elaine. Leave it.'

'But why not? I'm sure if I ask–'

'Your mother doesn't like me.'

'That isn't true! She does, I know she does. It'll be lonely for you. Rachel won't be home from school for another few weeks and–'

'I'll be fine. I've stayed there a few times before, they're nice.'

'Isn't it odd staying there without her?'

'No. It's fine. Really. I don't mind.'

'But, Agatha –'

Her mother's face appears around the door, hissing a whisper through two big, red, furious cheeks.

'I'm not sure your father's going to approve of you being locked away in here with all those confidential papers.'

'I'm not touching anything and he won't care anyway.'

'Really? Well, he may have something to say when the phone bill arrives.'

'No, he won't. He won't say a word. He never says a word. About *anything*.'

5
Winter Present
November

I'M REALLY MISSING MY night walks.

The compact silence as I draw near to the city when the streets seem that much closer, the sky that much lower and it feels like I'm wandering through the empty rooms of some vast interior space.

I miss the whiff of danger on the night air, the unidentifiable shadows – is that a tree or a man in the distance? Is that a nun's body floating downriver or a billowing length of riverweed?

I miss the way the sounds in my head are gradually softened by the beat of my footsteps. And the sense that I am the one in control somehow.

The dog beside me, toddling along; squirting, squatting, sniffing: undemanding and yet very much alive. I miss moving with him through the various shifts of darkness.

But – by order of the vet – the dog needs to take it easy now. Exercise should be gentle; damp and cold, at all costs, avoided.

'He's an old guy,' was how he put it, as he chucked the dog under his silvering chin, 'and us old guys, we need to take it handy – don't we, fella, hey? Don't we now, don't we?'

The dog, I believe, is relieved.

I hear him plodding up and down the stairs at intervals, or taking a turn about the hall and in and out of the downstairs rooms. If Lynette leaves my father's door ajar, he'll step in for a moment, sniff around for a bit but won't loiter. It seems the dog prefers me to my father and I can't help being pleased by this and then a little uneasy: it's as if the dog is me, somehow, and I have turned into my mother.

He stands outside my bedroom door, noses it open and shyly peeps in. If I'm lying on the bed reading, he comes over and studies my face. If I'm sitting in the dining-room watching television, he lies at my feet for a while before getting up, pottering around then heading to the door, where he sends me a last backward glance. He is telling me how the life of an old dog should be: a waddle around a warm house; a little tour of the back garden whenever he goes out for a iz; a dozen short naps in the daytime. After that, a long night of sleep, uninterrupted. On a fine day, *maybe* a stroll as far as the shops or around the estate – instead of all this being dragged around in the dark and the cold at two in the morning: night-walking for fuck's sake – I mean *really!*

'I get it,' I tell him, 'you're an old guy and all that.'

It's been almost two weeks but I know he still sleeps in dread of my step on the stair, the icy shiver of his chain in my hand.

It was something we did for a while when we were kids, sneak out of the house in the middle of the night and wander around the estate like ghosts on the edge of the world. My idea, as I recall: the one adventurous streak in an otherwise cautious nature. Rachel, myself, Brendie Caudwell occasionally, although she whined so much we tended to leave her out. The boys now and then. And Agatha. Until Agatha fell in love and stopped coming out. She claimed it was too tiring for her, but really she would have wanted to wait by her window for the tap of his coin, or his keys, or whatever it was that he used to announce himself.

Mostly these nights were uneventful – eventful nights would come later with the arrival of Patty. Although, once, we did meet Maggie Arlow. She was on her way home from a horsey function and had abandoned her car a few miles back. The road kept rising to meet her, she said – even when driving with one eye shut. She had no shoes on; her dress had split at the side; her face was scuffed with mascara. She linked me on one side,

Paul on the other. She kept rubbing the side of her face on his shoulder like a cat and saying, 'I tell you, if I was ten years younger, or you were ten years older.' Once she got mixed up and said it the other way around. 'I tell you, if you were ten years younger . . .'

Rachel was furious, snapping at Maggie before stomping off – 'He'd be a seven-year-old, then, and you'd be an even bigger, drunker, more disgusting pervert than you already are.'

I wanted to go home with Rachel that night – I was already scared enough of Maggie when she was sober. But Agatha had tugged on my sleeve three times, which was the signal to say she really, *really* wanted to stay and so I did.

Maggie invited us into her house. Dog hair and cat hair all over the chintzy sofas. A week's worth of rancid ashes piled in the fire grate. Limp rosettes pinned to the wall and a shelf of tarnished cups and trophies. A photograph of a woman dressed in old-fashioned riding gear, sitting side-saddle on a big bay horse. 'My mother,' Maggie said, raising her glass to the photograph, 'wherever the fuck she may be.'

She gave us musty sherry which I pretended to sip before pouring mine into Paul's glass. Maggie began telling a funny story, could hardly get it out she was laughing that much. Her hands shielding her face. They were all laughing then, except me. Laugh, I kept telling myself, for God's sake, why can't you just *laugh*.

Through the gap in Maggie's hands, I could see her grimaced mouth.

*

It was Fat Carmel who put the night-walking idea back in my head, a fortnight or so of sleepless nights after I first came back here.

There had been a funeral service earlier that day. A woman who lived in the cul-de-sac – 'You must have known her surely?' Carmel seemed surprised, even irked, when I'd said no.

You'd never set eyes on her in daylight, Carmel went on to explain, 'It was like she could only see in the dark. She would go walking all hours, in all weathers – you had to wonder if she'd been quite right in the head.'

From the flat above the shop, Carmel had often seen her setting off, this woman and her dog, just as she herself had been going to bed after a late night of stocktaking or cooking the books. And there'd even been times when, lifting the early newspapers from the pavement, she'd actually spotted the woman returning from her rambles, as if the poor creature had actually walked through the night. 'Always she wore a scarf on her head and carried a stick. The dog – a border collie. Put you in mind of the queen, she would, the whole shape and make of her. Although not so much toward the end, the flesh walked off herself: a skin-and-bone scarecrow and not much else really. Surely you know who I mean?' Carmel had almost implored.

I said – 'She probably moved here after I left. In which case I wouldn't have known her.'

But no, she was an old-timer, Carmel was certain. 'You could always tell the old-timers,' she said, 'never rrrude exactly, but then again never overly friendly; more closed into themselves – don't you see?'

I said – 'I haven't a clue who you mean.'

It was, of course, Karl's mother, Mrs Donegan. Mrs Donegan pounding the highways and byways. Mrs Donegan, year after year, mile after mile, trying to walk the poison out of her system.

And so, I simply substituted myself and my dog for Mrs Donegan and hers and, for a while, these night walks – until the vet ordered otherwise – were to become the best part of my life.

An Indian summer. The dog had seemed fit enough then, still up for the distance, although this may have had something to

do with the little red pills I'd been told to mix into his dinner –
steroids, I would later discover.

Each night we would leave by the back road, avoiding the
village and the sentry box that was Carmel's first-floor window,
and walk down into the neighbouring village, there joining the
river shortly after it skulks out of Arlows' land. We stuck to the
tow path, walking until my legs grew heavy, my mind light and
my sense of awareness at once blunted and strangely heightened.
This was the sensation I was after. It made me forget myself
– who I was or where I had been. I was somebody else now:
somebody young, more carefree and even maybe even cared for.

On the way back I often found myself nursing the girlish
notion that my father would be waiting in the hall for me, arms
folded – 'And just where do you think you've been at this hour
of the night?'

Even though – apart from that one exception – he had never
done any such thing in his life.

In my mind, my home then had still been New York. I was
going home any day soon. As soon as my mother's affairs had
been settled. As soon as I'd settled on a suitable nurse for my
father. As soon as he'd settled into his new routine or when his
old housekeeper had come back from her trip to Australia and
settled back into hers.

All September, I kept telling myself that. All September I'd
been telling Diana, long-distance. I used the word 'settled' a lot.

At first, she was all understanding, small gushes of sympathy
coming down the phone: 'Listen, sweetheart, if you need to
stay, then you stay. But let me say, if you're still interested in
selling your share of the business, I got people here pounding
on the door.'

'I don't remember saying I was interested.'

'Well, if you are. You know it makes sense.'

'I just need a little time.'

'You need time – you take it. So call me next week – okay?'
'I need more than a week, Diana.'
'I know, hon, I know. Just call me anyway, okay?'

The river route was a simple rectangle – down one side, over a
bridge, back on the opposite side. Yet there were times when I
lost my bearings and hardly knew which country I was in, never
mind what side of the river I should be on. I would find myself
becoming afraid and unable to grasp how I got to be there or
how I was ever going to find my way back. I could only think
of the night as a place then – a solid destination with a roof and
walls. On the way out I was walking into it; on the way back I
was walking out of it again.

The stone bridge – the last one before the first of the city
bridges took over – was where we stopped for a rest. I bought a
packet of cigarettes and planned on smoking one a night while
I leaned on the wall of the bridge. I felt it gave me an excuse to
be standing there.

The dog looking at me head cocked – what the hell is she
doing now?

'I'm smoking and, yes, it tastes vile.'

It made me feel sick and it made me think of my mother,
her late conversion to smoking, and so I soon knocked it on
the head.

Standing there, I had often looked down and noticed things
I'd missed moments before when I'd walked right by them, like
the swans asleep on the mooring ledge. And once, wedged into
a rowing boat and swaddled in a quilt, a tramp caught in the
milky light of the moon.

Suddenly it was early November and the dog reluctant to go
any further. As I pulled him along the river path, I remembered
the first night I'd brought him this way and how fit he'd seemed
then, trotting beside and, indeed, often ahead of me. The
blackberry bushes had been loaded with fruit then. Now the

berries had gone and in the river lights the naked brambles were rolls of barbed wire. Across the way, the boat clubs had been closed up for the night, sleeping canoes spooned into each other, and I stood there counting back through the weeks and realised that my mother had been buried three months ago to the day. Three months and ten days since I'd left New York.

I could hear the muffled chattering of the nearby weir. Trapped noise in a hollow place. When I closed my eyes, the sound grew stronger and I was reminded of another time when I'd stood alone in the dark and thought about the death of someone I'd once been close to.

That was over thirty years ago and I had just turned eighteen, the first time I'd helped Serena out in one of those sleek Manhattan art galleries. I was standing in the wings, waiting for the supervisor's bell to ring out; the tray, loaded with hundreds of flimsy bits on sticks, was a strain on my arms and I was worrying about how to keep it all aligned when the lights theatrically cut. And even though I had been told this would happen – it still caught me off guard. For a few short seconds, I was listening to a great noise without being able to see where it was coming from. And a terrifying ache of grief rushed through me, jamming the breath inside my chest so that I almost dropped the tray. It was as if everything that had happened over the past year and more had honed into those few seconds of me standing there in the darkness, trying to hold onto the weight of a tray. The bell tinkled and tinkled again. The lights came back up and I looked down on a moving collage of cackling faces, while in one elegant, synchronised movement trays of canapés appeared out of every corner and began gliding down all the flights of steel stairs.

Someone behind me was shouting, 'Go, go, go. Move it, move it, will ya, just move it!'

I remembered all this and then wiped it away and looked down at the dog. He was shivering hard. His weary, watery eyes looking back up at me. It was time to take him home.

The noise of the weir or the gallery, or both, stayed in my head then settled down into a low level tinnitus. There was the sound of calmer water now muttering alongside me. And other small nocturnal voices: squeaking, croaking, purring from trees and rushes. Behind all that the lonely sound of night trains being shunted in a nearby railway yard. I listened carefully to every note of this, knowing well this would be the last of these walks. Tomorrow I would take the dog to see the vet; tomorrow I knew what he was going to say.

The night walks had been more or less played out by then anyhow: the distance had been shrinking each time; the occasions had become less frequent. It was getting too cold. The dog was tired. I was tired. We were both too old for adventures. And it had started to become dangerous. The winter nights had brought an exodus of junkies and drunks out from the city. They were making little nests under the trees near to the river bank and in the carcass of a house that stood on the north bank.

I begrudged them the house. It was a house I used to see long ago from the top of the bus, when it still had a roof and windows and people. When I was a child I used to make a secret wish that I might live in it, as a grown woman. Because that's all I had wanted then: a house not joined at the hip to another house – nothing facing it but a straight road into the city. Nothing behind it but a cut of glistening river. When I was ten years old, it was the house of my future. A house filled with children I had no faces for; a man I couldn't begin to imagine except that he was talkative. I would have more than one person to rely on for company. I would have more than one friend – in fact, I would have to have a special room built to accommodate them. In my child's head I had it furnished from pictures I'd seen in my mother's magazines: long low sofas, a raised central fireplace, a basket chair that hung out of the ceiling. A double door would lead out to the back lawn, a short path to the river, where all my friends and all my children and my talkative, friendly husband and I could swim in the summer with the swans and the ducks and the salmon.

Now the smoke from the vagrants' bonfires was worming its way up through the trees by the house and from the house itself, creeping through its broken crown, the cracks in its walls, the gouged out sockets of its former windows. There was the noxious smell of burning fodder: old tyres, broken furniture. The swaying sound of drunken voices. The stench of open-air, makeshift latrines.

On the way back I stopped in a phone kiosk in the neighbouring village.

Back to her old self, Diana came on the phone – 'Where the fuck have you been?'

'Did you talk to Patty?' I asked.

'She'll sell, if you will.'

'Right. Let me think about it.'

'Don't you want to know how much first? Don't you want to know the offer they've made? The money, Elaine – don't you want to know the *money?*'

'It's not about the money.'

'Well, what the fuck is it about then?'

'Just let me deal with the idea of it first.'

'It seems pretty simple to me, Elaine. Do you want to stay there?'

'No – I don't know.'

'Okay then. So you want to come back?'

'No – I mean, I don't know. Look, if I do sell, I want Patty to get the greater cut.'

'What are you *saying?*'

'I want her to take my half share. I'll take her quarter. I'll sign over.'

'That's not how Serena wanted it—'

'It's how I want it. Look, I'll call you.'

'No. You're not disappearing on me again. I'll call *you*, day after tomorrow. You better have an answer then. What's your number?'

'I don't have one.'

'You don't have a phone in your house? Is that what you're saying? You don't have a—'

'I *do*. I can't talk on it – I mean, I can't talk in privacy. I want this to be private.'

'Well, get a cell phone then. Jesus, you can afford one!'

'I don't want a cell phone. Look, I'll call you. Soon. I promise.'

*

The nights can feel endless now. I listen to the symphony of snoring coming up through the ceiling of my father's room and try to remember if I ever heard him snore when I was a child. I get up and walk around the house. If my eyes aren't too tired, I might read. I get back into bed and count my breaths to a hundred. I get up and walk around again.

I give in and take a pill and then I sleep and then I dream. And when I wake it's morning and time to start over.

When I dream of a place, it's usually New York. The long, hard shadows above me, the side streets where a piece of light can occasionally fall like something lost out of a pocket. And the sky is a geometric pattern cut according to the rooftops of buildings. If they are buildings. They could be something else, of course – *I* could be something else. A mouse or a vole, maybe, zigzagging through the maze of trenches, sniffing for a familiar gap to squeeze through, never looking up because the cut-out sky is too far away to make any real difference to my tiny life.

When I dream about people, I dream about Agatha. I see her

in all sorts of scenarios; I speak to her. Sometimes I can't see her
at all, but I know she's the one who is leading me. She takes me
by the hand and tells me to watch my step. I hear her laugh; I
smell grown-up perfume and ask her about it. 'My mother,' she
says, 'sent it from London.'

I smell a heavy stench of tobacco on her hair: it smells of
wood and nuts and dirty socks.

'Maggie,' she tells me. 'One of her French cigarettes.'

'Liar,' I say, 'on both counts.'

She laughs, and then we both laugh.

In my dream, everything is dark but I feel the sun on my
face so I know it can't be night-time. Around me, I hear the
sound of bottles clinking in plastic bags. There are other voices.
Giddy voices. Boys, girls. The path is rough and slopes down;
ahead is the sound of a river. The smell of hash already burning.
Behind us, a whinny from a horse. Nearly there, Agatha says
and squeezes my hand, nearly there.

6
Summer Past
June

T<small>WICE A WEEK</small> A<small>GATHA</small> is allowed to come on a visit; twice more she's allowed to call on the phone. The days in between won't go away. Time will not budge: time is a big fat hippo stuck in a mud wallow. On such days, not even her journal can console her. She flicks back over the pages and finds it hard to believe that since coming out of hospital, so many days could have come and already be gone.

Agatha stays for exactly one hour – the hour between Elaine's afternoon nap and her evening medication. Those are the rules, her mother says, like it or lump it. For the moment she likes it. Elaine knows that in another few days she will be allowed to cross the road to visit Agatha and that when Rachel Shillman comes home from school next week it will be just like old times, the three of them in their own private capsule, sealed against the rest of the neighbourhood. Three girls, three houses, three back gardens until, without her mother really noticing, the restrictions will have gradually loosened into a general hanging around: the cul-de-sac, the wider neighbourhood, the riverbank, the valley. She feels a change coming on, a sense of something broadening, and wonders if it has to do with the new girl moving into the Osbornes' old house.

When Agatha comes for her visit, Mrs Hanley brings her across the road. Elaine will listen to the women fussing her friend up the stairs to her bedroom. Her mother anxious and inclined to be squeaky if there is the slightest hesitation on Agatha's part. Mrs Hanley quietly encouraging, although she must know that her niece would prefer a case of stairs with a

sturdy banister any day to an unfamiliar street or a room of
strange furniture.

When Elaine hears her mother squeal, 'Oh, careful, dear,
careful there, mind now, mind,' she knows Agatha is pretending
to falter just so they can laugh about it later on.

The two women leave; there is silence in the room. The girls listen to the footsteps go back down the stairs and then to Elaine's
mother asking – as usual – if Mrs Hanley has time for a cup of
tea and Mrs Hanley regretting – as usual – that she has so much
to do. The front door then closes. The kitchen door opens. Agatha and Elaine burst out laughing.

They are giddy together. Everything is funny. Everything
and everyone is there to be laughed at.

'What does my mother look like from a distance?' Agatha
begins. She is sitting across the end of the bed, back against the
wall.

'I've told you a million times.'

'Then tell me a million and one.'

'Young. Your mother looks young. Way younger than mine,
younger than most mothers I know, except maybe Patty's.'

'Patty Cake?'

'Patty Cake.'

'Okay, four more words about my mother.'

'Young . . .'

'You said that.'

'Slim. Hair. Tall. Walk. Blonde.'

'Not beautiful?'

'Sometimes.'

'Only sometimes?'

'Well, she can look a bit sour.'

'Sour! You never said that before . . .'

'You know – as if there's a smell coming from the drains or
something.'

Agatha screams out a laugh. 'Yes! Yes, that's right. I know exactly what you mean. Is that all? Impression then, what overall impression does she give?'

She doesn't want to say that Agatha's mother gives the impression of someone apart, someone who is always en route to some other place; that she has a way of either walking ahead or lagging behind everyone else. She doesn't want to say that she has noticed how Agatha's mother always seems to stay close to the door of whatever room she happens to be in, as if waiting for a chance to slip out.

'Well?' Agatha says,

'No. That's all.'

'I knew it. Shallow. Empty. That's why she's an actress, why she's good at pretending to be other people. She's like a jug, filling herself up with them.'

'I'm sure you're wrong.'

'Are you? Anyway. Your mother's turn. What does she look like then – five words.'

'Oh God, Agatha, *please* don't ask me that . . .' Elaine says, a remark that throws them into convulsions.

Agatha claims to see conversations. Words are blown like bubbles into a room, she says, some melt in an instant, others catch and float off – people then follow. The bubbles grow in number; they rise and fall, buckle – reshape. One careless flick of the hand and it's all over. She says that's why the floor is always wet at the parties her mother throws, hundreds of burst bubbles all over the floor. Either that or they've pissed in their pants.

'You talk more rubbish than ever,' Elaine says, 'you and your stupid bubbles.'

'I don't talk rubbish. I talk shit.' Agatha smiles and reaches out her hand. 'I hear you're skinny now,' she says. 'Are you skinny now? Let me see your skinniness so.'

Agatha uses these 'seeing' words about herself all the time:

'Let me see now, oh, I *seeee*. The way I look at is . . . I must watch out for that. Well, I don't see why not . . .'

When they first became friends Elaine used to worry that Agatha didn't realise she was blind. That she didn't know other people in the world could actually see the things they were touching. She was eleven then, Agatha just gone thirteen. Months later they had grown close enough for Elaine to tell her that and for Agatha to think it was funny.

'Actually, I used to see,' she said then, 'until I was five-and-a-half anyway. There was an accident.'

'An accident?'

'Oh but I never talk about that.'

Elaine didn't press her. There were plenty of things she didn't talk to Agatha about either. Her parents, the Hanleys, all that.

'All right,' Elaine says, 'here's my skinniness so.'

She places her arm on Agatha's outstretched palm, feels a cuff of cool fingers on her wrist.

'What's this I'm looking at here?' Agatha asks. 'Is it your neck?'

Elaine makes a choking sound and Agatha laughs.

She keeps her wrist and adjusts her hold slightly. 'Okay, which letter are we on today?'

'I'm not sure,' Elaine says, 'you keep hopping all over the alphabet.'

Agatha's mother wants her to be a teacher. She is teaching Elaine the deafblind alphabet so that when she goes to the interview for teacher training college she can say, I've already taught the alphabet to my seeing friend. A better reason, Agatha says, is that they can gossip about people, right in front of their faces. They can say anything they like and no one will know.'

'I know all the vowels and some of the consonants,' Elaine says, 'so when can I start making real words?'

She feels Agatha's fingers, like a nimble crab, clamber all over her hand, pinch the top of her index finger then make shapes against her palm.

'What? What does that say?'

Agatha does it again, this time a little slower, saying the words as she presses them out. 'Patience. Is. A. Virtue. You. Impatient. Cow.'

Elaine pulls her hand away and takes Agatha by the wrist, making three slow, uncertain moves, on her palm, the tip of her finger, the curve along the side of her thumb and index finger.

'B. I. C.' Agatha says. 'What's that supposed to mean?'

'When you teach me T and H you'll know.'

Agatha laughs and gives her a shove that topples her right off the bed.

Elaine steadies herself, then stands. 'That hurt, you know,' she says.

'Sorry.'

'That really–'

'Okay! Okay – sorry, I said. Ah no, Elaine, really, I am.'

Agatha reaches into the pocket of her skirt. 'I have chocolate. Swiss chocolate?'

She holds the bar out to Elaine, who stops rubbing her arm and steps forward. She breaks a piece off then gives it back to Agatha.

'And where, may I ask, did you get Swiss chocolate?' Elaine says, mimicking her father in court – or how she imagines him to be in court, because she's never actually seen him there.

'From a man, of course. I don't think I can remember his name.'

'You took chocolate from a man and you don't recall his name? And would you like to tell the court what you did in exchange for this bar of delicious Swiss chocolate?'

'I yodelled.'

'Might I remind you that you are under oath?'

'Under who? No, no, that definitely wasn't his name.'

Elaine laughs and breaks off another piece. 'How was your weekend with the Shillmans anyway?'

'All right. A bit quiet without Rachel. I played with Michael and Danny a bit . . . Ate a lot. You know, the usual. On Sunday night I made a fool of myself and started bawling. Oh God, when I think about it . . .'

'Why? What happened, Agatha, tell me? Quickly, I want to know.'

'He – Mr Shillman – was telling this story about that candlestick thing in their dining-room – a menorah it's called. It belonged to his grandmother. The soldiers took it from her during the war and years later his mother found it in the back of a secondhand shop. Anyway, I started crying . . . I just thought it was the saddest thing. Oh, never mind. I made a fool of myself – that's all. It's a mad house around there – I don't suppose they minded. Oh yeah, and on Saturday night Marvellous Martha got a bit tiddly and had to be put to bed.'

'What happened?'

'Nothing really, just came in pissed.'

'I want to know!'

'Elaine, you can't stay in a person's house for the weekend and then go gossiping about their private business.'

'Oh, I didn't mean to–'

'I'm just teasing you. More chocolate? So what about you? What have you heard, what have you seen? Give me all the dirty details.'

'Jackson.'

'You had sex with him!'

'Don't be disgusting.'

'I thought you were madly in love with him?'

'No!'

'No? I thought of all the men around here, you would do it with . . . ?'

'I only said that because you and Rachel made me pick someone out. Anyway, he's old. He must be at least forty. And I don't even like him. You'd have to like someone at least to have sex with them, wouldn't you?'

'Would you?'

'I heard him slapping the twins when I was out in the garden. Really, I mean, *really* hard. You could hear the wallops two houses away. I think they spilled paint or something over the lawn. But they're only four and puny. The screams!'

'Bastard. He probably rapes his wife too.'

'Agatha!'

Agatha lifts her legs up on the bed and edges her back to the wall. 'Lots of men rape their wives,' she says, 'Maggie Arlow told me. They're like slave owners – they pay for your food, so they think they own you. Quick dart in and out, any time they fancy, then up with their zip and off they go about their business – that's what Maggie says!'

'You've been talking to Maggie?'

'I'm starting to take riding lessons. Aunt Mary thinks it will be good for me to spend time around horses – if only she knew what Maggie will really be teaching me! I'm to learn how to groom them – well, help to groom them. Yesterday Maggie hauled me up on one of the old hunters and led me round the paddock. You can come with me, when you're better.'

'My mother does not approve of Maggie Arlow.'

'Don't tell her then. She won't find out.'

'Oh, Agatha, as if!'

Agatha sucks on the chocolate. 'They all smoke dope around there, you know.'

'Who does? Where?'

'The stables. Two stable lads. And this girl. I haven't spoken to them yet but I've heard them.'

'How do you know then?'

'I recognised the smell.'

'But how?'

'Some of my mother's actor friends, you see, and—'

'I don't believe you! Does Maggie know?'

'I doubt it. She wouldn't smell it over the horses. Not to mention her own smelly, ginny Gitanes breath.'

'She's not smelly – is she?'

'Yes.'

'Agatha, you think everyone is smelly.'

'Everyone is.'

'Am I?'

'Yes, but in a nice way.'

'Shut up. I am not.' Elaine says, holding her T-shirt out by the neck and taking a cautious sniff.

Her mother's voice comes singing up the stairs.

'Elaine? Eeeelaaaine? Eeee-laine?'

'Oh God, what now?'

Elaine goes to the door and opens it.

'Yes?'

'Would you and Agatha like some tea?'

'Would you like some tea, Agatha?' Elaine says, imitating her mother's voice.

Agatha shakes her head.

'No thank you,' she shouts down the stairs.

'Sure now? I have some lovely fruity cake. Ask Agatha if she'd like some fruity cake.'

'She has some lovely fruity cake,' Elaine says to Agatha. 'Would you like some fruity cake?'

'Tell her stick it up her fruity arse,' Agatha says.

'No thank you, just the same. We're fine.'

'Oh well, if you're sure . . .'

Elaine stays at the door for a moment. She notices Agatha is wearing sunglasses again.

'You're wearing sunglasses all the time now?'

Agatha stops smiling and begins to explain. Her mother's idea; she thinks the glasses make her more attractive. She has four pairs now – all identical – in case she can't find the other three and goes out one day and frightens the horses. There's a pair by her bed, another one on the shelf in the wardrobe, one in Aunt Mary's kitchen and, of course, this pair here on her face . . . She must look a sight without them, anyhow, otherwise her mother wouldn't keep pushing her to wear them.

In a sudden movement, she pulls the sunglasses off and asks, 'Better with or without – what d'you think?'

Elaine gets a fright. Agatha's eyes look so much worse than they did the last time she'd seen them up close. That had been at the Shillmans' New Year's Eve party. Then, they had looked like two stray eyes that happened to find themselves stuck in the same face. They didn't match, but they did at least look like eyes. Now they are hard and faded, deformed. She pretends to consider, as if there really could be a choice in the matter, humming and hawing, making as much sound as possible while she searches for the right words to use.

'If I had to choose, I suppose . . . Well, yes. The sunglasses, I think – yes, definitely the glasses. Simply because they make you look so much more glamorous.'

Agatha tosses her toffee-coloured hair away from her shoulders, then guides the wands of the glasses back over her neat little ears, settles them down on her well-shaped nose and smiles her beautiful smile with her perfect teeth.

Elaine can see the hurt in the slight tightening of the upper lip. She knows that Agatha has heard the lie in her voice and has sensed it on the air between them. She knows, too, that Agatha is hurt less by the fact of the lie than by the need for it.

Elaine can't think of the smallest thing to say that can pull them out of this moment. She goes to her dressing table, sits down, stares in at her own big red face, mutters something about the state of her hair and begins brushing it.

Agatha is the one to resume talking, a hard rein on her voice, holding it steady. Her mother doesn't know what the bloody hell she wants. One minute trying to make her look more attractive, the next dragging her aside and growling at her under her breath about modesty. Pulling her hem down, buttoning her up to the neck. 'Modesty! In front of who, like – Ted bloody Hanley?'

She bites down on her bottom lip.

Through the dressing-table mirror, Agatha looks different. Delicate-looking is the term Elaine's mother always uses to describe her, but Agatha doesn't look delicate at all. She looks grown up and maybe even beautiful. At the same time her voice has grown harsher, her temper shorter, her gestures more aggressive. That playful shove a few minutes ago that had knocked her off the bed . . .

She decides to chance a joke: 'Maybe you should arrive to breakfast wearing nothing but the sunglasses, completely naked. Give old Teddy a good heart attack for himself . . .'

Agatha doesn't laugh. 'Good old Teddy,' she says, 'pretending I'm not in the way. Well, trying to pretend anyway.'

'Agatha, they love having you there.'

'She does.'

'All your lovely new dresses and everything. They love spoiling you.'

'*She* does.'

Agatha sits, the sun of early evening on her shoulders, everything about her so still except for the fingers of her left hand which are picking and plucking at a piece of the quilt.

'Do you want to hear Rachel's letter – it came today?' Elaine opens the drawer and pulls out a bunch of envelopes. 'Listen to this . . . Her letters are so funny – I just love . . .'

'No.'

'No?'

'I'm not in the mood, Elaine.'

Elaine puts the letter back into the envelope and then cautiously returns it to the stack in the drawer.

Agatha says, 'I want you to teach me how to smoke.'

'I don't know how to smoke.'

'We should be able to at least smoke! *I* should at my age. I'm like a child, it's ridiculous. It's just fucking ridic–'

'I'm not really supposed to,' Elaine begins, 'my lungs, after, you know, being sick and . . .'

'Oh God. All right. Goody-goody.'

'I'm not a–'

'Well, Rachel will teach me – do you think? Or that American girl?'

'Yes, Patty or Rachel,' Elaine quietly says.

The sunglasses have spoilt the visit. Agatha's voice is agitated; there is also a sense that she might be looking for a row.

'Stuck here all summer,' she says. 'I can just see it now, weeks of Ted and Aunt bloody Mary and utter boredom until I'm packed off to blind school.'

'Nobody is sending you away to blind school. It's a teacher training college.'

'I'm only going because my mother wants it.'

'You'll have a proper job at the end of it. A career.'

'A career. Listen to yourself!'

'I'm only saying . . .'

'I hate blind people. Always feeling you up. I hate my mother too.'

'I know you do.'

'Dumping me on the Hanleys every time she gets a bloody part. All summer I'll be stuck here. All summer. I wish everyone would just leave me alone.'

'Agatha – what's wrong?'

'Nothing.'

'Tell me.'

'If they'd just leave me alone, I'd find my own way . . . I'd figure it out. But they won't, they *can't*. I wish everyone would just fuck off.'

Agatha thumps the bed and then knocks her head with her fist.

'I'm sorry,' she says, 'I'm tired. I'm a crank, I know. It's just that . . .'

'What?'

'I don't know. I'm tired. I'm tired.'

Elaine brings her a pillow. Pressing it into her hand first, so she knows what to expect, then settling it behind her head.

'Not you,' Agatha says, 'I don't mean you. It's not . . . I can't sleep in that glass room in this weather – it's too bloody hot. I've started to sleep in Aunt Mary's shed.'

'Are you allowed?'

'Of course not. I wait till she's finished reading her books and drinking her sneaky red wine and when she goes up to bed I go down the garden. It's cool in there at least. I like it. I bring my quilt.'

'You aren't afraid?'

'Of what, for God's sake – the dark?'

'No, I mean of falling or anything . . .'

'I'm not a simpleton, you know – I learn my way round very quickly. If I'm ever fucking let. Anyway, can we stop talking now. I don't feel like talking.'

'Then don't.'

'All right I won't.'

'Good. I'm sick listening to you anyway.'

'Are you?'

'No. But don't talk if you don't want to. But you still have to give me my lesson.'

Agatha holds the silence for a few seconds and then: 'What is it about the Shillmans – everything they have has to be from some place else?'

'What do you mean?'

'Swiss chocolate, Scotch whisky, French toast.'

'I don't know . . . His job, I suppose.'

Agatha sits up suddenly.

'What does he look like anyway, Shillman? Give me five words.'

'Brown.'

'Brown? Hair, face, eyes – what?'

'All three. Well, sallow skinned.'

'Because he's Jewish?'

'I don't know.'

'Is he handsome?'

'I don't know, Agatha, I've never really looked at him.'

'Well, next time, make sure you do.'

'Why?'

'I want to know everything.'

'But why, Agatha?'

'My mother. She fancies him.'

'She does not!'

'Her voice changes when he comes into the room. She'll be having sex with him next.'

'She can't! He's Rachel's dad.'

'She won't care – she's voracious.'

'Anyway, she's in London.'

'She'll be back for a weekend before the play starts. Aunt Mary is throwing her a party. She'll probably nab him then.'

'Oh, shut up, Agatha, she will not.'

'You know, she pities Aunt Mary for having Ted as a husband. Poor Mary, she always says, imagine having old Teddy Bear going at it on top of you.'

'Maybe she doesn't. Maybe they don't?'

'Oh, she does. They do. I hear the bed, whack, whack, whack against the wall. Lucky for her, it doesn't last long – that's what my mother says. But do you know what I think? I think, good for you, Mary, at least you have someone who stays with you.

More than my mother has anyway. Someone who cares enough
to sleep with her in the same bed every night. More than I'll
ever have, probably.'

'Agatha, you'll meet someone who'll fall in love with you. I
bet you'll get married.'

'Who'd marry me? Unless it's someone blind. The thoughts
of all that fumbling around and clawing . . .'

Agatha holds the pillow and slides sideways down on the
bed where she lies in a curve, sunglasses slightly askew.

Elaine sits on the dressing-table stool and looks at her own
face in the mirror: worried, embarrassed. The silence. She wishes
Rachel was here to break the silence.

Until Agatha sniggers. 'Whack, whack, whack,' she says.

And now they are screeching with laughter again.

*

When Agatha leaves, Elaine goes into the bathroom, wets the
corner of a towel then brings it back to the bedroom and tries
to clean the chocolate stain that her friend's hand has worked
into the nap of the quilt. In the end she is left with two stains: a
big water mark shaped like a pond and inside that, on the lower
right hand side, the smaller, darker mark of the original stain.

After tea, she sees Agatha and Mrs Hanley going out for their
evening stroll, Agatha's white cane sniffing ahead. Agatha and
her aunt are deep in conversation – about the party for Agatha's
mother, she supposes: what guests they should invite, what food
to serve, what they will need to buy.

Elaine remembers the time – the only time – her parents had
been invited to a Hanley party. Her mother had come home
early. After little more than an hour, in fact. She had said it
was because she couldn't possibly leave Elaine that long on her
own. But she hadn't been on her own: Mrs Preston had been
babysitting.

Mrs Preston had babysat a few times before, but only in the

afternoon when her mother had to go to the hairdresser or had some mysterious errand to take care of in town. Mrs Preston had one grown-up son who lived abroad. She had shown Elaine a photograph of him once – a big bald man with a red face standing behind the counter in a pub that she said he owned, in a town that was more than a thousand miles away.

The photograph had confused Elaine; she kept getting mixed up and saying – But don't you mean he's your brother? Or is he your uncle then? Your husband's big brother?

She could not get it into her head – the idea of Mrs Preston having a son who was practically an old man.

She had liked many things about Mrs Preston: her elegant way of sitting on the sofa and the way she smelled like lemon icing when you sat down beside her. More than anything else, the way she could draw like a demon. Whatever you asked for – horses, dogs, cats, houses. Thrilling versions of Elaine in costume: Elaine as a ballerina, Bo-Peep Elaine, Maid Marian Elaine. Elaine as a bride. Elaine with the Wimbledon cup held over her head.

One minute there would be a blank page on a sketch pad then Mrs Preston's hand would start scuttling around and, out of that page, a whole new life sprouted. For those few moments Mrs Preston would disappear. Elaine always wanted her to slow down so she could catch the pencil lines in the act, maybe learn a few of their tricks. But Mrs Preston never slowed down, her hand always moving as if it was drawing against time.

The one thing she had disliked about Mrs Preston was the way she took the sketch pad home with her, pretending not to hear whenever Elaine had asked – or even occasionally begged – to keep a drawing of herself, for herself.

The night her mother came home early from the Hanley party, Mrs Preston's head jumped up from her drawing and twisted towards the hall. She was on her feet then, flapping the cover of her sketch pad over and stuffing it into her basket. Her face all red as if she'd been caught doing something shameful.

She said, 'But it's early yet, Mrs Nichols, if you want to go back to the party, I don't mind staying in the least.'

'Not at all, Mrs Preston,' her mother had said, 'thank you just the same, but, really, enough is enough.'

At the sitting-room door, Elaine had seen her mother reach out, as if trying to catch Mrs Preston's hand.

'Oh no, no, Mrs Nichols,' Mrs Preston said, 'you've only been gone an hour, I couldn't really.'

'Of course you could,' Elaine's mother said, and Mrs Preston's red face nodded and mumbled a thank you.

A short time later, Elaine and her mother were sitting up in bed spying out the window, Elaine drinking cocoa, her mother sipping a tumbler of sherry and describing the party she had just left behind.

Her voice, light and girlish, had been barely recognisable. She used words Elaine had never heard her use before, such as 'super' and 'quite frankly'. She described people as 'sweet' as if you could eat them. And Elaine had wondered then if, as well as special shoes and fancy hair styles, adults had a special voice and special words they brought with them to parties.

There had been cheese cubes on sticks, her mother explained. Paté and olives, some of them stuffed with a red thing in the middle that made them look like green eyeballs and had quite put her off.

You could have punch from a big cut-glass bowl.

'Punch!'

'Yes, it's a mixture of drinks. It's called punch because it's so strong it can knock you out.'

'Knock you out – at a party?'

You could have red wine or white wine or gin and tonic. There were slices of lemon *and* lime. Some of the men drank whiskey and soda that came squirting out of a real syphon like you'd see in a hotel or maybe on the television.

'And what about you?' Elaine asked. 'Did you have *punch?*'

'Oh no. Certainly not. A mineral, that's all.'

'But why only a mineral?'

'Because it's not lady-like, in my opinion, to drink alcohol in public.'

Only a select few of the neighbours had been invited: Doctor Townsend and his wife, of course – she had a lovely cream frock on and as for her shoes! Mrs Jackson was, of course, done up like a Christmas tree and, frankly, ridiculous. Mrs Osborne had been there with her sensible cardigan and her monotonous voice. The Ryans weren't there – probably not asked and is it any wonder?

Maggie Arlow was half-drunk when she arrived, although she was wearing a super Chinese-style jacket. She was playing up to Terry Jackson in the most disgraceful manner. Of course, she wasn't the only one to go down *that* particular avenue. The Shillmans, of course, were very much at home, being similar types to the Hanleys, obviously well used to one another's company.

Most of the people had been extremely well-spoken even if one or two were not quite respectable. But then artistic people were often that way. Even so, everyone – apart from the neighbours – had an interesting side to them. Mary Hanley had introduced her around like a special guest. And as for Ted? He was so sweet. Well, Ted couldn't – just couldn't have been sweeter, frankly. He offered her a cigarette and when she'd said no, he'd offered her a different variety, in case the first had been a little too strong for her. Ted had said she was 'the perfect lady'. It had been the best night of her life.

'Better even than your wedding day?' Elaine had asked her mother.

In the dark there had been a pause, then a quickly mumbled – 'Don't be silly, of course not.'

When her mother fell asleep, Elaine had stayed at the

window. She could hear the party sounds pop out whenever the front door opened: laughing, talking, music. She saw the people who arrived late and the people who lingered at the door saying long goodbyes. She saw a man and a woman kissing in the shadows and then jumping apart when the Hanleys' porch door opened. And she began to understand why it was that her mother had left the party early. It was for the same reason she always seemed to enjoy looking at the photos from a holiday far more than she had ever seemed to enjoy the holiday itself.

It had been the middle of the night when her father finally came through the Hanleys' front door. She watched him shake Ted Hanley's hand on the doorstep, then turn and walk down the slope to the gate before coming back over the road with his hands in his pockets. In the streetlight she could see his stern, unhappy face.

She had tried to imagine him at the party – who he would have spoken to and what he could have said. If he had sat down on a chair or remained standing up all night. Or maybe he slipped off into an empty room and sat at a table on his own in the dark.

Ted Hanley had stayed on the doorstep saying goodbye to his guests; now shaking this man's hand, now helping that woman into her coat. How she had wished her mother had been awake to see him looking so pleasant. She would have just loved the way he was drawing the coat over the woman's shoulders, and the way he kissed her then on both sides of her face, the way the French were said to do.

It was natural to presume that not only did her mother love Ted Hanley but that she was a result of that love. Because she couldn't see the point of the man who had just passed under her window and through the front door. This man who ate dinner on his own, read newspapers on his own, went racing on his own. Even spoke to unknown people on his own private telephone. This man who watched television in another room.

7
Winter Present
December

THERE'S A BLACK GUY standing on the doorstep. I am taken aback by the sight of him and know this must show on my face.

There's a chance he'll think I'm racist but there's not a lot I can do about that. Unless I say something like, 'Listen pal, you're not the first black man I've ever set eyes on. Places I worked in New York? Every second person was black. And as for Paris, where I trained? Not one white face amongst the porter staff, which says a lot for the French and their so-called sense of equality – wouldn't you agree?'

I'm having this conversation in my own little head with this guy on my doorstep who is so magnificently, so unbelievably gorgeous it's almost ridiculous.

Sunlight shoves through the cracks in the clouds and at the same time it has started to snow again. Not real flakes as such – more like silver dust motes in this sudden gush of light. It flatters my visitor anyhow as he stands there in his white overalls, snow specks fussing around him. It gives him the look of a big black angel.

He holds out a business card. I take it from his long hand: fawn-coloured palm and round pinkish fingertips.

I read the card then glance up at eyes that appear to be lacquered with light – a deep green light – and ask myself how is that possible?

He takes a few steps back into the garden and lifts his face towards the roof.

I can see now he is well put together – far from slim but not too bulky either – comfortable, as if he's been upholstered in soft

brown leather. I can't help but notice his shoulders. I wonder
how old he is and reckon on twenty-eight. Then I wonder about
the shape of his feet and if he's married. Somehow I know he's
not gay. For a split second, I see him standing naked at the side
of my bed, my mother's lilac-coloured quilt crumpled behind
him.

He brings his eyes from the roof and looks straight at me.

'One moment, please,' I primly say.

I go into the sitting-room. My father, in his wheelchair in front
of the television, appears to be watching the racing at Chepstow, the sound so low he couldn't possibly be able to hear it.
I suspect he's just staring at the coloured shapes jostling about
on the screen. He's lost interest. Today's newspaper, like the rest
of the papers for the past week or more, lies untouched on the
bed, within its folds the racing section still intact. And he hasn't
eaten his lunch again.

'There's someone to see you,' I say, 'and you haven't eaten
your lunch again.'

'I'm not hungry.'

I'm a little surprised when he says this, as he has never struck
me as someone who was motivated by hunger but rather one
of those men who eat whatever is put in front of them. Besides,
with my mother, he probably never had that much chance to
work up an actual appetite before the next plate was shoved
under his nose.

'That's the fourth day in a row that you haven't touched your
lunch. Lynette tells me you're losing weight. You know, she
wants to call the doctor?'

He ignores me.

'Look, you can't carry on like this – you need your
nourishment, especially in this weather. You have to eat
something. I mean, you left half of your breakfast and last night–'

He turns his head and we exchange a brief and startled

look – it's as if the voice of my mother has just entered the room.

'It's okay,' I say. 'You don't have to eat if you don't want. Don't worry. Fine. It's all fine.'

I hand him the business card; he looks down and says, 'Fenton?'

The old lawyer's glint comes into his eye. His bottom lip pushes slightly forward, one unruly eyebrow gets ready to pop out of his forehead: I imagine these to be two courtroom gestures that have served him well over the years. There's a pause before his eye glides back to the witness. 'Am I to understand that he is, in fact, alive?'

I say nothing.

'Send him in so,' he says, smugly tapping the card off the side of his hand.

I lift the plate and begin to move away. 'You may find him a little changed,' I say.

I would just love to see his face when Othello walks into the room but I'm afraid I might laugh. And I don't like my father to see me laugh.

Lynette is standing with her coat on when I come back into the kitchen, patiently waiting to resume our conversation. 'It's snowing again,' I say. 'And you should see the guy who just walked into the sitting-room.'

'This weather,' she says, 'this country.'

'No, I mean it, you should see him.'

She looks at the untouched sandwich then gives her worried sigh. She thinks my father is pining for company, for conversation, for something. I wonder if she may be in love with him. When she talks about him, I sometimes have difficulty understanding just who she means. I wish she'd sit down and talk about something else for a change: tell me about what she does in the evenings, about the village in Malaysia where she grew up, about Hong Kong where her married sister is living. I want to distract her, to get her to change the record anyhow, if only for a moment or two.

'What I miss about New York,' I begin, '*all* I miss about New York, I sometimes think, are the seasons: the well-defined, no-ifs-or-buts about it seasons. I like knowing when it's time to pack one lot of clothes away and take out another. I like knowing which direction the heating bills are going. In summer the humidity will wipe you out; in winter the snow will move in and take over your life. But generally speaking, spring comes at spring time. Autumn in the fall. I'm not saying the weather is completely predictable – and we do have our treacherous days. But? At least you more or less know where you are. And, well, I miss that.'

Lynette continues to look at me, even after I've finished. 'Maybe that's why people here so insecure,' she finally decides, 'never know what come next.'

I look past her out into the garden. This morning started out with ice-spiked rain from a low grey sky. A while ago we had big fat snow clouds. Now it could be summer out there but for the veins of black shadow from the winter branches and the occasional confetti of snow.

'Too lonely,' Lynette is saying, 'need friends. Everybody need friends.'

'My father?'

'Of course.'

'You think so?'

'And no God.'

'No God?'

'No church. Church good place for people. Meet friends. One roof. All same. Before I come here, everyone say, ahhh, that good country for Christians. Where then? When then? I don't see. Old man and never one neighbour visit. To take for walk. To talk. Clever man and no one ask advice? In my country? In my country, a man like your father? He is honoured. Not like this way. A old forgotten no one, is all.'

She begins to put on her gloves, her cheeks reddened by her little outburst.

'Do you know, Lynette,' I say, 'he used to go to church on Sunday. Sometimes he even went to a Latin mass in town.'

'What Latin mass? Where? We could take him.'

'I think the church has closed down. There were gates on it anyway, last time I passed, big iron gates, a padlock.'

She shakes a sad head and begins to button up her coat.

'You think what I say before?'

'Before?'

'Community centre, senior socials? Whole day sometimes, all meals, breakfast time to tea. Games, singing. A tour in bus to interesting places.'

'Ah yes, the senior social days.'

I try to imagine my father sitting in the centre of a game of bingo or lifting his hands over his head for wheelchair Pilates or maybe playing 'Jingle Bells' on the piano for the Christmas sing-along. Then I try not to laugh.

'I'm sorry, Lynette, I'm afraid he's not really that kind of man.'

'I know,' she says, 'I know you say that.'

I think of the stony face on him whenever I enter his room, the strickening silence. And for a second I've a good mind to let her bring him. To allow him a day amongst people who are trying to make the most of the last scraps of their lives. It might give him a taste of what it would actually be like to live in a nursing home. To be spoken to by condescending voices, in overheated rooms. To be talked down to by people of lesser intelligence. To eat dinner at noon and supper at six, be put to bed at nine o'clock like a child. To have to watch afternoon soap operas on television instead of the racing from Chepstow. To be denied his piano and his evening whiskey. To be patronised and ignored and made to feel worthless.

'Lynette, my father is an unusual man.'

'Yes, yes, and I know that too.'

She lifts her large handbag. It looks far too grown-up for her. I half expect to see her clopping off in her mother's high-heels.

'What about cleaning lady,' she asks, 'she talk to him?'

'I suppose.'

'Nice woman, though? Friendly?'

'I don't know her. She doesn't start back till next week – she's been away, you see. In Australia.'

'But your father say she work here ten years before.'

'I wasn't here then.'

'A whole ten year?'

'I left here when I was sixteen years old.'

'Oh, that right. That right. But I thought in between . . .'

'I only came back when my mother died.'

'When or because?'

She bows her head. 'So sorry, I don't mean . . .'

'That's all right, Lynette.'

'How many time she come here a week – Missus, Missus . . .?'

'Larkin? Four, I think.'

'He didn't say?'

'No, he didn't say anything.'

'Few times a week, though – you think? '

'I imagine so, yes.'

'Not so much for you to do then?'

'Not so much. No.'

When Lynette leaves, I find myself examining the sandwich. I have to wonder what possessed me to make such a thing in the first place: plastic ham, plastic cheese, styrofoam bread, a gob of mango chutney in the middle. Would I eat this sandwich myself? Only if I was about to die of starvation and it was the last sandwich left on earth. I hate this sandwich and everything about it. I hate all the replicas of this sandwich that I have been making, over and over, since my return – so why make it at all?

The answer is simple: I make it because it's the sandwich my mother would have made. It's the sort of sandwich I ate in my own childhood and the sort I saw my father eat countless times when I was young. I made it for the same reason I've been making most of his meals: because I believe it's what he's used to – and I have it in my head that he's the sort of man who can only approve of whatever he's used to. So that's: beef, spuds, peas and cabbage – plop, plop, splat on the plate; a puddle of powder-made gravy. Fried fish on Friday and Wednesday, mash, peas; a puddle of powder-made white sauce. Chicken and roast potatoes on Sunday. An occasional cutlet of salmon and boiled potatoes without a speck of skin on their souls. Steak and chips on Saturday night. Porridge and toast for breakfast; egg and bacon on Sunday. Sandwich and yoghurt for lunch. Tea and cake in the afternoon. Brown bread and hot milk before bed. On Christmas day   and I can't begin to imagine the fun that's going to be! – I'm planning on going crazy and boiling the arse off a few brussels sprouts to complement his overcooked, cloth-dry turkey.

Quantity before quality has always been the motto of this kitchen and no one can say I've failed to respect that.

I am thin – even by New York standards. Too thin. In the past few months my palate has gradually died. I eat when it occurs to me to eat. Or I eat bits of whatever my father eats with a few concessions thrown in: olive oil, garlic, real cheese – when and if I can be bothered to go to the supermarket.

Three months ago, I came back to this house, walked into this kitchen, put on my mother's apron and picked up exactly where she left off. And now, without saying a word, he's telling me to stuff it. He's saying he'd rather die than eat another mouthful of her cooking. And I know exactly how he feels.

From the sitting-room comes the sound of men's voices. I had forgotten about our visitor and for a moment am unsettled. It's not that I'm unused to the sound of voices: radio voices,

voices on the television, Lynette's metallic stacatto when she's tending to my father. Even the voices of domestic appliances as they go about their daily business. But this is different, the voices of real men talking, and it snags on the routine soundtrack of this house.

I pick up the dog's bowl, drop the sandwich into it then open a tin of dog food and fold thick brown lumps into the mixture. The dog is behind me, panting with joy. I bring the dish to his corner and watch him snap it all up.

I don't want my father starving to death – not on my watch anyhow.

I want him to live. I want him to live till he runs out of money and can no longer afford to pay Lynette or the cleaner. I want him to live until he is beholden to me and my willingness to stay in this house.

I want him to live long and hard, and above all lonely.

I go round the kitchen and begin rooting through cupboards. Then I go out to the garage and venture into the misty depths of the freezer: a few small sliced pans, a single baguette, a stack of radioactive dinners in foil cartons. And a few odd-shaped blocks that look like body parts crammed into freezer bags on which I can see, without actually looking, my mother's handwriting in black felt marker: *use by this date.* I dig out the baguette. On the way back into the kitchen, I reach up to a nail in the corner, unhook a net of onions and a rope of garlic that I put there, in a rare moment of optimism, last week. Or maybe that was the week before last.

Back in the kitchen, I stand at the sink and wonder what now.

In the sitting-room, the muffled conversation continues: the roofer's rumble is low and steady; my father's contribution is lighter and more seldom. I can't make out the words but I can listen, as Agatha once taught me to listen, to the undercurrent of a conversation. Their voices move well together; there is an occasional collision but one always makes way for the other and it's clear they are getting along. After a moment, a new sound begins to edge into the frame and now it takes over. A weaving, velvety sound. Swift. Now swifter. Urgent. I listen until I've it figured out. It's the voice of the racing commentator, flowing along with the horses across the track, increasing in speed as they increase, finally bringing the race to its thundering, climactic shudder. A second or so of respectful silence before the men resume their conversation.

So that's what they're at. My father and this stranger – this male stranger. They are in there, in my mother's sitting-room, watching racing on her television.

Of course it's his room now; the room where he sleeps and plays his piano; where he eats and watches television: the room where he now lives. But I still think of it as my mother's sitting-room and I still think of my invalid father as something of a trespasser.

It was there she used to watch *her* television. It was there she closed *her* door after she'd placed my father's lone dinner plate on the kitchen table with his 'sweet', as she called it, a short stretch to the right. She wrote her lists and her letters in there, read her magazines and her raunchy novels. Smoked her cigarettes. Once when a diet instructor advised her to keep her hands busy and out of the cupboards she even knit me a bright green scarf and matching hat in there. And there was that brief heady period of afternoon sociability when she took to inviting 'the girls' round for afternoon tea – or I should say, afternoon biscuits and gin.

My father stuck to his own territory back then – the dining-room where his small black-and-white television was perched high in a corner like the television in a country pub, and where his law books were sardined into the bookcase at one side. Down the centre of the room the fully extended dining-room table, that had never felt the touch of a dining plate in its life, was where he dropped his ribboned bundles when he came home in the evening and where he plotted the strategy of his cases. There was his own private telephone on the table and a jokey mug with a picture of a lawyer on it kept filled with pens and pencils. Under the window, overlooking the back garden, was the sideboard that held his small pleasures: Scotch whisky, binoculars, racing form-books, music score books. And against the east wall stood his old upright piano, long since replaced by the baby grand that now darkly gleams at the garden end of the sitting-room.

In the evenings my mother would send me into him with the horse-shoe ice bucket for his pre-dinner drink and later again to collect it and wish him goodnight. There was a wooden coat-stand behind the door that I used to think was called a 'goat's stand' on account of the four large curled hooks like rams' horns jutting from the top of it, which were almost always left exposed. Except for those nights when he was delayed in court or had been in a hurry to get to an evening race meeting and hadn't gone back to his office, in which case, when I turned to leave the room, I would see his wig and gown lurking behind the door like a friend he'd brought home who was too shy to show his face.

The borders have all shifted now. The law books boxed away.

The coat-stand and the sideboard are both gone – I don't know where. I do know that the dining table is in the garage, folded back into itself and jammed against an oil-stained wall.

The house remains marked territory. The dining-room is my country now. The sitting-room, his island. The frontier of silence lies anywhere in between.

I fill the sink with hot water, press my stiff hands down into it and wait for the cold ache to soften. I try to picture the stranger in my mother's sitting-room, the where and how of him. Is he perched on the arm of the sofa, long legs straight out and ramped to the floor. Or is he standing straight, a respectful distance from my father's wheelchair, like a schoolboy in the headmaster's office. Is he listening at all, I wonder. Or only pretending to listen to my father's racing patter. Is he thinking – Jesus, all I said was I like a bet myself now and then, and I have to hear about every bleeding horse that has hit the turf since eighteen-hundred-and-ninety-two. Maybe he is biding his time till it's his turn to show off his racing knowledge.

I wonder how he dresses when he's not wearing those overalls. And if, when he goes out in the evenings, he chases women or simply stands still and waits for the stampede. I wonder what sort of an accent he has to go with that crumbly voice and if he takes sugar in his tea. When he lies in bed, hands behind head, is there a small blossom of wiry hair in each armpit? While I'm at it, I wonder about the shape of his buttocks – if they bulge out at the side, or if they have two slight indents just big enough for a woman to rest her knuckles in? I shake that particular thought right out of my head – I have got to, *got to* stop all this thinking about sex.

*

I went out with a black guy in New York once – about six months or so after I broke up with Michael. It was a one-off thing that hardly qualified as a date at all, seeing as how it lasted less than half an hour. Not that I minded – he was shorter than me and fattish, although he did have a beautiful voice. The date had been arranged by mutual friends. He was a doctor. A specialist, actually, in some remote part of the body that I can't remember now.

I probably looked like shit – although I had promised Serena that I would make an effort: hair, make-up, one of my pretty French dresses. Of course, in the end I didn't bother with any of that so, yes, I did look like shit.

He was something of a flourisher, as I recall – beckoning

to the chair where I should sit, helping me into it, drawing his hand through the air as he made his way to his side of the table. There was a touch of the matador about the way he cracked open his napkin.

'So,' he began, stroking and patting it carefully into place on his lap, 'I hear you're a chef? That must require a certain degree of passion. Now why don't you tell me all about *that*.'

I meant to be nice; it would have been so much easier just to have been nice – to have said, yes, I trained as a chef but am now a part owner of a catering business actually. I could have talked about the ups and downs of the job – how to get paid after an event or the difficulties of getting a canapé to be interesting and at the same time to hold its nerve until it has made its way safely into a mouth. I could have told him a little about my time in Paris – I'm sure he would have approved of that. Instead, I heard myself telling him that I found people who claimed to be passionate about food – *food* for Christ's sake – to be full of crap. I went on to say that, as far as I was concerned, nobody had a right to be passionate about food, apart from those who were feeling the lack of it – people sleeping on the street two blocks away, for example, or townships, cities and, indeed, entire countries on the great continent of Africa.

Quickly, very quickly, he decided I wasn't his type. He had been educated in Oxford, for God's sake! His father was a government minister of who-gives-a-fuck where. And here was a girl with dirty hair, who was drinking her cocktail far too quickly (and showing all signs of it not being her first one that day), lecturing him on the ethics of food and having the nerve to throw *Africa*, of all places, out on the table.

He was frightfully sorry but just remembered he needed to be in surgery in a couple of hours and had most regrettably left his notes at home. And so he left me sitting alone in a long, narrow uptown restaurant, the name of which I can no longer recall, nothing to do but watch his short, fat legs gurning off each other in their tight beige pants as he made his way back down the aisle.

It's a thing I've never understood about New Yorkers, this need they have to 'bring people together'. And not just for romantic reasons either. In fact, the romantic hook-ups are not the worst idea – it's one way of having sex with a stranger with no fear of ending up strangled in an alleyway because you will have friends in common just itching to see how you got on with each other. And so what if it doesn't work out? You can always blame the chemistry – whatever that's supposed to mean.

It's the other link-ups that have always annoyed me – the friendships of convenience (always of convenience): 'Now you ought to meet Marjorie – you guys are in the same boat. I'm *telling* you, you'll be the best of friends.' And then some nut calls and says – 'Well hi there, this is Marje . . . so . . . there's this new singles bar I'm thinking of trying this Saturday on Madison – you wanna come with?'

And you end up sitting at a bar in a blue lit cave talking crap to a man-mad, husband-seeking Marjorie who says, 'Oh how interesting' to every sentence that comes out of your mouth, while she looks over your shoulder and hungrily eyes the possibilities.

*

I'm standing at the kitchen sink, thinking about phoney New York friendships and one night fix-ups and how glad I am to be out of all that – I am probably even grinning at the memory – when a shadow falls like a blind over the kitchen window and I almost pass out with the fright.

The jangling sound turns out to be the ladder. And there's the black angel on the far side of the window, head lifted, eyes piously raised towards the gutter. Nothing between us but the kitchen sink and the glass of the window. I can see his fingernails and his watch; now the outline of his upper arms and elbows. And there's his Adam's apple: a dark, ripe fruit caught in the centre of his throat. Two long legs begin pegging up the rungs, now his knees, now the round toes of his boots are peeping in at me, finally the ridged soles of those boots, as he ascends out of the frame into heaven.

He has left a view of the garden behind, along with a few echoing strums from the ladder. The snow has been improving its efforts, big raggedy flakes now. The shed door is open, held back in place by the old push lawnmower and a large square terracotta pot.

In order for him to get out into the back garden without passing through the kitchen, he would have had to leave the house by the French doors in the sitting-room, which are always, *always* kept locked. And, in order to get at the ladder, he would have had to unlock the shed door, which is also always, *always* kept locked.

He would need to have had keys – my father's keys.

The same keys that are kept in a drawer by his bed. The same keys that I have to ask for, every night, putting my hand out like a child, just so I can lock up the house. The keys I have to give straight back to him as soon as I'm done.

I had to wait till a couple of weeks ago before he finally conceded and gave me his hall-door key so I could have a copy cut for myself. And Lynette still has to ring the door bell – unless I'm going to be out, in which case I'm told to leave the key under the concrete block where, as Brendie Caudwell quite rightly pointed out, anyone could find it and walk straight in. I doubt Mrs Larkin – ten years working here – even has her own key.

And now, here is this complete stranger, up there, walking along our roof, the whole bunch of them snug in the pocket of his overalls. Why? Because he's a man? Because he likes racing? Because he's not a nurse and he's not a cleaner? Or because he's not me?

I fume for a bit, tone it down to a low-level sulk then dry my hands and come back to the table where, leaning on the edge of it, I slowly begin to empty my head.

Releasing the onions from their web, I pluck one out of the rolling pile and weigh it on the palm of my hand. It's been a while since I've paid attention to the weight of an onion, felt the stiff skin of it on my palm, the scent of it under my nose. I play ball with it for a moment, sideways hand to hand, then straight up catch. My hands are steady. And now, I'm ready to begin my second tour of the kitchen.

This time I bring to the table: flour, olive oil, sugar. From the fridge, a good lump of butter and a silver nugget of foil holding a chunk of cheese – lightly coated with a whiteish mould but nothing that can't be cured by a swift, dry shave. Next I unscrew a head of garlic from the rope and sniff it. I know there's a bottle of cognac in the drinks' cabinet in my mother's sitting-room and some decent enough stock cubes in one of the kitchen drawers. I turn on the oven and unsheathe the frozen baguette from its plastic.

Down on my knees now, I begin pulling things out of an over-crowded cupboard: Mason Cash mixing bowls and biscuit cutters; flan-cases and jelly moulds, cake tins, wooden spoons, wire beaters, an old-fashioned electric mixer. There's a box packed with cookery books and, sitting on top of them, a plastic bag of recipes in pamphlets or in cut-outs from old magazines. My hand, no longer quite so steady, begins to sift through them.

My mother was not much of a cook really, despite her love of eating. She always favoured convenience foods – quick gratification and a minimum of mess – and took a child-like pleasure in the small miracle that could be brought about by the simple addition of boiling water to desiccated bits in a bowl: those off-white granules that swelled into mashed potatoes; the dried buck shot that transmuted into what she called 'real-live peas'. I'm sure she embraced the microwave cooker like the friend she'd been waiting for all her life. What she did excel at though, what she truly loved, was baking: for this she had a light hand and a patient, caring eye. Birthday cakes, Sunday cakes, scones, tarts, buns, bread, pastries – she never minded messing the kitchen for the sake of such things.

The scent of a cake shop always hung over our house, and I seem to remember her, here in the kitchen, baking most days when I was a child. I have to wonder now if that could possibly be true? And if so what did she do with all those cakes and buns – we certainly couldn't have eaten them all, despite her best efforts. Maybe she gave half of it away – but I don't see her walking up a neighbour's driveway, somehow, with a covered plate in her hands, and doubt she would ever do such a thing. Unless she had eaten most of it herself? I know I caught her once in the middle of the night, sitting on the step in the garage, stuffing her face like a maniac, chocolate wrappers all over her lap. Maybe she baked every day just for the pleasure of it and then threw the surplus out?

I sit back on my heels and look over the batterie of baking utensils spread all over the floor; these bits and pieces that would have kept my mother company every day of her married life. And I am struck by a sense of her loneliness. Whatever else I may think of her – no matter what may have been killed off or cancelled out by our mutual disappointment – I know this much about her and pity her for it: my mother was the loneliest woman I have ever known.

'Your mom must be, like, the fattest person in the neighbourhood,' Patty announced one evening in Serena's car when she was probably stoned. All the times she had listened in silence while myself, Rachel and Agatha carried on a conversation about how much we hated our mothers – something we three had in common – and yet, when she said that, I remember my eyes stinging with unexpected tears.

I reach into the cupboard again and, from the very back, drag out the large cast iron pot that once belonged to a grandmother I never knew. Then, one by one, I return all the obsolete baking aids back to where I found them.

The weight of the cast-iron pot when I lift it over to the sink, the motif of dust that it leaves on the front of my sweater.

I lower it into the sink, lather it with detergent and turn on the tap. I'm ready to lather up the inside too, but as I lift the lid I see there's something inside there and so pull the pot away from the reach of the water. I dry off my hands then take out an envelope.

It's a small white envelope, greying with age; when I turn it over the words *Mr and Mrs Nichols* greet me.

I can see this envelope didn't come through the mail – there's no stamp or address on it. It may have been handed to my mother but I feel it was more likely to have been slipped through the letter box in the middle of the night, or on a day when she was certain to be out. The envelope isn't sealed. There's something stiff inside it – a card obviously.

I spent an entire afternoon searching for this card a couple of weeks ago, after I'd come across that shoebox in the bottom of my mother's wardrobe. The shoebox was filled with memorial cards – maybe twenty-five of them: a lifetime of deaths, anyhow, that either she wanted to remember or that the relatives and friends of the deceased hoped she'd want to remember. The envelopes in the shoebox had all been opened – some more than others: tiny rips at the edges, flaps that had been unevenly resettled. I opened them again and laid the cards across her bed like some macabre game of solitaire. My maternal grandparents were there, and my father's brother who drowned when he was a boy. There was an old woman I didn't recognise but whose name seemed vaguely familiar. My father's friend, who died in India, and his second cousin, a priest, I remembered from a wedding photograph simply because he had a hare lip which made him stand out. There were neighbours too: Mr Preston who died only four years after I left – the photograph taken when he was a young man with two solid arms stretched over the back of a sofa. Mr Slater who lived to be ninety-four and who, without his hat, looked like a vagrant – a photograph I can't help but suspect his wife chose out of spite. And Mr Caudwell with his fat, red face, even fatter and redder than I recall, dunted down between the braided beak of his police commissioner's hat and the epaulettes of his uniform.

That day, I had been searching for one particular card because I knew it had to have existed. I also knew it would have been given to my mother by whatever means, even if it was only to make a point. And so, she had kept it after all. Maybe out of superstition, or maybe out of compassion – even if she couldn't quite bring herself to put it into the shoebox with the rest of the respectable dead.

I'm not saddened by the card in my hand and this surprises me a little. In fact, I feel warmed by it, almost glad. I think about opening the envelope, inching it out and what I would see. First the black border, then the words *In Memory of*, beneath that, the photograph.

I wonder which photograph they chose in the end.

I put the envelope into the back pocket of my jeans. This is not the moment; this is not even the day.

Now I turn on the radio, edge the knob over the wavelengths, past the news and all the opinions of the news, until I arrive at a sound that pleases me. I know this one actually – this is 'Winterzeit'.

I heard it at the first recital I was ever at in New York (or anywhere else for that matter) where I was taken on my very first date by a skinny law student with the gentlest of kisses. Simon Fischer – I was even in love with his name. Then, as we sat holding hands in the cheapest seats of a dimmed auditorium,

I heard only hope and love in Schumann's music. Now when I listen, I hear madness and darkness in an isolated landscape; I hear the beginning of the journey to death.

Outside in the garden, there is the rattling of the ladder being folded and carried back to the shed. But I don't care now about the ladder, about the keys or even the beautiful black angel.

I'm about to go somewhere else.

I know what I'm doing now, and I know the season. I know where I am. I'm in my mother's kitchen, in my father's house, peeling onions for French onion soup.

8
Summer Past
July

MR RYAN, THUMP THUMP-THUMPING cartons of stationery into the boot of his car, calls up now and then to his son Thomas.

'Byebye Tomtom. Tomtom byebye.'

Thomas, she imagines, dressed in his turtle pyamas, splayed on the box-room window.

'Byebyedada. Dadda byebye.'

Downstairs in the front room, Jilly brays like a donkey. Elaine knows by the way she is dragging her wordless voice round the room that she's trying to communicate with her father.

Byebye Tomtom. Tomtom byebye.

'Answer her, you bastard,' Elaine mumbles, 'could you not just, for once, *answer* her?'

Around this time every morning, Elaine starts to feel bad about Jilly and Mrs Ryan. Shortly after she'd come out of hospital, she'd fallen into a routine of having breakfast with Mrs Ryan, waiting for all the men to leave for the day and taking her cue from Mr Slater's departure. She would then sneak down the back path in her dressing-gown and slippers and squeeze behind the broken fence that divided both back gardens. Her mother, lost in the noise of the hoover, or – as had more recently become the case – still in bed with one of her 'merciless' headaches. Tommy, up since dawn charging around, would be worn out by then and enjoying his post-breakfast snooze. Mrs Ryan in the kitchen or, in this warm weather, out on the patio, getting Jilly ready for another day in a life she didn't appear to know she was living.

But then one day, not long after the arrival of Serena and

Patty, Elaine had been about to pull the fence back when she
heard a sound coming from the Ryans' patio. She could see Jilly
up there, as usual, lying on her day-bed, the basin of water her
mother had been using to wash her on the ground with the
yellow sponge bobbing on top of it. And poor Jilly, dead-eyed
and face all twisted, right arm extended with her hand angled
on the end of it, as if some one had been trying to screw it
off her wrist. Mrs Ryan sitting at the patio table, crying. One
hand over her mouth, trying to shove the short, angry sobs back
down her throat. In the other hand, pressed down on the table,
had been a sheet of blue writing paper. Mrs Ryan crying! Elaine
hadn't known which way to turn – should she go in and try to
console her? Should she allow Mrs Ryan absorb whatever bad
news she'd just read in that letter and come back later on?

And that's what she had always intended doing, if not later
that day, then certainly the next one.

But when she had stepped back into her own kitchen, there
had been her mother, an identical page of blue paper in her
hand. 'Will you just look at that?' she'd said, holding the page
towards Elaine but then snatching it back and reading it aloud
herself, in a mealy-mouthed New York accent.

'Serena Greene and her daughter Patty would be so pleased
if you could join them tomorrow for a . . . wait for this: a
mother-and-daughter afternoon – did you *ever* hear anything
so ridiculous in all your life!'

Since then, there have been four mother-and-daughter afternoons.

The second one took place in the Shillmans' house on a
beautiful day in the garden and went on late into the night, way
after all the daughters had gone home anyway, along with Mrs
Hanley who 'unfortunately had so much to do and could only
stay for an hour'.

As soon as they had walked into the house, Mrs Shillman,

hand on hip, had said, 'Now look here, there's lemonade for the kids, and there's tea and there's coffee – if that's what you want. But in this heat, I say: let the grown-ups have a proper grown-up summer drink – anyone care to try an Italian Bellini?'

Some time after midnight, Elaine opened the bathroom window to hear three voices still floating around in the dark: her mother's, Mrs Caudwell's and Mrs Shillman's, and had to wonder what it was about drunken people that made them think everyone else was deaf.

Jilly and Mrs Ryan had not appeared at any of these parties and, as far as Elaine knows, they were only ever invited to that first one, and that was probably only because Serena Greene hadn't yet realised that the daughter in the Ryan house was a big broken doll.

'You're my big doll,' Elaine used to whisper to her, when she was seven or eight years of age, and Jilly – so small for her age – was a few months older. She loved brushing Jilly's cotton-wool hair with a baby brush, tying a bib around her neck and feeding her, then pushing her along the Ryans' back garden path in her special pram with the little engine attached to the wheels. Or even pushing her out front as far as the cul-de-sac corner. Until Jilly grew too big and too ugly to believe in as a doll, and Elaine grew too old to bear the jeering of the bigger boys, like Gerry and Peter Caudwell.

She listens now to the morning chorus of car engines: the smug purr of the professionals; the rat-tat of all the in-betweeners; the chug of those cars that work hard for a living – Mr Jackson's station wagon, Mr Tansey's showroom specimen. Mr Ryan's car with the cartons of stationery stacked neatly inside. And Jilly erm-ermming them all on their way.

Soon Mrs Ryan will be wheeling Jilly out to the patio. Not long after that, she will be settling herself down at the patio table, her teapot and toast, her last night's newspaper.

She wonders if Mrs Ryan, as she turns over a page, ever glances down at the broken fence at the bottom of the garden and waits for it to tilt.

Elaine takes the usual few seconds then to imagine herself getting up, throwing on her dressing-gown and going down her own garden path and then coming up the Ryans' garden with an excuse already tumbling out of her mouth. Except there is no excuse. Mrs Ryan knows well where she's been all this time: she's been going to mother-and-daughter afternoons, she's been wearing make-up at the Hanleys' garden party that Agatha's mother couldn't be bothered to come to in the end. She's been sunbathing in back gardens, practising her smoking skills and going out places; she's been talking and talking and talking – to friends, to boys, to complete strangers. She's been learning how to drink and how to fit in.

She decides to stop thinking about Jilly and Mrs Ryan. Pulling her journal out from under the bed, propping herself up with her pillows, she considers the cars of the neighbourhood.

Out of all the houses around, only two of the men don't own cars. Mr Owens who 'only' works in a shop in town – as she's often heard it said. And Mr Preston who has a withered arm and can hardly be expected to hold onto a steering wheel. The third non-car man is Mr Slater but, as he is retired, he is excused.

Preston and Owens live facing each other on the right-hand curve of the cul-de-sac. They take the same bus to work every morning, yet never walk to the stop together – one always leaving a little behind the other, as if by prior arrangement. She knows this has something to do with cars, or maybe the shame in the lack of a car. Cars are significant in this estate – she has always known that. Cars are manly possessions.

And out of all the houses around, only three of the women

own their own cars: the newlywed nurse who lives near the village; Mrs Tansey whose husband is a car dealer; and Mary Hanley from across the way. Dinky, sweet smelling things that zip around corners and make her think of powder-puff boxes on wheels. It is generally accepted that Mrs Shillman could have her own car if she so wanted, but as her husband is usually picked up in an embassy car or else he's away, she gets to use his car almost as much as he does.

Other women can, and sometimes do, drive, but only if a husband is not using his car and only at his convenience. In Mrs Donegan's case to go the supermarket on Saturday mornings or to run her children to music classes. And in Mrs Caudwell's case to clean her mother-in-law's house every Sunday, bring her weekly groceries and a fresh change of sheets.

Maggie Arlow also has her own car: a long, low affair from Sweden, dented all over and muck-caked at the bottom which the men regard as something of a disgrace. But Maggie is not of the estate as such and so lives by different rules.

And now there is Serena.

Serena refers to her car as a nervy little pony although it's not all that small – just smaller than the sort of car she is used to – and it's only really nervy when she jerks on the gear stick – something else she needs to get used to. Serena's car, like herself, smells of jasmine with an occasional slash of turpentine.

The house gives off a similar scent – jasmine and turps in varying degrees. Upstairs is more jasmine; downstairs more turps. In the dining-room where she paints her pictures, the air is clogged with it.

'I'm not calling it my studio just *yet*,' she said to Elaine, at the first of the mother-and-daughter afternoons. 'I'll call it my studio when I've managed to finish one Goddamn picture that's worth the price of the paint.'

Agatha, Elaine, Rachel and Patty: Serena calls them her four little heartbreakers. Although so far none of them – apart from Patty – appears to have caused so much as a hairline crack on any heart in the neighbourhood.

Patty is different. And that, as Rachel Shillman points out, is the crux of the matter. She is a novelty. 'I'm not saying that Patty isn't attractive.' Rachel then adds, 'And no, I am *not* jealous. Although obviously I'd prefer to be walking around with her figure than this . . . whatever this is that I have to cart around with me.'

When she says this, she pulls two big handfuls of fat from out over her jeans, then lets them spring back into place.

As it turns out, Patty is almost nineteen years old, which Rachel says, from the boys' point of view anyhow, just adds to the attraction.

Karl Donegan's spots seem to swell up at the sight of her, and the eyes on Jonathan – as the boy with the tired eyes turns out to be called – glisten with sudden light.

Paul is forever trying to get her to talk to him, complimenting her New York clothes and asking endless questions about what it's like to live there.

She answers his questions like she answers most questions, with a shrug, unless the question is very direct and then she'll snap it straight back.

'So what about your dad?' Paul asks her.

'What about him?'

'Why isn't he here?'

'They're divorced.'

'Oh? And where does he live?'

'Right now?'

'Yes, now.'

'New York.'

'And he didn't always?'

'Didn't always what?'

'Live there – you said *now* as if he lived somewhere else.'

'Oh right. California.'

'Is that where you lived before?'

'Sometimes.'

Agatha says, 'You know, Patty, listening to Paul trying to get you to talk, it's like he's following you through a big house and you're slamming door after door in his face.'

When she says this Patty just gives one of her half-smiles and shrugs. Then Elaine has to tell Agatha – 'She smiled and shrugged' – in case Agatha thinks Patty is ignoring her.

Patty is the only girl in the neighbourhood who would be allowed to have boys in her house without supervision, but she never asks them inside. When they knock on the front door, she comes out and leans on the door frame. When she gets bored listening to them, she goes back inside.

Her mother calls out, 'Would the boys like a Coke or something?' And she shouts over her shoulder, 'No, Mom, they're fine.'

One day, when there happened to be only Elaine and Patty in the back of the car, Serena said, 'Oh look, there's Paul, he looks a bit lonesome, let's ask him along?'

And Patty said, 'Oh nooooo, Mom let's *not.*'

Agatha says: 'The boys are too young for her that's why she's no interest.'

'Too young for her maybe – but what about us!' Rachel yells and flings herself back on the sofa.

When the girls are lying on Patty's back lawn, the boys sometimes come out to Paul's back garden, next door. First there will be the sound of their voices through the wall. Then a few jokes are lobbed over the top. Paul's head might appear, followed by his body, and then Karl and Paul and Jonathan will be sitting on top of the wall, swinging their legs and talking down.

They do this a few times before they begin dropping down into Patty's garden and sitting on the lawn with the girls.

One day this happens when Paul is on his own. Patty looks up from the pillow she's made of her folded arms. 'What are you doing here?' she asks him.

'I just . . .'

'I don't want you in here right now,' she says.

'You're joking?' he says, his face becoming uncertain and then turning bright red.

'Why would I be joking? If I wanted you here, I would have invited you over.'

Elaine wonders if that's what she might expect when she gets to Patty's age, a sort of sophisticated world weariness.

'You mean a general not give a fuckiness about anyone or anything,' Agatha says.

'Well, I call it plain ignorance,' Rachel says. 'I mean, to speak to Paul like that. It was just *awful*. We should have all left with him. And I would have done, only I was paralyzed with embarrassment. One thing's for certain, he will never, *ever* show his face near her again.'

But the next day, Paul's face was back again, grinning over the top of the wall.

Elaine watches Patty and thinks she is like a cat, spending hours on the back lawn, following the heat of the sun with her army sleeping bag which she spreads on the warmest spot in the garden. Sometimes she'll turn over on her stomach and read and then she might actually move, swinging the lower part of one leg from the knee.

The sleeping bag belonged to her father when he was young and in the army.

'He fought in the war?' Paul asks.
'In more than one,' Patty says.
'Did he kill people?' Rachel asks
'What do you think?' Patty says.

She never sits at a table and eats a meal like anyone else, but carries her food around with her: a hot dog eaten in her hand as she walks up the road; a sandwich brought up to her bedroom; a bowl of cereal at two in the afternoon as she walks down the back garden. A bag of popcorn sitting on the wall in the evening, when most people are at home eating their dinner. And one Friday night when she was in Elaine's house, she opened the fridge door and began drinking the Sunday-morning orange juice straight from the carton, nearly giving Elaine's mother a heart attack.

Patty really only comes alive when she's playing tennis or riding a horse. Or when she gets involved in one of her deep, meandering conversations that Elaine can never quite follow. She goes to bed in the middle of the night and gets up in the middle of the day. She often looks like someone who is only seconds away from falling asleep.

Serena says that's because of her relaxed disposition.

Elaine's mother says it because she's a spoilt, lazy lump.

Paul says it's because she's a really deep thinker.

Agatha says it's those dickie cigarettes she's been smoking with the stable lads in Arlows.

*

Sometimes when she's finished painting for the day, Serena will come to the back door in bare feet. She'll stand for a while, taking gulps of fresh air as if she's smoking an invisible cigarette, then call out, 'I'm going out in ten minutes, anyone wants to come with – be ready or be left behind.'

If anyone is missing – and it won't be Elaine – Serena will tell Patty to go call them. 'I don't want to leave any of my heartbreakers out,' is what she'll say.

Rachel is absent most because she has to babysit: days when their 'girl from the country' is off or when Mrs Shillman has to go to a function or maybe is at the golf course giving Elaine's mother golf lessons.

'Lessons in how to drink, more like!' Rachel shouts out one day, making everyone laugh except for Elaine.

If Elaine's mother is out with Mrs Shillman then, when they come back from their drive, Elaine will usually call round to keep Rachel company before it's time to go home.

Rachel says, 'You don't have to feel bad. If it wasn't your mother she was out with, it would be somebody else. She hates staying in, that's all. She hates being a housewife. She hates having kids. She thinks we hold her back. There's no need to look so shocked – that's just the way she is.'

Agatha is sometimes missing too – afternoons when she has to go out with her aunt or evenings when she says she's too tired. But Elaine is a constant. She is there every day of the week from the moment she sees the first sign of life across the road: the front door left open to let in the air and let out the turps; or the first twitch of the curtains on the sitting-room window; or the milk bottles lifted from the porch. And it doesn't even matter that Patty is still in bed, she's happy to talk to Serena, and if Serena needs to go out, or wants to go and paint, Elaine will tidy the kitchen and fold the laundry and just hang around until it's time to call for Agatha, who these days rarely gets up before noon.

'You'll wear out your welcome in that house,' her mother says.

'They like me being there. And anyway, I'm not the only one.'

'Well, I don't know how she puts up with it – all those teenagers hanging about. It would drive me insane.'

'It's not that kind of house,' Elaine says, 'and we don't just hang around, she takes us out places. '

'Well, you might tell her that people round here, we like to know where our children are. Yes, we do. And I'd appreciate it if, in future, you could let me know next time she decides to *take you out places.*'

'I would let you know, if you were ever here.'

*

Elaine likes being with Serena. She likes her almost as much as she likes Agatha and Rachel. Sometimes, she secretly prefers her. Agatha is often moody. And Rachel only ever wants to talk about Paul Townsend and how she can get off with him – something Elaine thinks is just never going to happen. Serena requires no effort, except that you listen to her, which is almost always a pleasure. When Serena talks to her she never feels stupid. She feels grown up and intelligent and, above all, chosen.

'We're alike, you and me,' Serena says, 'two sensitive, artistic people.'

Or, 'Well, you get it, don't you, Elaine? You understand me – you know what I mean.'

'Oh yes,' Elaine agrees, 'I do, yes.'

She tells Elaine how she came to this place 'of all places' to find her artistic self. Mrs Osborne was a second cousin of a woman in Serena's art class and Serena wrote and asked if she would consider renting her house for a few months. Mrs Osborne then sent her some photographs.

'A place like this, there are no distractions and artistic people are so easily distracted. When I found out about the house, and the big north-facing window in the dining-room – the light from the north is so important for us artists, you see – I thought I'd use my savings, allow myself a summer here and if it happens it happens, and if not . . . Well, then I'm just going to have to go back to New York and get a job. Or something.'

She tells her about her divorce and her dating life; about the house she grew up in; about her friends in New York: their love affairs, their triumphs and disgraces. Listening to Serena talk so freely, Elaine often thinks, is better than reading a book: the way she wraps a story around you and people you've never met become so real, and the rest of the world and everyone in it just disappears.

The late night conversations can be less satisfactory if Serena is tired or maybe has had a few drinks. Then, she tends to dip out of the conversation, lowering her voice as if about to reveal a dark secret. But the secret usually turns out to be a let-down: a few hasty half-sentences on a big blank page.

'Patty, you see. Problems. Unsuitable – you know? One boy in particular – well we won't go there. But. Let me tell you something now. Let me tell you. Her father. Blamed me. *Me*. I mean, come on! Anyway, say nothing, tell no one. Know what I mean?'

*

She loves when they all go out in the car with Serena; the way everyone just knows it's okay to take off their shoes and place their bare feet up on the dash or across each other's laps in the back seat.

And the way they won't know where they're going until they get there.

When she was small she once got sick in her father's new car.

They were on their way to church, the breakfast her mother had forced her to eat, the smell of the new leather seats, her father's aftershave. They hadn't yet pulled out of the drive when the unwanted breakfast came rocketing out of her mouth, her mother's hands held out to catch it, as if it was a ball.

'To this day, I hate the smell of aftershave,' she tells Serena while she's helping her to unload the groceries. 'If I ever get married, it will have to be to a man with a beard.'

Serena throws back her head and laughs. 'I swear,' she says, 'you are the funniest kid.'

In the house, Serena can be a vague presence: a voice calling out that 'there's food in the icebox, please help yourselves'.

Or a different sort of voice yelling at a canvas: 'For Christ's sake, what's the *matter* with you! Honestly, I could just rip you apart with my teeth!'

She's a blur crossing an upstairs window. A back view mixing paint on the kitchen counter. A figure bent over a foot on a bathroom stool, painting toenails before a date.

But in the car, Serena becomes more solid. When she cuts a corner, the bangles on her left arm shudder. When she bends to light a cigarette, her long earrings get caught in her hair and whoever is sitting up front has to release it, which is why Agatha always has to sit in the back.

As soon as they pull away from the kerb, she slams a music cassette into the player. On the way home, the music stays off and then it's time to practise what she calls 'a little light or even meaningful conversation'.

When she says this, Patty rolls up her eyes and looks out the window.

Elaine knows that this could easily have been her first summer of sitting on the edge of the green. She knows this for all the summers gone by when she has watched the older girls come out after tea and sit like a row of giggly puppets, watching the boys play football. Sit and wait until the evening sky turns mauve and the boys slow down and gradually begin to drift in their direction. Even someone as beautiful as June Caudwell had once been a ringside puppet before starting secretarial college and finding a proper boyfriend to go on proper dates with in town, and before she became all exotic and went off to work as an au pair in Brussels.

It had not been something Elaine had been looking forward to, sitting watching the boys for hours at their football. And yet she knows she would probably have ended up doing it anyway – like so much that has happened to her over the past few years such as monthly periods and training bras, she had presumed it was another one of those things she would just have to put up with.

But when Serena takes the girls out, the boys stop playing football and stand with their mouths open, watching the car pull out of the drive; even the much older boys smoking at the corner near the shops turn their heads and watch them drive by.

Serena gives the horn a beep, and the girls give a little wave out the window and keep their laughing down to a snigger until they're out of the village and turned onto the main road. Serena hits the cassette and a big American voice swells into the car. They allow it a few seconds grace – before joining in: 'You're so Vain' or 'You Ain't Goin' Nowhere'.

When this happens Elaine feels something soar up inside her. The music, the movement, the sound of their voices, the sense of belonging. Sometimes it overwhelms her. This is my real family – she thinks then – these are my friends. I would die for any one of them.

There are other, smaller moments of joy: like when Serena takes them into what she calls 'the city' and they go for coffee in a proper café where scenes from Italian life are painted on the wall and the waiter makes jokes to them and people on neighbouring tables say hello and Serena places her cigarettes and lighter on the table and covers her eyes with her hands and says, 'If anyone wants one – I'm not looking . . . If anyone asks – I didn't see a thing.'

And as they all sit there together, Rachel and Patty smoking with ease, Agatha improving day by day, Elaine just taking one or two drags of Agatha's cigarette because she still can't smoke without feeling sick, drinking real coffee and eating dark cake, she lifts her head to watch pass by the parade of all the lives she might one day lead: students in cheesecloth, office girls in cotton dresses, women with handbags and high heels.

On the way home, the light or meaningful conversation.

Rachel is by far the chattiest. Rachel, followed by Patty who, for all her tutting and eye rolling, will eventually join in and even sometimes take over. Elaine and Agatha sit together on the back seat, Agatha pressing letters onto Elaine's hand as Serena urges them to join in the conversation. Elaine figuring Agatha's words out – O. NO. NOT. THIS. FUCKING. OR-DEAL. AGAIN.

*

Her mother says: 'I'm not sure about this mixing of generations. I mean, I don't know how the other women feel but I certainly don't want my daughter listening to all that adult conversation.'

Elaine doesn't bother to say: I've already heard all of your so-called adult conversations, between your shouting on the phone and your roaring in the Shillmans' garden in the middle of the night and your shouting in the sitting-room with Martha Shillman over your Geee and Teees after-golf. Even from behind closed doors, I've already heard them.

Her mother says it again. This time to Mrs Shillman, who is sitting in their kitchen. 'I'm not sure about this mixing of generations, Martha, after all . . .'

Mrs Shillman is smoking in short, sharp puffs, her right foot is constantly wagging. She says through her teeth, 'It's a break from the kids I need. Not a whole bloody afternoon watching my Ps and Qs in case Big Mouth goes back and blabs every word to her father. Do you know what she told him? Do you know what she actually said? She said . . . I could kill her, I really could. She said that I had a drink problem – now isn't *that* lovely, Sara, I ask you? From my own daughter. And of course, he was delighted! Gives him one over on me, you see? As if he's sipping bloody cocoa every night of the week.'

'Oh now, Martha, that's just ridiculous, surely he wouldn't pay any attention to – I mean the very idea! It's just too ridic–'

'I'll give them drink problem, all right,' Martha says.

*

She is in Serena's kitchen making cheese and toast, while Patty writes a letter to her father with her looped wrist and secretive hand. She is listening to Serena on the phone in the hall to a friend she has made at meditation class: 'Of course, I agree with you, totally, you are so right. Absolutely. That's okay, sweetie, of course it is. I agree, uh-huh. You did right. Of course, I mean it. Oh, whenever suits you. I'm here for you, you know that. I agree, absolutely I do.'

And she remembers Mrs Shillman, a few weeks ago, saying Serena was 'very agreeable'. There had been something snide in the way she had said it, although Elaine hadn't been able to work it out at the time. It occurs to her now that Serena does tend to agree with everyone – no matter what they say. Mrs Shillman probably thinks this is because Serena is some sort of hypocrite. But Elaine knows that's not true: Serena just wants everyone to feel better. Serena just wants to be kind.

Some day, she will say so to Martha Shillman. She'll say it right up to her face. Her words will be assured and crisply delivered; they will put Mrs Shillman back in her place.

'Well, Mrs Shillman, not everybody is the same, you know. Some of us like to make people happy, whereas others, it would seem, prefer to make them *un*happy.' Some day, she just might say that.

She is arranging the cheese onto the bread when she sees, through the hall, her mother's shape on the porch window. Elaine puts down her knife and takes a step back.

Serena says goodbye to her friend on the phone and opens the door.

'I won't come in, Mrs Greene,' her mother is saying, 'I just wanted to say – you know the way Mrs Hanley is having the, you know, the thing tomorrow afternoon?'

'The mother-and-daughter afternoon, do you mean?'

'Yes, that. Now, I know I haven't had my turn yet, mine will be next week, but as I'll be extending my invitation tomorrow at Mrs Hanley's, I thought I should let you know that, well – and I hope you don't mind – but I'm going to exclude the children from my invitation. You see, I'm not sure it's fair on Mrs Townsend – as she has no daughters. And if we start inviting all the boys too, well, goodness knows where that could end up.'

'Oh, you're so right,' Serena said, 'I really only wanted the girls to get to know one another, and they've certainly done that by now. But I totally agree with you. Absolutely, I do.'

*

On a rainy day, the women sit in the Hanleys' garden room and look at each other. Her mother says: 'Did you cut those flowers from the garden, Mrs Hanley? They really are beautiful and so perfect for that vase.'

'Thank you, and I really wish you'd call me Mary,' Mrs Hanley says. 'Now, which will it be – tea or coffee?'

'Tea would be lovely,' her mother says.

'If nobody objects, I think I'd like a drink . . .' Mrs Shillman says, sounding as if she may already have had a few.

Mrs Hanley hesitates before saying, 'Of course. Please, help yourself.'

Elaine's mother gives a wittery laugh.

Serena and Patty are last to arrive. Serena brings a plate of home-made French biscuits shaped into hearts. They're called *palmiers*, she explains, and puts the plate on the table beside Mrs Hanley's Swiss roll and chocolate digestives. Mrs Shillman says, 'And we didn't bring a thing! Really, Serena, you're showing us up. I feel quite mean now, I really do.'

Serena says, 'Oh, I'm sorry. I thought everyone . . . I mean, it's just something that's done where I'm from . . .'

'Something that's done! Now you're making us *all* feel mean. *And* bad-mannered at that.'

Mrs Shillman's eyes are glassed; her bottom lip is pouted.

Mrs Hanley admires the French biscuits. She takes some of them off the plate and places them beside her slices of sponge cake. Then she picks slices of cake up and puts them on Serena's plate alongside the remaining *palmiers*. She adds some chocolate digestives and then hands the plate to Elaine.

'Agatha,' she says, 'why don't you take the girls into your room and have a chat? There's a jug of lemonade and glasses on a tray in the kitchen, if you wouldn't mind bringing it, Rachel?'

'Yes, why don't you just all go and do that now!' Mrs Shillman says loudly with a large sweep of her arm.

Rachel turns and looks at her mother.

'And what are you looking at?' her mother says, the words sounding a little sticky in her mouth. 'What the hell are you looking at now! Go on. Have a good look. Don't forgot, now, to take it all in. Do you want a pen and paper in case you'd like to make a few notes?'

Rachel's face goes up like a balloon. She turns away from her mother and goes through to Agatha's room. The girls follow in silence. They lie on the bed or on the floor and listen to music. The rain dribbles down the glass ceiling. They don't speak for ages until Agatha says, 'Has anyone got a smoke?'

Patty stands up and goes around the room opening all the windows. She pulls a pouch out from the back pocket of her jeans. 'I can do better than that,' she says.

When Elaine comes back into the garden room, the women have already gone. The cups have been cleared, the plates taken away, the ashtrays emptied. The flowers Mrs Hanley cut from the garden are balls of coloured fire in the grey rainy light.

9
Winter Present
December

I'M BACK IN MY old room. The room of my childhood and teen-age years. The room where I slept until I was sixteen years old. Every trace of me has been removed from this room: here there is nothing to suggest the least of my former existence. I know it's been a long time – but still, you'd think there'd be some little thing.

I imagine my mother bagging my life, resisting the temptation to sniff and poke, to open a copybook, read a letter, examine more closely that curl of hair hidden in the blue plastic pouch. In her rush to be rid of me, suppressing her very nature.

Did she give my things to charity, I wonder – what were my things then anyhow? A few clothes? Anything half-decent would have been put in the suitcase for New York. Apart from that winter coat that had cost her a packet a few weeks before I fell ill – by the time I'd recovered, I was swimming in it. There had been talk of having it altered. It owed me, she'd said, another winter.

I imagine her, mourning the waste as she folded it like a shop assistant would fold it, edge to edge, before easing it into a black refuse sack. Bagging it all, bit by bit, week by week, so the neighbours wouldn't notice.

There was the box of books: those Mrs Hanley had given me, a few later additions bought with my pocket money. I'd been on a Steinbeck spree, as I recall; Steinbeck and Sartre.

Until Jonathan introduced me to the Russians. The elation of being singled out (he thinks I'm clever, like him!) Followed by the immediate deflation (oh no, if he thinks I'm clever, he can't possibly fancy me).

I stayed up all night to finish one, just to have something to talk to him about the following day. A slow, dense wade through the words; tangled names I practised in the middle of the night: Raskolnikov, Razumikhin. *Crime and Punishment*, a title that would turn out to be somewhat significant.

What else? The cassette player I'd been given for Christmas – the last gift from my parents to me, although we weren't to know that then. And a few cassettes Karl had loaned me which I pretended to enjoy just to feel part of something. For much the same reason, the posters on the wall: rock stars I might yet learn to admire; political ideals I might grow to understand.

Always that bit behind; I wasn't sure of anything then – I was only starting out.

And of course the journals! Every thought in my stupid little head laid out in their pages. Now those she would have definitely thrown on the fire. She may well have done the same with Mrs Hanley's books – flicking through the pages, finding those sentences I'd underlined – deciding on reflection that, after all, they had been a corrupting influence.

Lastly, the furniture – there would have been no reason to get rid of every stick of it, but I know that's exactly what she would have done. Did she saw it up like an axe murderer – the laundry basket lined in pink plastic? The dressing table and matching stool? What about the bed – how did she get rid of that? *Why* did she get rid of it at all? My old bed was far superior. My old bed was sturdy and large. A bed you could bounce on. The bedspread was candlewick. The curtains, a greenish gold. When you looked out the window you always saw something. When you lay on the bed you could hear things.

Now, a car comes into the cul-de-sac in the night and it's enough to jolt you awake. The clanking of the recycling truck terrifies the ear.

An alarm goes off two blocks away and it's like someone is screeching right into your brain. Mostly, though, there is silence.

This has nothing to do with peace – in fact, it's the opposite.

*

I am used to New York noise, to being lulled to sleep every night by it and brought safely with it back into the morning. No matter what heartache or headache has been going on in my life, no matter which part of the city I've been living in, the white noise of New York has reached in and rocked me to sleep in its steel-plated crib. It's been that way almost from the start – I say almost because for the first five or six weeks I had forgotten what it was like to sleep in a bed.

We were staying in a small midtown hotel then, while Serena searched for a suitable place for us to live.

Every night, she carefully bladed a sleeping pill: one half for me, the other for herself. I saved all mine in the zip compartment of a vanity case my mother had given me when I was ten years old – a reward for coming first in an essay competition called 'Summer Sundays with my Family'. A five-page fabrication in bright blue ink, heaving with lies I came to almost believe.

In daylight, I would often pass out like a drunk – once when we were visiting a friend of Serena's in her swish uptown apartment, I dropped my coffee cup mid-sentence and slid off her sofa.

Another time, on the subway, in a graffiti-smothered car, I felt myself disappear into the wall as if I was just another one of the scribbles. When I came round I was slumped over a Chinese woman who was squawking like a chicken, while I clung on to her lap and had to be prised off by her husband.

'Jet lag,' I heard Serena apologise, her voice sounding as if it was submerged under water. And then sharper, and definitely not submerged, Patty: 'For Christ's sake, Mom, how could it *still* be jet lag?'

Serena and Patty slept with their heads hermetically sealed: eye masks and ear plugs, a helmet of orange-coloured sponge curlers – so this was where their beautiful wavy hair had come from?

I would lie in the dark, listening to their breathing, and try to think of a way to escape on my own – I wouldn't need long, just enough time to find a private corner where I could take the stash of half-pills, lie down and quietly die.

That was my plan; my only plan then. After everything that had happened, I had no interest in staying on in the world.

In the morning, I would watch in a sleep-deprived daze as Serena and Patty did their exercises, lying on the floor, making scissors shapes in the air, courtesy of a contraption they carried in their luggage called a thigh-trimmer. I hated them then, their callous indifference, their ability to care about things like hair waves and trim thighs.

Sometimes, I was starving and gorged on food all day; other times, I could hardly lift the fork, never mind get it to go into my mouth.

I was forever biting my tongue and stubbing my toes; it was impossible for me to hold on to the shortest conversation. I heard Serena say: 'I'm really worried about her. Do you think I should take her to a doctor? A therapist maybe?'

And I heard Patty reply, 'Oh, do what you like with her. I don't care, I really don't care!'

And then one night I went into the bathroom, opened the window and listened. Below me, the sounds from the street. Horn honks and brake screams; cars twanging across man-hole covers; chimes from a nearby subway station. Behind all that, the slender whistles of doormen calling taxis to hotels and apartment buildings. Sirens catcalled across the city. Ambulances gulped nervously at street corners and junctions. A whine from a long-forgotten burglar alarm. Things clattered and whooshed and churned and farted and pinged. Wheels forever turning in this factory of outdoor noise.

I took the cover and pillow from my bed, returned to the bathroom, lay on the floor and listened.

My eyes shut down, my senses eased off, my thoughts were smothered. Distinctive, discordant sounds, almost but never quite blending. And yet there was a sort of promise running through it too.

The first time I would hear an orchestra tuning, I would think of that big city sound.

And so I was sleeping again and, physically at least, could begin to recover. I had a dream one night that a swarm of large insects had invaded the city; I could hear their metallic wings stridulating outside on the street and, terrified, woke myself up. When I looked out the window it was a caravan of rattling supermarket trolleys as scores of homeless people pushed their few possessions around town, in search of a soup kitchen or night shelter.

Human voices sometimes intruded. All night voices: talking, laughing, disagreeing – in that slightly whiney, reasoning tone that I would come to recognise as a New York argument.

Or foreign accents – usually drunk – that would sometimes break into a song of homesickness and longing. Mostly, it was a general late night chatter: friends, lovers, work colleagues, cops, night porters, junkies. Accents I'd only ever heard on the television. In fact, I sometimes woke in the night and for a moment imagined I was back on my mother's sofa, where I'd fallen asleep with the television set still on.

We stayed at that hotel while Serena searched for, and found, one apartment after another, before finally getting the go-ahead from her ex-husband. She explained to me, 'Well, you know how it is – don't you, honey? He who pay gets to say.'

She was talking to me as much as ever; talking and forever explaining herself – a habit I was finding increasingly wearing as well as irritating. I had long stopped being interested in what

Serena – or anyone else, for that matter – had to say. I wanted nothing to do with words or the commerce of words required for a conversation. Words were heavy, cumbersome things to me then.

'You need to talk, sweetie, you need to let it out,' Serena would say.

'We're here for you now – you know that, don't you? If you think I'm too old to understand, then you can always talk to Patty.'

But Patty wasn't talking to me – except to remind me, every now and then, that she was never going to speak to me again.

She took up a sulk the minute we got on the plane and has pretty much stayed in it ever since. She was civil enough in front of others – or at least no ruder to me than to anyone else. But right from the start, Patty made it clear that I was there only because my father was paying her mother to be my caretaker. I was not welcome in her life: not in the room we shared in that midtown hotel, not the apartment we would later move to, not the neighbourhood we were living in and certainly not in New York. At first I felt the weight of her resentment; later I learned to ignore it and, to be honest, I was grateful, too, for the solitude it allowed me.

They had an argument in the lobby of our hotel, Serena and her ex husband. They didn't scream at each other; there were no tears or slammed doors like the rows I had heard several times coming from the Ryan house or the Shillmans'. Not like the half-drunken snipes I had witnessed in the hallway of the Jacksons' while I waited to be paid for a babysitting job after they'd come home from yet another unsuccessful night on the tiles. Nor was it one of those bitter, impenetrable silences such as I'd known in my own house.

They just spoke very loudly to each other: loudly and slowly, as though each believed the other was deaf and maybe a little slow off the mark.

It was a small, respectable hotel – the reception desk on one side and on the other, in an alcove, a half-moon bar counter and sitting area where people on leather sofas read newspapers and drank coffee. Everyone around listened in on the argument – the bartender, the bellboy, the woman on the desk, two businessmen having a meeting at a nearby table. I couldn't get over that, the way Patty's parents, and even Patty herself, didn't seem to care that people could hear every word. Nor did the onlookers even try to disguise their interest. One man sitting at the counter turned his stool right round so he could get a better view – as if he'd paid for a ticket to the event.

It was the first time I'd met Serena's father. The first American man I'd seen up close and in action. He was not a handsome man; he was stocky and his feet seemed a little small for his body. His movements were abrupt. But I do remember being struck by his physical confidence, his startling masculinity. The way he looked right into your eyes when he spoke or turned his head to follow the sway of a woman's backside as it moved through the lobby. And the way he stood up suddenly as if about to make an announcement, and then did: 'I don't have time for this, so let me just say again – I don't want Patty having her head turned by a load of phoney arty types: you better find some place else.'

Serena said, 'Oh, come on now! You're being a little unreasonable – don't you think? It's not *in* the village as such, it's more . . .'

He said, 'I'm not paying for it. You wanna live with pigs. You pay for the stye.'

'She said, 'What are you *talking* about – pigs? You know, this is why we divorced – your intolerance, your blatant disregard for my feelings . . .'

'I'm not here to talk about my intolerance and I've certainly no interest in your feelings. I don't want my daughter living there. Look what happened to you, for Christ's sake, mixing with all those phoney assholes.'

Then he flicked a slice of money off a wad and threw it on the table. He leaned down to Patty, cupped his two hands around her face, kissed her and said, 'Call me if you need anything, sweetheart – okay?'

'Nice meeting you,' he said right into my eyes and I felt my face steam up and my heart give a disturbing little pop. Then he turned on his dainty heel and was whipped out of sight by the revolving door.

She settled on an apartment in the mid-fifties. It was on the sixth floor and had a working elevator. It was close to a secretarial college where Patty would enrol in October. There was a doorman who would whistle you a taxi. You could walk a couple of blocks before coming across a destitute person sleeping in a bin or a doorway. There was a committee that made sure all the residents behaved nicely and that the public areas were maintained. Everyone knew one another: Mrs Rose across the hallway; Doctor Philips down the way. A retired college professor lived on the floor above; an art gallery owner on the floor below. In the building there were five small dogs and two Persian blue cats. The apartment itself was large; the kitchen had a huge oven. It allowed us a bedroom each. Large and quiet and entirely respectable.

'I hate this apartment,' Serena said. 'I hate the neighbourhood. I hate the walls, I hate the windows, I hate him.'

*

Now, I wake each morning to a sense of unease. I keep my eyes shut until I find the wherewithal to let in the light. I am always wary, if not exactly afraid. It's this silence, I think, this hard, intransigent silence.

I look across the street and can't tell who lives in the Hanley house now, who owns the Townsends'. Elbow-height hedges have been replaced by tall trees. Gates, solid and high, are electronically operated. Cars come and go. From the upstairs rooms, specks of electric light show through the sparse winter foliage but I couldn't say whose hand has turned on the switch. I can't tell if the Hanleys' garden room is still in place, or if Doctor Townsend's surgery still exists – it could be a computer room now, or maybe a home gym; it could be completely razed. I don't know if Agatha's old room is still there – her glass prison. The walls are too high and I can't see over. When visitors call, they speak into an intercom built into the pillar, then the gates cautiously part and a car is slowly sucked in.

Other houses in the neighbourhood have cut themselves off to a lesser degree: no house seems to be without a burglar alarm and a few have electronic gates – there is a general security awareness around here that didn't exist when I was a child. But the Hanley and Townsend houses are different: both gates are identical and look pretty old, as if they were put up at the same time – while the Hanleys and Townsends were still living there, most likely. In which case the reason for the gates would not be to keep out intruders, but to keep themselves in.

Since I've been back, I've hardly seen any of the old neighbours. Apart from those faces I found on the memorial cards in my mother's shoebox, I don't know for certain who has died or who has moved away, who has gone into a retirement home.

I drive past some doddery old guy and he could be anyone. Sexpot Jackson or fussy little Tansey. I see a car parked outside the local hairdresser's, a zimmer frame protruding like an overbite from its open passenger door, and I wonder who owns the fading blue rinse on the other the end of it – Mrs Preston or Jackson or Owens?

Mrs Ryan is my only real contact from the old days, the only person around here that I could come close to calling a friend – although I'm not sure she would care to return the compliment.

Sometimes I think I see it in her face when we sit opposite each other at her pinewood kitchen table. We don't talk about the past as a rule, or at least we have learned how to skate round the edges. But it's there, like a leaked fart in the room that we both pretend not to notice.

The first time I called in to see her was a couple of days after my return, when I arrived with my excuses warm in my pocket.

She said, 'Elaine – my goodness!' and stepped aside to let me in, then proceeded to fill up every minute of the visit with other subjects: the recent government cuts; the ridiculous amount of new television channels; the price of electricity; her garden; her hip surgery. Anything. In between she asked me questions about New York – simple, narrow things that could just as easily have been applied to any small town in almost any country: the cost of living, the size of apartments, the transport system, the food.

She was still going on about New York over an hour later as she showed me out.

'Tell me,' she said, 'is it as cold there as it looks on the news?'

'Colder,' I said, which seemed to make her happy.

My ears were ringing after that first visit, but I was grateful too that she hadn't given me the smallest opportunity to lie about my mother's funeral.

Almost four months ago, in New York, the phone woke me up just before dawn and not long after I'd gone to bed.

A voice on the end of it told me that my mother was dying in hospital and that if I wanted to see her I should get on a plane.

'Does she want to see me?' I asked the voice.

'How do you mean?'

'Let me put it this way, Nurse,' I began, 'has she *asked* to see me? Actually asked? Because otherwise . . .'

'Elaine, dear, it's Sally Ryan.'

'Sally Ryan?'

'Yes – you know? Sally Ryan from next door.'

'Oh God, I'm so sorry, of course, Mrs Ryan. How are you? I presumed you were a—'

'I hope you don't mind but you see your phone number was in a little book in the drawer in the hall and I just thought well I thought I'd better what with your father after his cancer – you know about his cancer – of course you do oh he's recovered in almost every way except of course he can't *walk* . . . and there's the oh now what do you call it yes colostomy bag and the wheelchair I've been helping out since your mother went into hospital but Mrs Larkin well she's going to Australia at the end of next week and will be gone for quite a while and he needs to find a nurse now wouldn't you say and a housekeeper I suppose too a temporary one though because Mrs Larkin swears she'll be back in a couple of months and I wouldn't like to think of her out of a job she's been saving so long for this trip her son you see and there's a grandchild now as well as other relatives all over Australia and New Zealand too I believe I've been doing what I can a bit of shopping and that but I've just had my hip done you see and . . . and I think he's a bit awkward with me in the house to be honest you know how it is and in any case I'm not sure how to go about getting a nurse that might suit him and well your mother God help her is so bad now that the doctors are saying it's only a matter of . . . Elaine? Elaine – are you still there?'

'What? Yes, yes, Mrs Ryan, thank you for letting me know. Of course I'll come. I'll come right away.'

I put down the phone and opened the blinds. Then I stood for a while watching the dawn spit orange fizz all over New York. And all I could think was I never even asked about Jilly – that is, if Jilly was even still alive.

And so I got in a taxi and got on a plane and then got off it again. Anything in between was a Xanax-blurred, vodka-tinged muddle of colours and queues and shrill overhead voices. I was in a different airport then, standing at a car hire desk and wondering what I was doing hiring a car when my parents' house was probably only a twenty minute taxi ride away. I decided maybe it would be as well to have a car in case things got awkward and I needed to stay in a hotel. Or even if things didn't get awkward and I needed to make myself useful. My father, now wheelchair bound, probably no longer had a car. There would be errands to run, arrangements to make. Yes, much better off with a car.

And so, glowing with my own efficiency and all round good sense, I got in the car and began to negotiate my way out of the airport. A road sign appeared in front of me – at the next roundabout I would need to turn right and stay southbound to get to my parents' house. I circled the entire roundabout once then I circled it a second time. Third time round, I turned left and headed due north.

I turned left and stayed northbound for hours, only stopping when I needed to – once at a gas station, another time at an isolated roadside bar that turned out to be closed down and where I ended up peeing round the back, between old beer kegs and crates of empty bottles. When I could go no further without driving the car right into the sea, I found a hotel for the night. Next day I began moving west. And there I stayed, just another Yank of a certain age on a solo vacation. During the day I went touring; in the evenings I ate dinner and sometimes drank a little too much. If I happened to fall into a conversation, I invented myself – once I was a teacher, another time a librarian. I was here on my own because my friend and would-be travelling companion had broken her leg a few days previously, but had insisted I go anyway. I always felt the need to explain or even apologise for my lack of a companion and each time had to wonder what it is that makes us so ashamed of being alone?

I had coffee by the fireside of a country house hotel on a day of relentless rain and hooked up with an elderly Swedish couple. Later we went for a walk through the sodden grounds where the woman slipped and fell on her back and stayed there laughing in a patch of wet grass, her old face in an anorak hood, plump and crumpled with joy, while her husband and I, now also laughing, tried to haul her back up on her feet. That evening they invited me to join them for dinner. And I remember looking at them and thinking – here I am with these two elderly, laughing strangers, while my own mother is dying in hospital and my father is inching around an empty house in a wheelchair, and I can't honestly remember when I last had this much fun.

In a grim hotel in a dismal town, I hooked up with a hefty Lithuanian barman. He had a hairy back and gave an even-sized grunt each time he shoved himself into me. 'Shove away,' I thought, 'just don't take all night.' I was too drunk to care and, besides, the sex wasn't the point – and I'm not sure what was really, except that I needed to feel the weight of a man on top of me, crushing me.

Every day I checked the death notices and waited. And then one morning, in the corner of a musty dining-room somewhere on the north-western seaboard, I found out that my mother was dead.

Greatly missed by her daughter Elaine . . . I read and almost laughed out loud.

Greatly missed! After thirty-four years I was over it.

I folded the newspaper, ordered more coffee and sat for maybe an hour. I remember the room: thin salmon-coloured tablecloths, red plastic carnations, one to each table; thick brown velvet drapes coated with ancient cigarette smoke. But I can't remember myself in the room – how I was feeling or what I was doing. I may have been sobbing – although I doubt it. I may have just sat there staring out through a veil of soft rain at the steady, grey sea.

And then, two days later – as if there was the slightest chance of making it to the funeral – I drove back down country like a maniac.

*

I call in to see Mrs Ryan about twice a week. We have tea – sometimes she'll have cake or I'll bring in some biscuits. Often we'll just have the tea and she'll smoke two cigarettes. Shortly after the second one, she'll begin to yawn and then I'll know it's time to think about leaving.

For the first few weeks I called on the same days, at around the same time in the afternoon, and then she asked me not to do that any more.

'Oh it's not that I'm on a timetable or anything,' she laughed, 'I just don't want to start expecting you – you know?'

And I thought of the fence at the end of the garden and wondered if it was still there and, if so, had it ever been mended.

I always liked Mrs Ryan, a calm-eyed, timid sort of woman with a touch of steel in her bones. Like Maggie Arlow, she had always seemed somewhat removed from the other women, although for entirely different reasons. When I was a kid, I used to go to the shops for her and she would insist on giving me something for my trouble, pressing a coin or a bar of chocolate into my hand and showing far more gratitude than this small deed warranted.

In her heartache over Jilly, she had been very much alone and, I suppose now, the fact that I visited Jilly, spoke to her and even played with her in my own clumsy, one-sided way, stood me in good stead with Mrs Ryan. She didn't have to feel ashamed of her daughter in front of me anyhow, and that must have meant something.

The night of the 'unfortunate tragedy' – as Serena came to call it – it was to Mrs Ryan's house that I ran in the middle of the night, banging down the door and waking her. She calmed me down, hugging me until I stopped jerking like a caught fish. Then she had me breathe into a brown paper bag. Mrs Ryan was the one to call the ambulance and then she held my hand while she spoke on the phone to my father and, without letting go of it, led me down her back garden and up mine, towards his dressing-gowned figure standing stark against the fluorescent light of our kitchen.

Since the first visit, I've known Jilly was dead, but it takes a few further visits before I bring up the subject again – not out of any indifference on my part but because of the frantic way Mrs Ryan hops from subject to subject like a basketball player trying to block an opponent, and I simply can't get past her.

One evening she opens the front door and, instead of leading me into the kitchen, invites me to follow her into the sitting-room. There is a fire in the grate. Two glasses of sherry are waiting on the coffee table, along with a plate of neatly sliced cake. She hands me a glass, raises the other one and wishes me a happy birthday. I can't believe she has remembered and I don't know how to feel about this but, in any case, I have to turn away. My eye catches on a photograph across the room; I go to the sideboard and lift it. For a moment there is silence.

'That was taken the day before she went into the home,' Mrs Ryan finally says.

'The home?'

'It became impossible to mind her.'

'Of course.'

'I still have the dress – you know. God, the trouble I had getting it on her. The way she was all folded into herself. And all angles. The elbows on her! And as for those knees! I managed in the end – though I don't suppose she even noticed.'

'But you did.'

'Oh yes.'

I come back to the sofa, and sit beside Mrs Ryan, accepting a piece of cake. She lights her first cigarette and begins to explain.

'I never went to see her, you know – years and years of

looking after her and I never went near her. You probably think I'm a terrible mother?'

'You must know I think the opposite.'

'Too painful you see. People forget how painful it is . . . how seeing her there with all the others . . . She died a year later. Forty-five years of age. This used to be her room – do you remember?'

'Yes, I do.'

'Her bed over there – so I could get around it. You used to love pressing the button on it when you were a little one. Up down, up down. And the wheels on it. You used to help me to push it.'

'I remember.'

'Poor old Jilly. You know – they told me she'd be lucky to reach puberty? All those years, I kept her alive. I wonder sometimes . . . Oh well.'

'And what about Tom?'

'Tom? He lives at the other end of the country.'

'Married?' I ask

'To a witch,' she says and laughs her head off.

'And Mr Ryan?'

'Oh, he left me, years ago – you heard that surely?'

'No, I never hear anything. I guessed though.'

'Did you?'

'Well, he's not here – is he? And if he'd died you would have said.'

'Oh no, he didn't die. Just did a flit with a typist out of his work.'

'I'm sorry,' I say.

'Hooo-ooo,' she laughs again, 'no need to be.'

She lights up her second cigarette.

'You weren't upset then?'

'More embarrassed than anything, I'd say. Embarrassed by myself for a start. My own stupidity.'

'But why? You had no need to be—'

'Of course I had. I wasted my life. We only get the one. And I wasted it. Giving it up, to this . . . to this man I hardly knew. I was twenty-one when I married. I had my few friends, a job I liked. Started at seventeen and was promoted twice, you know. In those days, you had to leave work when you got married. Yes. Give everything away. Your job. Your independence. Even your name. And when he left, I thought – well what a waste of bloody time that was! A stupid, shameful waste. I'll admit, though, at first I was a little worried about money. How would we manage? But we did manage of course. The new one, you see . . .well, I didn't imagine she'd be keen on him throwing too much our way and the thoughts of having to chase after it, month after month . . . I was cute, though – I told him stuff your maintenance, just sign over the house.'

'And he did?'

'Oh yes, of course he did, anything for a quick get away. I remortgaged it too. Up to the chimneys. They'll let me stay here till I die, then the bank will own it. I leave nothing behind. Do I give a damn? No, I don't. But if you're asking me did I miss him, the answer is no, Elaine. I didn't. Not in my bed. And certainly not around the house. He blamed me for Jilly, you know, never forgave me. Like it was a trick I played on him. Do you know what he said to me during our last conversation – I mean, after he'd just told me he was leaving? "I only married you anyway because you were pregnant." Wasn't that a lovely thing to say, as you walk out the door? I wouldn't mind but there was no need. I wasn't stopping him from leaving. I wasn't shouting at him nor calling him names. "I only married you because you were pregnant." And do you know what I said right back up to him? I said, "And why do you think, now, that I married you?"

'And that was the truth. If I hadn't been pregnant, I'd have dumped him. I'd well gone off him by then. Well, when you're young, you think sex is love – don't you? Different nowadays –

you can test each other out in the bed and no one thinks the worst of you. Get each other out of your systems. Ready to finish with him and then I found out Jilly was on the way. Poor Jilly, the way he couldn't even bring himself to look at her.'

If I was to talk to anyone about what happened all those years ago, it would probably be to Mrs Ryan. I have come close to it once or twice, but have always stopped short of the door. She is elderly, and I'm not sure it would be fair to burden her in order to unburden myself. I could trust her, at least – and it's good to know that. Just as she once knew she could trust me.

When Mrs Ryan found out she was pregnant on Thomas, apart from the doctor, I was first to know. I knew even before her husband did. I saw her coming out of the doctor's surgery on the far side of the village, when I was on my way home from school one day.

He was a new doctor, young and thought not to have enough experience. I remember being a little surprised to see Mrs Ryan leaving his surgery as, like the rest of the women in our estate, she usually went to Dr Townsend.

I said, 'Oh, hello there, Mrs Ryan,' as she came out the gate. She looked at me, stupefied, and then her eyes filled up and out dropped all these big tears. I followed her brisk walk around the corner and sat down beside her on a garden wall. When she'd stopped crying, she told me she was pregnant. She was afraid, she said. Terrified, was the word she used. Afraid the baby would be like poor Jilly, afraid of her husband and what he might say.

'But it's not your fault!' I began and then blushed at the dark blurry image that had come into my head of a man and a woman doing something strange and dirty in a big double bed. She laughed and touched my hot face with the tips of her fingers.

'Do you know what I wish sometimes?' she said. 'I wish I

could just start all over again. Not all the way back to when I was a baby. But to your age, say – that age when everything is still possible. Before . . .'

'Before what, Mrs Ryan?' I asked her.

'Ahh, before all that other stuff,' she muttered and then blew her nose.

She didn't ask me to keep it a secret, but I did anyway. A few weeks later, my mother stepped away from the back bedroom window.

'Do you know,' she said, 'I could swear next door is expecting again.'

'Expecting what?' I asked.

'Oh, really, Elaine,' my mother laughed, 'I forget sometimes how innocent you are.'

When I was in hospital, Mrs Ryan came to see me one day. She brought me a comic and a bottle of Lucozade. The comic was too childish for me – but she would have no way of knowing that.

She would have had to get two buses to visit me. She would have had to pay someone to babysit Tom and for the special nurse to come and mind Jilly.

*

There is a stiffening in the air when I leave Mrs Ryan's house, a sense of returning snow. After more than an hour in her oven-warm sitting-room, I need to cool down. And besides, I don't feel like going back into my father's house, closing then locking his front door behind me for another long night. I give Mrs Ryan a few seconds to lock herself into her house, then double back and begin towards the village.

The sixth of December – until Mrs Ryan wished me a happy birthday, I had forgotten what date we were at. For days Christmas trees have been showing in windows. There was a time around here when it was almost obscene for a tree to display itself until the week before Christmas Day. Even then, it had to confine itself modestly to a corner of a sitting-room: a private pleasure for family and visitors. Now, it seems, the whole house gets tarted up, gardens included; shrubs spangle, doorways twinkle, house fronts are garnished with jewellery. On the gable end of one of the newer houses, a Santa Claus figure is scaling a rope-ladder.

The road is deserted. The stars in their heaven are made lesser by the brassier lights down here on the earth. The waning moon with its lopsided face looks like a stroke victim.

I come close to the village. Up ahead, two men are sitting on the window ledge of an empty shop that used to be the barber's where outdated pictures of men in quiffs and crew cuts sat in the window. Tonight the men sitting on the ledge are drinking cans of beer and I see now there is another one having a piss into the shop doorway – one hand on his dick, the other holding a can. He is a few steps away from the lane that runs behind the village shops, but obviously prefers to use the doorway and have the streetlight highlight his aim. These are not kids nor do they appear to be homeless. These are grown men – almost middle-aged in fact.

I hang back and wait for the pisser to finish.

The night air is cluttered with smells from local fast food takeaways: tainted oil and stale spices. Monosodium glutamate. Indian, Chinese, old-fashioned chip shop. The pavement outside these shops is lightly sheened with grease. Carmel's shop is also along this parade – a cave of cheap sweets and processed food. She tried selling fruit for a while apparently and even had a go at a few vegetables, she told me, but in the end decided there was no call for such nonsense. Seven shops make up this village: the three takeaways, a bar, a turf accountant's where you can put on a bet all hours, even on Sunday, and finally a funeral parlour. For anyone interested in an early death with the minimum of effort, this village would be an ideal place to live.

The iron shutters are down on Carmel's shop. Above it, the

light in her flat is on. And there she is, a large figure – or part of a large figure – in a window, dressing a very small artificial tree that she has carefully positioned for all to see.

I don't mean to call her Fat Carmel – even if she was the one who invited me to do so, maybe the second or third time I walked into her shop. She'd already told me about her mortgage troubles, her brother's shingles, her ongoing battle with shoplifters and gypsies. Only then did she introduce herself.

'My name is Carmel,' she said, 'but feel free to call me Fat Carmel, everybody else does you see on account of the other Carmel, the skinny one, who works in the chippie.'

'Oh, I'm sure that's not true,' I mumbled.

For a moment I have a rush to the head and consider knocking on the door to Carmel's flat. Maybe it's the birthday blues, but I feel a need for company. And even if I don't pay much heed to what she's actually saying, I enjoy listening to her speak. Carmel can take a word and roll it around in her mouth like a big soft jelly sweet. Words such as 'no-*terrr*-iety' or 'Rizzzzla' or even a whole collection of words – 'and what do you think but didn't the little bugg*ar* have the box of chocolates stuffed down the back of his trowwwzers'.

In the end I decide I'm not up to the effort of knocking on her door, of climbing up the linoleum staircase, of walking into her gas-fired room and having to admire the little Christmas tree with its child-like decorations and then, five minutes in, having to deal with the inevitable onset of panic as I search, and then fail, to find a way out.

I by-pass the turn for the village, carry on to the end, following the pavement on its loop until it turns and I'm on the opposite side of the road. My life is a continuous series of loops. The valley, the river walk, the thoughts in my head. Loop after loop. Twenty-five minutes it takes to walk this particular one – from the rear of the Esso station at this end, all the way up to the motorway wall. We are cut off on both ends. The only way out by car anyway is through the village. You can walk by the narrow laneway at the side of the Esso of course, or via the side steps that lead to the motorway bridge. Otherwise – I don't know, you could always go into Arlows' land, scramble down the hill towards Hoxtons' bridge, dive into the river and swim across to the other side, to freedom. A little extreme of course for a woman of my age, and highly unlikely. Still, it's a nice thought to carry around in my head on this crisp winter's night at the start of my fiftieth year.

The silence. I can hear my own pulse, my brain ticking over, my tapping footprints. The local bar comes into sight and I stop to consider it – heavy wooden double door; broad windows filled with amber light. I imagine for a moment going inside and finding a quiet corner. There would be convivial background noise – chatter, gurgles, glass-clinks, laughter. Time disappearing down a hole. There would also be neighbours and I can imagine, even now, that a woman on her own would stand out in a place like this. And there would be whispers – even if they only existed inside my own head, I would still hear them. I'm about to forget the whole thing and then I remember the small back lounge.

On a long ago summer's evening, I stood in the doorway of it and tried to be invisible while Rachel tried to deal with her mother. Rachel was crying, the young barman near to tears too. The only one who appeared to be unmoved was Mrs Shillman and this struck me as odd, considering she was the only one disgracing herself. She was berating the barman because he'd phoned the house and asked that someone come and collect her. She was too drunk to walk, was what he'd said, never mind drive the car home.

'I'm sorry,' the barman was saying to Rachel, 'I thought your father was in, I saw the embassy car earlier, you see, drive by with him in the back while I was—'

'No,' Rachel said, 'you couldn't have. He's not home yet, I don't know where he is.'

'But I saw the car coming back a few minutes later. Just the driver. And he wasn't in it. I was lifting the kegs out you see and–'

'No.' Rachel sniffled. 'No. You couldn't have.'

Mrs Shillman at the side, waving a cigarette around like a baton.

'Give. Me. My. Fucking. Keys. And let me tell you now, I'll be writing a letter of complaint tomorrow. Dragging my daughter into a public house at this hour of the night. She's not allowed into public houses, I'll have you know.'

'But I thought . . . I was sure . . .' the barman began again and then just gave up.

The cigarette flew out of her hand across the room, landing close to my feet. I picked it up and brought it back to her. I'm not sure she even recognised me.

Rachel promising: 'Let's just go. Come on, let's just go home. I won't tell. I promise I won't tell, if you'll just come home with me now. I promise . . .'

Between us, we lugged her home, making several stops, Rachel crying all the way; Mrs Shillman, joining in halfway up the road, through her tears, kept saying: 'I'm so. I'm just so. Oh God, I'm so . . .'

And where was my mother, I wonder now. Why was she not there, as she usually was, floundering around in the background?

But the back lounge itself, I remember it as a compact room – cracked leather seats, a gold-faced grandfather clock. There was a stone fireplace filled with dried flowers. On a winter's night, it would hold a bright fire. Nobody really went into it – an old man or two. Sometimes a few women from the pitch and putt club. I check my pockets and am almost beside myself with joy when I find enough there for a drink or maybe even two.

I push open the door and immediately regret it.

It's like I've stepped into some sort of a barn. A barn pretending to be a pub – like one of those places you see in an airport. A big curved counter: two lone men sitting a few stools apart. Another one, strolling out of the gents, makes his way to a different part of the counter, comes down on his stool like a cowboy coming down on his saddle. All around are vacant tables, steps leading up to platforms, everywhere visible. Not a shadow or corner to mope inside. A few men standing and staring up at a football match on a screen the size of a small cinema. I'm holding the door open; the barman is looking at me. Two of the men at the bar have turned their heads – the third one, the cowboy, stays as he is and stares down into his pint.

I step inside, begin walking, chin at an angle as if looking for someone who is waiting for me. Then I see the ladies' toilets and duck inside. A few minutes later and I'm back outside.

The moon has gone in now; the houses have darkened. It has turned deathly cold. Back on the loop, I keep walking until I end up at the motorway wall.

I climb the steps to the bridge. Steel platform clanging under my feet. Steel cage over my head. I stop halfway and look down on the motorway. Flat tops of cars pass beneath me. Resting on the decline at the side of a slip road, a pile of dumped black plastic sacks glisten in the lights like a colony of seals. Something catches my eye. I look up and am startled – what is that, anyhow? What? Actually it is me. Or rather an imprint of me, pasted large and black against a big motorway sign. A cut-out shape thrown into relief by the headlamps of speeding cars. I am huge. I am huge and visible to every driver and any passenger who happens to be travelling in any one of those cars. The lapels of my coat, the bracket of my elbows, the outline of the top knot I'd forgotten I tied into my hair earlier on. They don't have my face nor my age; won't know if I'm pretty or plain; clever or stupid. But they have my existence. For some reason I am fortified by this: the fact of my huge existence silhouetted on a sign high above the motorway. Happy birthday to me.

I come back down the steps of the bridge and begin retracing my steps. Before I realise it, I've gone past Mrs Ryan's house and then past my father's house, have turned into the cul-de-sac and am walking around its horseshoe-shaped pavement. And now here I am, after all these years, standing outside the Shillman house, my hand on the gate.

I can't say I feel anything. Maybe a vague sense of embarrassment in case anyone should look out from one of the neighbouring houses and see me standing here. Otherwise, I am fine.

In any case, it hardly seems like the Shillman house: the old windows have been replaced, the porch has been removed and a new set of steps lead up to the front door – also new. The house is almost ready for reoccupation. It seems smaller than I remember, smaller and insignificant. It is, after all, just another bland suburban house, like any one of a million.

I look at the garden. The driveway has been cobble-locked. The lawn on one side smothered with pebbles. The side entrance door has not yet been replaced: I can see lengths of pipe lying on top of one another and then disappearing into the black gape that leads through to the back garden and round to the back of the house. I imagine going in, crossing the back garden to the shed, pushing the door to, seeing the haversack there, slumped in the corner.

I push the gate open and step inside.

10
Summer Past
August

HER MOTHER SAYS, 'SHE'S not your only friend, Elaine. You are
not her nurse, you know. And you need to broaden your hori-
zons, you need to mix more with . . .'

'With what?'

'You know, people who are not . . . well, people who don't
need to be . . . Oh now, you know what I mean. First it was Jilly,
and now it's . . .'

'No, I don't know what you mean actually.'

'Looked after. That's it. Ted Hanley's mother has just had a
stroke, you know. Mrs Hanley will have to visit most days. It's a
good hour's drive away. Agatha won't want to go with her. She'll
expect you to be available to her . . .'

'She can come over here.'

'Here? Oh no, I don't think so. I couldn't take that
responsibility.'

'Why not, for God's sake?'

'Martha Shillman thinks you hide behind her, you know.
That she's a cover up for your shyness.'

'Martha Shillman should mind her own business!'

'All I'm saying is there are other girls in the neighbourhood.
You have Rachel. And there's Brenda Caudwell, for example –
she has the door worn out knocking on it. She'd be glad to be
your friend.'

'Oh God – Brendie bloody Caudwell!'

'There's Patty, she's a little older of course, a little well-up for
my liking but . . .'

'And there's Agatha.'

'Yes and Agatha, of course. I'm not for a minute suggesting you drop her. But you know, you should really go to that tennis camp next week.'

'I don't like tennis.'

'You like it in school.'

'I'm gone off it.'

'Now you're being ridiculous. You won't go because Agatha can't go. Am I right?'

'No!'

'While the rest of them – Patty and Rachel and, yes, even Brendie Caudwell – will be there. Serena will be driving them. And collecting them too, if they want, although I'm sure they'll be staying late most evenings. Even some of the boys are going, Paul and that tall lad – what's his name, you know the one with no mother? Jonathan, that's it. Meeting new people. Making more friends. Going to the dance at the end of the week. They'll all be there . . . everyone, in fact, except you.'

'And Agatha.'

'And Agatha, indeed.'

*

Agatha says: 'Go if you want, I don't care. What do you think of my hair this way?'

'I don't want to leave you on your own, Agatha.'

'Oh, please, I'll be fine. Karl's mother did it for me. It's called a chignon. She used to be a hairdresser – did you know?'

'Mrs Donegan? No, I didn't. You were in their house?'

'And I will be most days until Granny Hanley snuffs it. Does it make me look older?'

'Why are you not going to the Shillmans'?'

'I don't want to. Well, does it . . .? Does it make me look older? It feels very sophisticated anyway. She's going to teach me how to do it myself.'

'Is she?'

'Yes, it'll take maybe a million times before I get it right but it'll be worth it. And it makes me look older?'

'Yes, I suppose.'

'But not old-fashioned?'

'No! Agatha, the tennis? I'm trying to tell you – Serena will collect us every day, she'll probably bring us out afterwards. And Paul is going. And Jonathan. And . . .'

'I'm not standing there like a fool on the sidelines, listening to you lot play tennis.'

'Fine. But if you're not going – then I'm not.'

'For Christ's sake, Elaine. If you don't go, how do you think that makes me look? Like an invalid, that's how. A burden. I'm well used to being on my own. Do you have to be so . . .'

'What?'

'Clingy.'

'Clingy!'

'Sometimes. You really are.'

'Clingy, Agatha? You're saying I *cling* to you? Just because I show a bit of concern.'

'I don't want your concern, Elaine. And I certainly don't want your fucking pity.'

*

Her mother says, 'Now? You mean this minute, *now*? You can't go now. Your dinner is on the table.'

'Serena is taking us for a drive.'

'But it's lamb chops. They won't keep. They'll be ruined if they're reheated.'

'They're all waiting for me in the car.'

'Lamb chops. After all the trouble I've taken?'

'I have to go.'

'Lamb chops. They cost money, you know. And now what am I supposed to do with them?'

'Eat them yourself,' she says and runs out the door.

*

On the way home from the drive Serena begins to draw Agatha

out and suddenly she is telling a story. Elaine is sitting up front next to Serena. Agatha is right behind her; Rachel is at the far window. Patty, in the middle.

The story is about her mother's actor friends and a fat woman who wanted to play Ophelia. They were rehearsing a play in an English country town. It wasn't *Hamlet* as such. It was sort of a take on *Hamlet*. Or maybe a take on Ophelia. Agatha says, no matter how many times she heard it, she'd never been able to work out which.

While Agatha tells her story, a stillness comes over the car; there is only her voice and the ticking of the engine.

The story frightens Elaine. It makes her feel, not only as if she is there with Agatha, backstage in this country theatre, but almost as if she is Agatha. The musty smell; the taste of dust on the air; the ropes on the ground like snakes underfoot. And all these peculiar people moving around so that she is always in the way; a constant obstacle to the passage of others, never knowing which way to turn, until in the end she sneaks off to sit on her own in the dressing-room.

Her mother gone off somewhere, getting her hair done – or so she had said. Elaine could imagine her standing by the door beforehand, waiting on her chance to slip out. Agatha could hear the lunch break being called then she heard the cast and crew go out. She kept expecting the door of the dressing-room to open, to hear a voice asking if she'd like to come with them. She could hear their footsteps thudding down the backstage stairs. She could hear them bitching about each other. (He keeps missing his cue! What do you expect, she never gave me the line!) The iron slam of the backstage door then.

The dressing-room was large but Agatha knew her way around it. On two walls there were rows of costumes on rails, a smell of sweat, old perfume, mothballs. A feel of velvet, fur, satin. There was a long shelf with a kettle and biscuits and cups. The mirrors and dressing tables were positioned in the centre of the room so you could walk either side of them. The mirrors were trimmed with bulbs. Agatha knew the dressing-room was dark because whenever one of the cast came in they always made a comment like, 'It's pitch black in here.' Or, 'Oh my God, I can't see a thing.'

When the lights were on, there was a buzzing sound overhead, and the bulbs on the mirror were hot to the touch when she trailed her hand along them. That day, there was no buzzing overhead, and the bulbs on the mirror were cold. Yet she felt there was somebody else in the dressing-room. She said, more than once, 'Who's there? Is there somebody there?'

'And was there – was there somebody there?' Serena says.

'Oh yes,' Agatha says.

'And they didn't reply? They didn't say a word?'

'Not a word.'

'Oh, how cruel,' Serena says, 'to pretend like that, how–'

'Shhhh Mom,' Patty says, 'will you let her just tell it?'

'I could smell her.'

'*Smell* her?' Serena asks.

'Oh, I do that. Elaine always says I'm like a little animal, the way I smell people.'

'Oh, Elaine . . . you do not?' Serena says, throwing a look at Elaine for a second.

'Oh, but I don't mean –' Elaine begins to explain, but Agatha has taken everyone away again, back with her into the dark.

She could sense something blocking the space on the far side of the room.

'You can do that?' Serena asks.

She could hear her breathing. Yes, it was a woman, definitely a woman.

'Well, thank goodness for that much, anyhow,' Serena says.

'Mom, will you just keep quiet!'

'The breathing was odd,' Agatha says, 'gasping and grunting.'

'But what was she *doing*?' Rachel asks

'At first, it sounded as if she was doing exercises, push ups or something. But then . . . the grunting, you see.'

'What? What?' Patty says. 'Was it, like, something disgusting?'

'There was another sound then, like a long fart maybe.'

'She was going to the bathroom!' Patty decides.

'In the corner of the dressing-room?' Rachel says. 'Why would she do that?'

'She was . . .' Agatha pauses. 'She was trying on Ophelia's dress. And she . . .'

'She ripped it!' Rachel says.

'Yes. She was fat, you see, and knew she would never get to play Ophelia.'

'But if it was dark,' Rachel says, 'she wouldn't even be able to see herself in the mirror.'

'But that was it,' Agatha says, 'she didn't want to see herself. She just wanted the feel of the dress.'

'And she definitely knew you were there?' Patty asks.

'Yes, but she didn't care about that. She just presumed, if she stayed very quiet, that I wouldn't hear her, and even if I did, how could I say for certain it was her. Later when Ophelia – the real Ophelia – discovered the ripped dress, everyone thought it was me. Even my mother, who ended up paying for it to be fixed.'

'But didn't you say something?'

'No.'

'But why?'

'Because. Well, because I don't know really.'

'Oh, how cruel,' Serena says again.

After Agatha's story, they drive on in silence and then Serena swings the light into Elaine's corner of the car. She says, 'You've studied *Hamlet* in school, Elaine – right? So what do you think, maybe Ophelia was already a little crazy to start or did, I don't know, life – men – whatever – make her that way? What do you say?'

Elaine feels her mouth dry up and her hands dampen. She turns her red face to the window with a mumble.

Serena says, 'Well that's okay, honey, you don't have to talk if you don't want. Another time maybe?'

They are almost home when Patty asks, 'How fat was she anyhow? The Ophelia woman. Was she fat like Elaine's mom? Sorry, Elaine, but your mom is, like, the fattest person in the neighbourhood.'

'Patty!' Serena says. 'That's extremely rude.'

Elaine keeps her face to the window. Through the side-view mirror she sees Agatha and Patty, silently shaking with laughter.

*

'I see how she does it,' Agatha says, later on, as Elaine walks her back to her house.

'Do you really?' Elaine mutters.

'She coaxes a few words out of one of us, sprinkles them like crumbs on the ground and then the rest of us follow.'

'Oh, for God's sake!' Elaine snaps.

'What? For God's sake – what?'

'Nothing.'

'What?'

'Always saying things, just to be clever. '

'No, I'm not.'

'Yes, you are. To make yourself sound more interesting. I bet you made up that whole Ophelia story.'

'I did not.'

'I bet you did.'

'You're just needled because I had something to say for myself for a change, instead of always sitting there like a big stuffed toy. Is that it? Because now you're the only one who hasn't contributed to Serena's bloody conversation sessions?'

'I am not needled. I just find it so false sometimes the way you go on.'

'*What?* What are you talking about?'

'All that crap about conversations. First it was bubbles, then slamming doors, now crumbs . . . Why can't a conversation just be a conversation?'

'Because that's how I see them,' Agatha says.

'No it isn't. How can you see something that isn't visible? They're just sounds. How can you *see* them? And anyway you couldn't see them – you're blind.'

'How do you know?' Agatha says, her bottom lip beginning to give. 'How do you know what does and doesn't go on behind my eyes?'

Agatha starts crying.

'I'm . . . I'm sorry, Agatha,' Elaine says. 'I didn't mean . . . I shouldn't have . . .'

Elaine reaches out to take her arm but Agatha shrugs it away.

'Why don't you just fuck off,' she says through her teeth, 'fuck off and leave me alone.'

Elaine reaches out again. 'Agatha, listen . . .'

Agatha grabs a lump of Elaine's upper arm and twists it.

Elaine pushes Agatha's shoulder with the heel of her hand.

Agatha's hand sweeps back then flies down, slapping Elaine right across the face. Elaine feels the slap shudder right through her head. She lifts her own hand then and smacks her right back.

*

Her mother says, 'Fighting like fish-wives out on the street. Anyone could have seen you.'

'But she hit me first. She hit *me*!'

Elaine covers her face with her hands and rocks on the kitchen chair.

'But to raise your hand to a blind girl, Elaine. A *blind* girl. God knows what the Hanleys will say. Do you think she'll tell? Do you think they saw? Mary sits in the back room of an evening, doesn't she? Or does she still sit out in that shed reading? Was Ted's car there?'

'No,' Elaine says into her hands. 'No, no, no.'

'Oh well, that's something, I suppose.'

Her mother begins rummaging in the kitchen drawers. 'Look, we'll put ice on your face, in the morning we can cover it with make-up.'

She lifts a corkscrew out and lays it on the draining board.

'A cup of sugary tea is what's needed now. A piece of apple tart. You're shocked more than anything else. Deep breaths now. Deep breaths,' she says and pulls a bottle of wine from the fridge before putting on the kettle.

And a few minutes later: 'If you ask me, you're better off without her. It's worse she's getting. Do you know she's been sleeping in that shed? Yes, Mrs Hanley only just found out. Sneaking out in the middle of the night, sleeping on her own, down the back of the garden like a cat. Her mother is not right in the head either, you know. She cares nothing for Agatha, never did. There's things I could tell you about that woman, and I will when you're older . . .'

And another few minutes again: 'Oh, do stop that crying, it's ridiculous carry on. Agatha is Agatha – just because she's blind doesn't mean that she can't be a little bitch.'

Elaine stands up and looks at her mother.

'You shut up about Agatha. What do you know about Agatha? You never liked her anyway. I see the way you look at her, as if you're afraid of her or she makes you sick or something just because she's blind. Well, you should take a look at your own big, fat disgusting self in the mirror sometime, see how sick you make other people feel!'

Her mother says, 'Really! To speak to me like that. To speak

to your own mother like . . . Well, there's a pair of you in it, if
you ask me.'

Elaine waits for her mother to go upstairs, slam the bedroom
door and lock herself in. Then she goes into her father's study
and picks up the phone. But Mrs Hanley says Agatha has a
headache and is too tired to come to the phone.

*

She watches Agatha from her bedroom window. She watches
her as she leaves the house first thing every morning with Mrs
Hanley – except for the two 'Sadie days' when their cleaner, Sadie, comes in. When Mrs Hanley is with her, they walk into the
cul-de-sac, Mrs Hanley carrying a small bag of Agatha's things
for the day. A short while later, Mrs Hanley returns, goes back
into the house for a few minutes then comes out again with
her handbag, gets into her car and drives off to take care of Ted
Hanley's mother.

On a Sadie day, Agatha doesn't leave the house until lunch
time, when Sadie walks her round to the Donegans' before
returning alone and going down to the village to catch the bus
home.

On three of these mornings, Ted Hanley is the one to take
Agatha into the cul-de-sac. He brings her in his car and it only
seems to take a few seconds before he's whizzing back past
Elaine's window and has turned the corner out of the estate. It's
as if he just opened the car door and booted Agatha out at the
side of the road outside Karl Donegan's gate.

In the afternoons, she has sometimes looked across the
road and thought she saw movement behind a window. She
has stood for a while, watching and waiting, wondering if she
should go over and see if Agatha has come back to the house
and is in there, alone. But in the end, she has put it down to her
imagination or maybe to simple wishful thinking.

She sees other things: Patty brushing her hair in the garden to the stroke of one hundred; Mr Slater coming home from town with a package under his arm; Serena speaking to him as she gets out of her car and him lifting his hat slightly to her then crossing the road with a dirty big grin on his face. She sees Rachel give Jonathan money to buy drink because she's the only one who always has money and he's the only who always gets served. Rachel steals the money from her mother's purse when she's drunk. She steals it out of spite, she says. Steals it and then immediately gives it away or spends it on everyone else.

She sees Jonathan coming back up the road with Karl walking beside him, carrying his haversack full of drink like a bag of loot on one shoulder.

*

She thinks about Jonathan more and more. She thinks about his tired eyes and his curly hair and the book he always carries in his pocket. For a long time he was the new boy, a slow shadow coming round the corner. Now he's Paul Townsend's best friend, leaving Karl Donegan dawdling in the background.

He has greenish eyes and bony fingers and a chipped front tooth. He has no mother. His father comes and goes at odd hours. He has one sister who is married and lives somewhere else. If she ever comes to visit him, Elaine has never noticed.

She thinks she must be in love with him. She feels it in every inch of her skin whenever he's around. She finds it more and more difficult to speak to him. She would like to be able to ask someone – is love not a pointless thing if you can't even bear to look the one you love in the face or can't imagine ever being able to relax on your own with him long enough to even kiss him? She would like to ask – how do you kiss anyway? And if it's true that French kissing means using your tongue – just how exactly do you go about it?

She can't ask Rachel because she would think it was funny and then the whole neighbourhood would have to hear about it. She can't ask Patty because she would only make her feel like a fool. She can't ask Brenda Caudwell because she probably doesn't know.

And she can't ask Agatha because Agatha is still not speaking to her.

One evening when her mother is out and her father is away on circuit, she walks into Serena's kitchen and sees his long skinny legs through the window dangling on the wall in the back garden. Paul's shorter rounded ones swinging beside him. Patty is lying on the grass on her stomach, one hand shielding her eyes against the last blare of the sun.

Serena, at the kitchen counter, face through a magnified mirror, is colouring in her mouth. She turns to her, fluffing up her long wavy hair with a flat, long-toothed comb – 'Tell me I look cute,' she says.

Elaine finds the word 'cute' an odd choice for a grown woman but tells her anyway.

'So . . .' Serena says, 'I hear you're coming to the tennis camp after all?'

'Yes,' Elaine says.

'It will be such fun. Won't it be such fun?'

'Yes, it'll be fun.'

'No Agatha again?'

'No Agatha.'

'You should go talk to her.'

'I've tried.'

'Try harder. It's more difficult for her, you know, and she needs to hold onto her pride. She's probably very lonely. I'm sure, once she hears your voice . . .'

Serena gives her a big happy smile, then gestures to the window, stiff-headed, as if afraid her hair will unfluff. 'Why don't you go join them?'

'I will now,' Elaine says, 'in a minute.'

She lifts the dirty dishes from the counter and carries them over to the sink then, leaning into it, looks out the window. Now Karl Donegan's head has appeared over the wall; he hauls himself up and sits on the ledge, beaming. The boys are doing all the talking. Patty gives so little in return: an occasional toss of her hair, a word or two, a cocked half-smile. Sometimes she appears not to be listening at all. But the boys keep talking. It's as if they are trying to sell her something.

She hears Serena running up the stairs. The toilet flushes, the bathroom window opens and her voice calls down to the garden that she's going now and that Elaine is in the kitchen.

Elaine closes her eyes and backs away from the sink. She doesn't want to see the boys' bored reaction or Patty's indifferent shrug.

She waits for the clip of the door behind Serena, the small growl of her car as it pulls out of the drive. Then Elaine leaves the house, goes into the Hanleys' and knocks on their front door.

Ted Hanley opens it, a newspaper in one hand, a chunky glass of whiskey in the other.

'Oh, hello,' he says, as if he's trying to remember her name or where he might have seen her before.

'Is Agatha in?'

'No. She's not here, I'm afraid.'

'Not in?'

'No. She's gone around to Karl's about twenty minutes since.'

He begins moving away from the door. 'They're probably around in his house. I'm sure they won't mind if . . .'

She wants to say – you're a big fat liar. I know she's not with Karl. I know she just told you to say that.

But she nods and says, 'Thank you, Mr Hanley,' then crosses the road and lets herself into her empty house.

*

Rachel says: 'If it's any consolation, she's dodging me too. Won't even come to the phone. When I bump into her at the stables her face goes all funny and she'll hardly speak to me. I wouldn't worry about it. Let her stew in it for a while, Elaine.'

'I shouldn't have slapped her,' Elaine says.

'No. But she'll come round – you'll see. She was always a bit moody – we know that.'

Rachel is carrying her riding helmet like a basket over her arm. She pulls a packet of cigarettes out of it, then a lighter.

'I have to say – it's bit mean on us. It's not as if we did anything on her. And my mother, old bitch that she is, was always very nice to her. We've offered loads of time to have her – but no, it's only the Donegans for her now. I said to my father – it's your fault. You should have seen his face! I was just teasing him about that time he made her cry – you know the menorah story – and then he had to drive her home, she got so upset. Anyway, that was weeks ago . . . Ah, come on, cheer up, Elaine. Here, see what I have!'

She pokes her finger into the lining of her riding hat and pulls out a folded note. 'Nice big one,' she says, holding it up. 'This will buy a lot of fun. Agatha just has a snot on. Don't mind her. Now why don't we put the snot to the other side of her face. Show her we can have just as good a time without her. Let it filter back to her through Karl. She'll soon wonder what she's missing.'

Another few days and she has had about enough of Agatha's huff. She decides to call and see her in the middle of the night when Agatha can't pretend to be out. She knows Ted is spending every other night at his mother's house now and that Mrs Hanley will be sleeping in her room at the far side of the house. If she knocks at Agatha's window, she'll have to listen to her. She'll have to believe how sorry she is.

But when she gets to the side of Hanleys' house, the glass room appears to be empty. She peers in all the windows but

Agatha isn't there. She waits for a few minutes in case Agatha is in the bathroom but there is no sound from the glass room. She turns to go home, but then remembers the shed.

Halfway down the Hanleys' back garden path, she hears dull thumping noises coming from the shed. Another few steps and she sees shadows through the window. The lamp is on – Agatha wouldn't need to put the light on. In fact, she would keep it turned off in case Mrs Hanley noticed. A taste comes into her mouth, like a taste of fear. She senses there is someone in the shed with Agatha, someone who is trying to hurt her. In her mind she sees a sudden image of Agatha lying on the floor, someone on top of her, holding her down. Agatha – she has to save Agatha. She rushes to the window and looks in. And there is someone lying on the floor, but it isn't Agatha. It's a man. Agatha is sitting on top of this man. Agatha naked. Agatha naked and rocking on top of a man; his big hands holding her slight hips, pushing them back and forward, making them rock.

She wants to run away but can't seem to move, can't stop looking in through the window. If Agatha could see, they would be staring right at each other. Elaine's eyes burning, Agatha's eyes hard and distant, like two river-washed stones.

She knows the man. She knows him but can't allow his name into her head. He is a man, that's all. A half-dressed man. He is wearing a shirt and a loosened tie. His trousers are in a crumple on the floor; his underpants clinging on to the legs of them. His shoes on the floor, his jacket thrown over Mrs Hanley's bookcase. The man's eyes are closed; he is making a horrible face. Elaine feels sick. She gates her mouth with both hands, turns and runs back through the Hanleys' back garden.

At her bedroom window, she waits. A few minutes pass – hardly any time at all – before she sees him turning the corner. He must have got out over the Hanleys' back wall, crept along by the back

of Serena's house, then the Townsends' before slipping out onto
the main road and coming into the cul-de-sac on the opposite
side of the road to the Hanleys'.

She watches him now, moving along, slyly tightening his tie
as he goes. His walk is leisurely. He moves past the Ryan house,
then her house, then on past the Jacksons' before disappearing
into the left-hand curve of the cul-de-sac.

In the coming days, she will search back through the moments.
She will look through her journal and try to find them, pressed
between the pages like forgotten tokens. She will hold each one
up to the light and examine it. She will pull out each moment;
she will lay them all out end to end then add them all up. She
will say: I should have known. I should have known. I should
have seen it.

11
Winter Present
January

THE SMELL OF BRAISED onion crouches over the landing and as I come down the stairs there are other stray whiffs: red wine, bouquet garni, bacon, beef. On a tray on the kitchen table, last night's empty plate sits like a small triumph.

I go to the drawer, pull out the list, put a tick beside Boeuf Bourguignon – another one down.

I am leaning the list on top of a large, thick brown envelope, as yet unopened since its arrival yesterday by registered post. Later today – or probably this evening – I will open and read it and then sign whatever needs to be signed.

For the moment, though, my only concern is with this list here under my hand. As soon as I've crossed the last item off it will be time to start another list. The second list will be less time-consuming; the second list will have nothing to do with food.

This list-making business – it's a habit inherited from my mother.

She had one for all events and every eventuality: weekly menus, laundry, household chores, plans for diets - plenty of those. She probably even had a list of all the lists she intended making. My whole childhood was dictated by lists. It helped her make sense of her life, I suppose, brought to it some small sense of purpose.

My present list is compiled from memory. It consists of dishes I mastered a long time ago, so that my name could earn its place on three French diplomas: *le premier, l'intérmediaire, le grand.*

My time in Paris – tuition fees, equipment, travel and living expenses – all paid for by my father. I can't begin to imagine what that would have cost, though I doubt he would have minded. Whatever else about him, I could never say he was mean with his money.

I clear then re-set his tray for breakfast.

In all, I remembered twenty dishes – seventeen of which made it onto the list. Some I've repeated for the sake of convenience: coq au vin, cassoulet, navarin of lamb. Some I've yet to attempt: foie gras with mustard seeds, turbot with beurre blanc – tricky ingredients and certainly not to be found around here. I have deliberately omitted escargot and frog legs. Even if Carmel sold them in her shop, I would still leave them off – with all the things one can eat in the world, I have never really seen the need for such nonsense. I feel much the same about Vichyssoise: cold soup tastes – well, like cold soup, at any time of the year.

Today is Friday – a good day for fish. I feel well today, lifted even. I look down the list and see all my smug crossed lines and little ticks and feel better than I've felt in a very long time. Later on, I will go shopping. I will borrow the car and go into town. I will buy cinnamon for his porridge, a jar of honey. Bakery bread. This time, I will look for a fishmonger's. The one I went to that time with Serena – if it's still there, that is, and if I can remember how to find it.

We were shopping for her art exhibition party. The party that was supposed to have taken place a few days later, but of course never did. She took me to lunch. Showed me how to eat real spaghetti without using a knife. Later we went to the fishmonger's.

I wonder now what happened to all that party food afterwards? Did she give it away? But under the circumstances, who would want to take it? Did she just leave it there to rot? The estate agent arriving a few weeks later, opening the fridge door to a rotten sludge of shrimp cocktail and vol-au-vents.

She didn't buy the fish – she ordered it in advance and asked to have it delivered on Friday morning: shrimp, smoked salmon, crab meat. The boy behind the counter, confused by her order, had to go off and look for his boss who came in from the pub next door with a rim of foam around his mouth.

Then we went looking for the delicatessen. I was supposed to be helping her to find it. She didn't exactly get cross with me, but she was surprised at how little I knew my own city, a girl of my age. Over-protected, she said I was, over-protected by motherly love.

Eventually, we found ourselves at the end of an alleyway, dim and slightly buckled, tight little jewellery shops all in a row. A smell of roasting coffee. There was a wrought iron gate with a church tucked behind it – I remember that came as something of a surprise. A woman came out blessing herself, little button face in a coloured headscarf, shopping basket weighing her down to one side. Never heard of a shop called Deli, she said. We kept going to the end of the lane where, stepping out of the dim alley and into the light, we found it.

Through the window, a confusion of shapes. I had to lean in, make a cave of my hands against the glass in order to see. Even then, I wasn't quite sure what I was looking at. Row over row of odd-shaped jars, stuffed with odd-shaped things, all the way up to the ceiling. In the dim light, other heftier shapes were hanging from hooks. Each piece an individual: no two things the same, nothing appeared to belong with anything else. A world away from McKenna's grocery store, with its fluorescent-lit, repetitive order. When the door opened, the warm gust of salami on my face.

I am thinking about Serena since the envelope arrived. I am thinking about her more than usual. Last night I dreamed about her. In the dream she was talking to me on the telephone. She said 'No, no – white anchovies only. Tell them we need white anchovies. Grey sea salt. Red mullet, yellow polenta.'

Serena still talking in colours.

From Serena, I learned to be particular about food, but I've never really been keen on that whole food-as-a-vocation concept.

I'm not saying I regret the job – there were things about it I loved: the planning and preparation; the algebra of this many ingredients and that amount of time. The pleasure in nursing everything along to the finishing line. The camaraderie, the concerted effort. The babel of insults, the magnificent swearing. But in the end what are you left with, really, but an edible picture on a plate? It's a brothel arrangement: money for temporary pleasure and seldom worth the price in the end.

If there was ever passion on my part, it was a cold sort of passion. If there was love, it was warped.

I did it for the white noise of a busy kitchen, the barely controllable chaos: the sense that I was just about keeping hold of the galloping stagecoach. I did it because the concentration required to run a kitchen fills up every nook and corner of the mind.

For fifteen years after my return from Paris, I did it – until I couldn't seem to speak without shouting and, under my skin, my nerves were constantly wriggling. After work, I sometimes found myself buying drink for bums in all-night dives or waking up beside a colleague that I neither liked as a person nor had ever found remotely attractive. Or I would sit alone on my night off, staring at the expensive walls of an apartment that I rarely saw in broad daylight.

And yet for all the noise in my life, all the pandemonium that surrounded it, on the streets and in the restaurant, all the agitation that went on backstage in the kitchen, I often felt like a nun in a convent who keeps tending to her duties: the matins, the masses, the evening chanting, the reading and teaching, the praying in her cell – day following day, night after night, going through the ropes, without truly believing in the God she was serving.

I did it until Michael found me in New York and left me six months later with this realisation: no matter how much noise there is in a room, there are some voices that will always be heard.

And so when Serena called on me for help, I had no difficulty accepting. Besides, it was a good proposition. From her first timid offer to cater for Dr Philip's retirement party in that apartment off 57th, she had built up a strong business. But she was growing tired – I could see it on her face, hear it in her voice – the cancer, already sniffing around in the dark. She still loved what she called 'the artistic side of the business' but wanted someone to help her shoulder the rest. She was lonely too, of course. Her second marriage had broken up; her best friend had moved to Alaska. She hadn't seen Patty in over four years.

What Serena really wanted was someone to sit down with at the end of the day and help her look back over the hours. I owed her, I guess, but I was ready too.

She said, 'I hope I'm not tugging you, sweetie. I wouldn't want to do that.'

I said, 'Serena, of course you're not tugging me.'

But of course she was, just as she's tugging me now, five years after her death.

And now, after all the years of study; of testing and tasting; for all the tricks and turns I have learned; the diplomas earned that still hang on the wall of Serena's old office. For all the consultations and the blazing rows; the numb ears suffered from hours with the phone clamped to my head. All the backs of spoons licked, all the slit fingers, all the knives sharpened – here I am, spending my days cutting chiffonade sage leaves and hand-crushing peppercorns and worrying about where I'm to find ingredients – for one grumpy old bastard in a wheelchair.

And yet, I know he's enjoying it. The clean plates tell me so, the slight puffing around his middle, the rounding of his face. Once or twice, we have even come close to discussing the menu – well, referring to it anyhow. The first time I made *magret de canard*: 'I'm doing duck tonight and was wondering if you'd prefer it well-done.'

A little bristle from his newspaper, a vague clearing of his throat then, without looking up, 'What? Oh, I'll leave it up to yourself.'

Last night he said thank you *again*. God only knows where all this could end.

Lynette is ecstatic. 'Soon, he will be fat,' she cries. 'Oh, he will be so fat!'

*

The phone rings and I jump. The phone in this house so seldom rings and mostly I forget that we have one. It's Lynette's voice on the other end.

'So sorry,' she says and begins to explain how her car wouldn't start. How she's at the garage right now but will have to take the bus and will be late by at least an hour. Two buses she will need to cross the city. (I had no idea she lived so far away.) She is full of apologies; there is a sort of plea in her voice, as if I'm going to have her whipped when she arrives. I want her to stop saying, So sorry, so sorry . . .

'It's fine, Lynette, please take your time.'

I would like to tell her that I can manage without her today; that she should go take care of her car. That I can see to my father myself. Do whatever needs to be done. But I can't seem to bring myself to say the words.

As if she knows what I'm thinking, she says: 'Just do usual, though. Breakfast and pills. Put chair beside bed. He can get in. I take care all else. His little worries, I take care.'

'Well, if you're sure, Lynette. You see, I was going to go into town today. I have a few things I really need to . . . I'll leave the key under the brick then if you're sure.'

'Soon I be there. I stay late.'

'There's no need to stay late.'

'I stay.'

'No, Lynette, please, really. There's no need.'

'He pay. I stay.'

I put down the phone and think of Serena again. So sorry. So very sorry.

The porridge is cold by the time I come back to it and so I clump it out into the dog's bowl, top it up with a little boeuf bourguignon I've kept from last night and take the dish over to him. He looks at me tiredly but doesn't get up.

'Brekky time,' I tell him, 'come on now. Have a sniff, go on. You know you want it . . . Come on, Boy. Come on. *Please?*'

Back at the stove, I start a new pot of porridge and wait for it to thicken about the spoon and burst into slow, lazy bubbles.

I glance down at the list again: only three more dishes to go.

When the tray is ready, I carry it into his room and lay it down on the coffee table. There's no need to tell him that Lynette will be late – the phone is right outside his door and I know he's heard every word of the conversation.

In my head the list grows: unwaxed lemons. Salted capers. Eggs.

I draw the curtains back and open the top window.

Then I help him to pull himself into a sitting position, the way Lynette taught me to do at the start of September – a lifetime ago. Hooking him underarms with my arms, hauling him backways, I can smell his breath, he can smell mine.

I wait while he edges himself into a sitting position. As he does this his colostomy bag gives a small coy slosh. His breath stinks of sulphur and pills, overnight garlic. His pyjamas are clammed to his back. But these are his little worries and Lynette's little worries – not mine.

Salami. Smoked bacon. Swiss cheese.

I straighten his bed and fix his pillows around him then lift his tray from the coffee table, pulling the little side legs down and settling them into his quilt. I spread the napkin across his chest. Then, from a shelf over the television, take down three bottles of pills. I peck out this morning's dose and place them into the plastic container which I leave beside his plate. I take his handbell from the window ledge and put it within his reach.

Throughout all this, we exchange not a glance nor a word. It's as if none of this is happening: the tray, the bed, his breath, the bulging colostomy bag – they simply do not exist. And neither do we.

On my way out, I switch on the radio.

Mushrooms and balsamic vinegar.

I get to the door and say, 'Would it be all right to take the car this morning?'

'Of course,' he says to his porridge.

Back in the kitchen, I survey last night's havoc. I am a messy cook, a cook that expects to always have someone two steps behind, cleaning up after her. The sink is the aftermath of an earthquake. The floor is an upheaval of things I dragged out of the cupboards last night. My mother's pamphlets and cookery books are strewn everywhere. Yesterday I was getting ready to dump them but was waylaid by such titles as *100 Recipes for Slimmers. The Joy of Cooking. A Summer of Low Fat Meals. Recipes for a Happy Family. Woman's Way Tricks with Mince.* And most intriguing of all: *Woman's Own Ten Things to Do with a Sausage.*

It would take me an hour to clean up. But the bit is between my teeth now and I don't have an hour to spare. I have to drive into town today. I need to drive into town today.

Mrs Larkin can clean it up – that is, if Mrs Larkin is in today. I can never be certain because she tends to do things in her own Mrs Larkin way.

For the first few weeks, she came in the mornings. Then one Friday morning, she just didn't show.

On Friday afternoon, the doorbell rang.

I said, 'I thought you came in the mornings?'

'It depends,' she said, taking off her coat and carefully arranging it on the hanger. 'I explained to your father – he knows.'

I'm not all that sweet on Mrs Larkin. I just don't like her being in this house, the fact that she knows it better than I do and appears to be so at home here. I don't like the way she wears her good coat to work and hangs it so carefully on a hanger, nor the way she changes her high heels for a pair of slippers that she keeps on a shelf under the stairs, along with her perfectly laundered aprons. I don't like her carefully made-up face, nor her discreet shade of lipstick; the way she keeps opening her mouth as if she's about to say something and then appears to change her mind before abruptly moving off. And I don't like the fact that she now has her own front-door key.

I come across her sometimes when she's towing the hoover around the house and I know she's looking at me from the side of her eyes.

I don't know anything about her – if she's still married, or if she's a widow, where she lives even. Sometimes she arrives on foot; sometimes she gets out of a fairly decent car. I don't know why such a woman would work as a cleaner and maybe that's what I don't like most of all.

I stand for a while and consider the kitchen, then decide to leave it. A few weeks ago, I wouldn't have dreamed of leaving it in this state, but I'm done trying to impress Mrs Larkin.

I write a note: *Please leave cookery books etc. as they are. Am in middle of sorting them.*

I let the dog out, bring the phone into the sitting room and place it beside my father, then go upstairs and begin to get ready.

*

Since my return, I've only ventured into town on a few occasions and that was by taxi. Sitting in the back seat, watching the suburbs give way to the city, it was like I was a kid again, going for my weekly hospital check-up. I kept expecting to see Mr Slater's ghost flapping along in the distance.

I never brought much back: a few bits of cheese, a bottle of wine, a few softback books. Sometimes I just wandered around. I could just as easily have gone by bus. But to stand at the bus stop in full view of the traffic – neighbours driving by (Is that . . .? Surely it's not? My God, it is! What does she want here? What does she *want* . . .?)

I have taken his car to the supermarket a few times, always asking for permission first – as if there's the remotest chance he'll be using it himself. He won't be driving again, nor will he ever sell his car. To sell it would be to admit defeat. And so the car will remain on the driveway until he dies, or even beyond then.

The first time I took it out, it had been sitting on the drive for such a long time. The windows were filthy, the body work coated in dust, the doors reluctant to budge. The seat groaned when I sat into it. A cobweb was laced across the rear-view mirror. An old car, a car that had been left to rot in all weathers, a car that had been all but forgotten. And yet, at the first turn of the key, it sparked up.

I'm looking forward to driving it into town, to sitting in the traffic listening to the radio like anyone else. To twisting it up through the corkscrew ramps of the car park, all the way to the highest floor where I can look over the city, try to find my place within it. Then coming out and walking around in broad daylight.

Away from this neighbourhood, I could be anyone.

Somebody's wife. Somebody's mother. I could linger on the upper floors of a department store, I could be any other middle-aged woman, looking at all those clothes that I can afford at last, but no longer really want.

I could have coffee somewhere, maybe fall into a conversation. My son, you see . . . My daughter always says . . . . My husband, you know. My mother.

I could be part of one of those conversations that I have so often overheard. Later I would look for that delicatessen. That hidden church. The fishmonger's. Buy turbot. Foie gras. Mustard seeds.

*

On the way into town, I get caught in a traffic jam and for some reason start thinking about Paris. Or the last time I saw my mother anyway, which was in Paris, where we stood late at night, watching the boats pass under the Pont Neuf arches. It could be one of those songs, something crooned out over a lounge piano or wrung out of an old man's accordion. I sing it into the car: *The last time I saw her was Paris . . .* but it sounds neither funny nor ironic and so I stop.

The two of us standing there, leaning over and looking down on the river; boats sliding beneath us. The piped music. Lights on water, lights on boats, the flashing lights of cameras, the happy waving hands of Japanese girls. And our silence.

A week before I was due to receive my final diploma – *le grand* – Serena phoned me.

'Your mom wants to see you. She wants to come to Paris.'

'Here? She wants to come here! To see me *here*? Why though? *Why*?' My voice panicked and getting ready for tears.

'I don't know, she just called.'

'Maybe she wants to be here when I get my diploma? Would that be it? Would it? Serena – did she say?'

'She didn't. Well, you know how she is when she calls? On and then off again.'

'Does she . . . does she want me to go back – do you think?'

'I don't know. I really don't know, sweetie, I don't.'

'Oh. Oh God. What'll I do? Do I have to?'

'No, of course you don't have to.'

'Do you think I should?'

'I can't answer that question.'

'Well, your opinion then – at least give me that?'

'You're twenty-two years old, sweetheart. It's your mother we're talking about here. You're going to have to do whatever it is your heart tells you to do.'

'Oh, Serena,' I said, 'I don't even know what that *means*.'

I told my room mate, a beautiful and enthusiastic Dutch girl called Mina, whose robust good humour often wore me out. 'That's wonderful!' she cried. 'I'm so happy for you. You must cook for her. Then show her all the sights. She will come to the ceremony! I will take photographs of you! We can put the best one in a frame. Later you will go to dinner. You must feel wonderful, after all!'

'Yes. Wonderful.'

'How long has it been?'

'Oh, about five months,' I lied.

For once Mina looked sad. 'A long time so.'

'Yes, a long time,' I agreed, half-wishing that I'd told her the truth was more like five years – just to see her reaction.

Serena was to call me back at the end of the week; I would let her know my decision; then she would call my mother and in turn let her know if I wanted to see her. But of course, my mother got there first.

A few days later, there was a note in my post box written on hotel notepaper.

E – I'm staying in the Hotel du Louvre, if you'd like to meet there the day after tomorrow at 6.30. If that doesn't suit you can phone me at the hotel. Leave a message if I'm not in – S.

I called Serena.

'It's like one of those fucking notes she used to leave on the kitchen table,' I whined. 'After five years, this is what I get. And I still don't know what to do.'

'If you don't go, you could regret it. But on the other hand . . .'

'Serena, that is no help to me. No help at all.'

'I know. I'm sorry. I truly am. But if you do decide to go–'

'What?'

'Be careful.'

'What do you mean be careful?' I asked her.

'Just be careful. Protect yourself. Before you leave your room, I want you to imagine yourself putting on your invisible armour.'

'Jesus, Serena!'

'And remember I love you.'

'Please, you know how I hate you saying that.'

'I know, sweetie, I know. But I do.'

I had one sleepless night: I would go. I wouldn't go. But then, why wouldn't I go? No big deal. And just why the fuck should I go anyway? Of course, I would go, even if it was just to let her know *exactly* what I thought of her. Go? How could she even have the nerve to ask? I certainly would not!

And even if I could bring myself to go, how could I face her after the terrible thing I had done?

The night was halfway through when I realised I was simply terrified of my mother. Terrified, as if she was going to take out a big stick and beat me. Terrified that I would start crying and disgrace myself. That it would turn into one of those early phone calls, with me pleading to go home and her coldly telling me to pull myself together.

An hour before I was due to get up, I finally fell asleep. I had a dream we were in a big bed together, the bed in the middle of the lobby of her hotel. She kept squeezing my face and trying to make me eat sweets. I'm not opening my mouth, I kept saying, and she answered, Yes you are, otherwise, how would we all be able to hear you? Everyone in the lobby looking at us. Patty's father waddling across the floor. 'For Chrissake, give your mother a kiss . . .'

I woke up crying and when I eventually managed to get out of the bed, I don't know what got into me, but everything had somehow changed. I had erased the past five years from my mind. And here I was now, making plans for our few days together. We could do the whole tourist thing – if that's what she wanted. We could retrace her steps from that holiday she had before she was married, when she'd bought her *le chat qui fume* ashtray. We could walk from her hotel to Notre Dame – she would want to go to Notre Dame, I was certain. We would stroll down the leafy quayside – stop to look at the books in the stalls. 'They are called *bouquinistes*,' I would tell her, 'here since the sixteenth century. The only city in the world that has bookshelves for river walls,' I would jauntily add.

She would tell me a little about that holiday she had when she was maybe my age – what she had seen, and what had changed, who she was with. I would take her to dinner every night, small, discreet little bistros, where we would be the only ones speaking English. I would show off my French, my knowledge of food. She would be impressed, proud even. At college I asked my tutors for advice and even made a list of suitable bistros. Beyond all that, I could see nothing.

In the lobby of the Hotel du Louvre, there were other women

sitting alone, on sofas and soft chairs, women waiting on taxis, women waiting on men. There were other women smoking. In fact, there were two or three other women who fitted more with the image in my memory. She had shrunk to about half her former size. She wore trousers – I had never seen her in trousers before – and heels. Her hair was a different colour. She looked nothing like the woman I remembered, and yet I would have known her anywhere.

From across the lobby she had seemed so much younger. Up close – when I finally brought myself to look at her – her face, without its plumpness, was wrinkled, her neck had begun to yield.

We didn't embrace. She waited for me to come right over and stand before her, and then she half-stood as if she'd only that second seen me. But she must have seen me – I was the only one of my age in the lobby. We barely looked at each other. This awkwardness will pass, I told myself, we'll settle down, everything will become normal. She had been shopping: carrier bags at her feet from department stores on Boulevard Haussman; a large stiff bag at her back bearing the Lafayette logo. 'Oh, just a little gift to myself,' she said and patted it, but made no attempt to explain or show me this little gift. I asked her if she'd like a drink before dinner.

'Oh, I don't drink any more,' she said.

I ordered tea and we talked about Paris. She asked me which area I lived in and if I was enjoying the 'cookery course'. She said she'd been to the Louvre that morning but had been a little disappointed in the *Mona Lisa*. 'The size of it, for one thing,' she said. 'And sly looking, I thought. Not beautiful at all.'

It was a conversation between strangers. No, it was less than that – strangers will offer a little glimpse to one another: something from their past, the name of a family member, a neighbour. There was none of that. She did ask after Patty once and I told her Patty had moved to California four years ago, as soon as she'd graduated from secretarial college.

'Oh yes, of course, I knew that.'

And I did ask after my father, once.

'Oh, busy as ever, you know. Busy.'

I longed to ask her about so much else: the Hanleys, the Townsends, the Shillmans, the Caudwells. I longed to know what had happened to Karl and Paul. Mr Slater even. Anyone at all. But I knew better. Instead I told her about the bistro that had been recommended to me.

'Far?' she said in a dreamy way and it occurred to me that she may have been on tranquilisers.

'About a twenty minute walk, but a nice walk, along the river where the bookstalls are, we could—'

'Well, I'd better change my shoes so.'

She didn't invite me up to her room, just gathered her bags and said, 'I won't be long.'

As I waited, I thought about an evening a long time ago when I was a child, shortly after Brenda Caudwell had broken the news and sent it flying through the school that, at nine years of age, Elaine Nichols slept in the same bed as her mother, while her father slept in another room on the opposite side of the house. I had been simmering about it for days and then one evening had marched into the sitting-room and made the announcement that, in future, I wanted to sleep on my own.

'Your own bed do you mean?'

'My own room.'

'Oh, now, don't be silly.'

'I'm not being silly. I want my own room. We have enough of them. And if you won't let me, then I'll just have to ask Daddy about it, that's all.'

Abruptly she had turned away from me and said, 'Shhhhh. I'm watching this.'

And for the next few minutes, she pretended to be engrossed

in a television programme. I stayed standing right by her
armchair and waited until she spoke again.

'Well now – where were we? Oh yes. You can certainly
have your own room. Of course you can have your own room.
That's no problem at all. If you're sure you won't be frightened
of monsters and murderers and ghosts and witches and all the
other scary things that come in the night.'

'I won't be frightened.'

'Are you certain about that now? Because once we make the
move, there is no going back.'

She looked at me carefully and I carefully looked back.

'I want. My. *Own*. Room,' I growled.

She slept on the sofa for a couple of nights then quietly
moved into the spare room at the back of the house. Gradually
she began to speak to me again. My clothes were washed and
ironed, my room made spotlessly clean. My meals were always
on the table. Snacks continued to be offered in between. But it
would never be the same between us.

The first day I started school, my mother had taken me there
by the hand. By the time I was nine, nothing had changed:
every morning, I walked tall in the midst of the herd of mothers
and infants and occasional senior infants, while children my
own age ran loose around us or maybe held the hand of younger
siblings they themselves had been entrusted to take to school.
And at the end of each day, when I came through the gate, I
would find my mother standing under the trees across the road.

But after she moved into her own room, I would go to school
on my own, and the space that she had for so long made her
own, across the road under the trees, would remain obstinately
vacant.

12
Summer Past
August

THE FIRST TIME ELAINE gets drunk, she gets sick all over Karl Donegan. She remembers:

Sitting by the river on a midsummer's evening. Patty showing Jonathan how to roll a joint. Rachel and Paul arguing over who owns which bottles and how many should be left in the haversack. Brenda Caudwell standing with her face scrunched up, angrily squirting a can of fly spray at the midges. A voice saying, 'I can't believe you actually brought a can of fly spray down here . . .'

Karl lying on his stomach, arms stretched into the river, holding a big brown bottle in each hand into the water to cool them down. His T-shirt slipped up his back. Somebody saying: 'What's that bruise on your side?'

'It's nothing,' Karl says, pulling the bottles back out of the water.

Elaine cranes to see it. 'It looks like a map of Australia,' she says and then vomits on top of it.

The vomit stinks of rotten apples; a sour fizzy liquid pours into her nostrils and down the back of her throat; she feels she might be drowning in it.

'Oh, I'm sorry, sorry, I'm sorry, I'm sorry, oh.' She can hear her own voice some way behind her, gulping out the apology.

Karl taking off his T-shirt. His back embroidered with acne, some of it already melted into his skin. He wipes her mouth with the clean side of the T-shirt then leans into the river and swishes it around. He pulls out the T-shirt and bangs it off the stones,

'This is the way they wash clothes in India,' he says.

Jonathan nodding as if he's agreeing with everyone, even when no one is saying anything. Then he takes the joint off Patty and sucks on it.

'That's it,' Patty says, 'hold it in, hold it in. Now, you've got it. Now.'

She remembers:

Karl coming back from the river in his belly, making a pillow of his jacket in the long grass, telling her to sleep it off and that when it's dark he'll bring her home.

Karl sitting down in front of her, leaning forward; he is holding a bottle by its neck. A picture of a woodpecker on the bottle's label. The woodpecker swinging to and fro. The sky beginning to spin; the long blades of grass swaying. The skin on Karl's back: yellow red, purple. The scars in between, little fishes.

When she wakes up, her brain is throbbing and her throat is raw. Karl is lying down beside her, counting the stars. Everyone else has gone home. It's late, he tells her. The middle of the night.

'I have no key,' she says. 'I'll have to wake my mother.'

'Do they lock the back door?' Karl says.

'My father does, but he's away.'

He stands up and holds out his hand.

Karl takes her round the back of the cul-de-sac through a grassy patch and behind a few bushes. He makes a stirrup of his hands and helps her climb over a high wall. And now she finds herself crouching in a gap between two high walls: the Caudwells' and the Shillmans'.

'How did you know this was even here?' she says.

'You're not the only one who knows how to sneak around,' Karl says.

Her mother is still up. They can see over the wall, all the way up the back garden, right in through the kitchen window. Her mother and Mrs Shillman and another woman Elaine recognises as a golfing friend of Mrs Shillman's. The two visitors move towards the door as if they are leaving, then they change their minds and move back again. They sit down, stand up. Light a cigarette. Drink something. Sit down again. Drink again.

'They'll be a while yet,' Karl says.

'Oh God,' she says, 'I'm so thirsty I could die . . .'

Before she has even finished her complaint, Karl has climbed the wall and disappeared into the Shillmans' garden.

'Karl!' she whispers. 'What are you doing!'

He makes a long shhhhh at her, through the wall.

He's back then with a plastic bottle filled with cool water.

'It was clipped onto Michael's racer. I filled it from the garden tap.'

'Jesus, Karl, are you mad? What if someone heard you?'

'I didn't make a sound. I could be a cat burglar, you know, if I wanted.'

He tells her how, a few weeks ago, he and Paul stole the key into Dr Townsend's surgery and went looking for drugs.

'What!'

'We didn't find any. Actually, we didn't really look. Once we got in, we couldn't stop laughing and so we got out again.'

In the dark she is tempted to tell him about Agatha and what she has seen in the shed. She gets as far as saying, 'Karl, if I tell you something . . .'

But instead she tells him about the time she was night-walking with Rachel and Agatha, and they saw Dr Townsend come home in the middle of the night so drunk that he fell out of his car.

Then she tells him about the time they got over the back wall of Hanleys' and saw Ted walking round the garden room wearing nothing but a pair of purple Y-fronts and for ages they called him Purple Balls Hanley.

Karl laughs when she tells him that; he laughs so much the tears run out of his eyes. He lights a cigarette and holds it low to the ground and then he tells her about his bruise, the shape of Australia.

'My mother must look like a whole atlas,' he says; 'he hits her and then I hit him. He's bigger than me, well for the moment, but I'll still have a good go. One day I'm going to break his fingers and that'll be the end of him and his fucking orchestra.'

She nearly dies the way he just comes out with all that.

'Your father hits your mother . . .?' she begins. 'That's terrible, Karl, that's just . . .'

Karl puts out the cigarette. 'Light's just gone off,' he says, 'are you right?'

*

The second time she drinks, she starts crying like a baby. She cries because Agatha is blind and because even if they make it up she can never be her friend again and be Rachel's friend at the same time. She cries because her mother is fat and she knows other people jeer her. She cries because she feels lonely, as if she is bricked in behind a wall and can hear everyone outside, but nobody can hear her. She cries because Jonathan doesn't love her.

And she cries because Karl's father hits Karl's mother and men rape their wives and go off with other women and sometimes even go off with their daughters' friends.

She cries and she cries. People ask her – why are you crying, Elaine? She says, 'Nothing, nothing.' Or she says, 'I don't know. I don't know.'

Before she starts crying, Patty is kneeling beside Jonathan, cutting his hair with a nail scissors. She lays each curl on the palm of her hand, then lifts the palm to her face and stares into it, turning her palm towards the fading light, then away from it, smiling at each curl as if it was a live thing and as if she really loved it. Patty picks each curl up in the pinch of her fingers, raises it over her head and slowly lets it drop on the ground.

'Jesus – what's the matter with *her*?' Brenda Caudwell asks.

'She's dropped acid,' Paul says.

'Dropped what?' Brenda says, looking around.

*

The third time she drinks, she doesn't get sick. She talks and talks and makes everyone laugh. They are in the Shillmans' house.

Rachel makes them drinks from the cocktail cabinet. She opens all these bottles and puts ice into a shaker then puts on music and dances around like a South American. Then they all start dancing around. Until a group of older boys comes knocking on the door, some of them with girlfriends; boys who are practically men. One of them says, 'Is this the free house?' He has black hair on his hands. Peter Caudwell walks through the gate and Brenda has to rush through the kitchen and sneak out the back and over the wall. Elaine goes with her to give her a leg up.

'Fuck him, anyway,' Brenda says. 'And I was really looking forward to trying out that acid stuff.'

When she comes back in, Paul Townsend is falling backwards on top of the cocktail cabinet. He falls like a shot cowboy. Bottles from all over the world topple and bounce on the black rag-rug. Two bottles fall on the side of the fireplace; one smashes, the other spews out a thickish green liquid. Two of the older boys pull Paul out of the cabinet and steady him up. Paul leaves a big crack right through the middle of the glass. 'Oh no!' Rachel screams with her hands on her head. 'I'm in such trouble now, I'm in such trouble.'

'It's okay,' Karl Donegan says, 'It's okay.'

'How is it okay? How? How? Look at the place. That's my mother's Indian kaftan that girl is wearing. They're my father's Cuban cigars. I'll be killed, I'll be– Look at the cabinet. My mother's cabinet. She spent a fortune on that cabinet!'

'Don't worry,' Karl says. 'We'll get rid of everyone, clean up.

I'll say I tripped on the rug and fell on the cabinet. I'll say I broke it.'

'I don't want you to say you broke it!' Rachel screams at him. 'Why should you take the blame?'

'I don't mind,' Karl says. 'Really, I don't.'

*

Another row with her mother.

'Have you been drinking? Elaine – answer me, please, is that drink I smell off your breath?'

'Is that drink I smell off yours?'

Her mother grabs her by the arm and squeezes it.

'I thought I told you to stay in tonight. I thought I told you you weren't allowed to go out after six o'clock in the evenings.'

'I'm not staying here on my own. While you go off drinking with Martha Shillman.'

'I'm not out drinking! She's teaching me golf and we go into the club house afterwards for a bite to eat and maybe one or two– How dare you question me anyway? How dare–! For once in my life, for once in my life I have a hobby and you'd begrudge it me.'

'I'm here on my own all day. And now you want me–'

'I thought you were in Serena's.'

'I don't like going there any more.'

'You don't like Serena?'

'It's Patty, always sneering and saying mean things, she said you were the fattest person in the neighbourhood.'

Her mother lets go of her arm.

'You won't even let me go to the stables during the day. And now you want me to stay in every night too.'

'You have to be punished, Elaine. After what you lot did to the Shillmans'. The place destroyed and that Karl Donegan smashing the good cocktail cabinet.'

'He didn't smash it. He didn't go near it!'

'Bad enough, Elaine, you telling lies on your own account,

but lying for your friends too. You are staying in for the next two weeks and that's all about it. And you can forget about any tennis camp too, mi*ssss*. You can put it straight out of your head.'

'I'm not staying in this house on my own. I hate this house. I hate it.'

*

At the end of August, they hear the truth about Junie Caudwell. And then immediately afterwards, the truth about Agatha: one truth leading into another.

Maggie Arlow is the one who tells them about June. She tells them about June first thing one morning when she's not even drunk. Elaine is on her way to the shops when she looks over the wall and sees everyone by the stableyard archway. Only Jonathan is missing. She sees Agatha is there and almost walks on by because it feels too awkward. But then Rachel spots her and starts waving like mad and so Elaine decides to wander in. When she gets near, Paul puts his finger to his lips and nods his head towards the yard.

Maggie inside shouting at one of the lads – 'You fucking simpleton.'

And the rugged mumbling of the lad trying to defend himself – 'Buh bu dubbedy, bud bu.'

'What? *What?* I can't understand a word you're saying!'

'Buh bu, dub bu.'

'Oh, just get out there now and clean up that mess, or you're back on the train this afternoon to whatever arsehole of the country you were shat out of.'

'Someone has a big fat hangover,' Rachel says.

Brenda Caudwell says, 'How do you know?'

'By the look of her.'

Brenda tuts. 'How can you know just by looking at her?' she says. 'That's just ridiculous.' She turns to Elaine. 'You can't tell if someone has a hangover just by looking, can you, Elaine . . .?'

Elaine says nothing.

They can see through the archway into the stableyard, Maggie crossing from one side to the other, still shouting at the stable lad. Brenda is holding an envelope; she lifts it to her mouth and sniggers.

Agatha is also holding an envelope in one hand, in her other a cigarette. She takes a pull and then says, 'Oh God, I don't want this. Does anyone . . .?

Brenda shouts out, 'I'll take it!'

And then Elaine takes a small breath and says, 'I will.'

Brendie said it first, but Agatha holds the cigarette out towards Elaine and, for the first time in weeks, says her name.

There is the hard wet scratching of a yard brush; the clean, hard clip of horses' hooves on stone. There is the savoury stench of horse-piss on hay. There is Maggie. She comes out from the tackroom and begins towards them.

'Well?' she says when she gets there.

She is short of breath; her eyes look startled; her face is ruddy, her mouth clenched as if she's eaten something that's slightly off.

'Back in a minute,' she says suddenly and then rushes into the house.

'What did I tell you?' Rachel says. 'A stinker.'

They wait.

'You're not even smoking that properly,' Brenda says to Elaine, then, 'I mean to say, what a waste. I wouldn't mind but I baggsed it first.'

'Shut up, Caudwell,' Agatha says and Elaine tries not to show her pleasure.

'Yeah, shut up, Caudwell,' Elaine says, 'you're always moaning.'

Maggie comes back out of the house. Her short dirty hair stands up in peaks.

'Doesn't she look like a man?' Brenda Caudwell says under her breath. 'She looks like that postman – do you remember him, that old pervert with the bandy legs? One time he flashed his dickie at our Peter.'

'He *what*?' Karl laughs

Agatha asks, 'Does she? Does she look like the old postman?'

Rachel says, 'Oh God, yes, she does, shut up, shut up, she'll–'

Maggie is standing in front of them now.

'What's so funny?' she says.

'Nothing,' Brenda says. 'I just want to pay for last week's lessons and to book in for next week.' She hands the envelope to Maggie and then walks around and stands behind her.

Agatha says, 'I want to pay too but I'm not feeling well today so I won't be able . . .'

'You're looking a bit peaky, all right,' Maggie says and lights up one of her French cigarettes.

Behind Maggie's back Brendie Caudwell is making faces. She is imitating Maggie's crabby expression. She has put her hand under the waistband of her jodhpurs and stuck her index finger out through the top of her zip. She is doing a little dance and wagging her finger pretending that it's Maggie's dickie.

Elaine can hear Rachel behind her, trying not to choke. Maggie looks at Rachel's big red face then at Karl, who chews his lip and stares at the ground. Paul has walked off. Elaine is about to follow him. Then Maggie swings around suddenly and glares at Brenda. There is a split second between her swinging around and Brenda's freezing. Brenda looks at Maggie with a blank, innocent face.

Maggie turns back and asks Agatha if she needs to go to the doctor.

'No, no,' Agatha says, 'it's just a bit of a bug or something. I'll be fine in a day or two.'

Maggie finishes her cigarette, throws it down and screws it into the ground with her boot. Then out of the blue, and without even looking at Brenda, she says: 'And how is that sister of yours doing, Brenda?'

Behind Maggie's back, Brenda stops grinning. 'Who, June?'

'You only have the one.'

'She's fine. Thank you.'

'Brussels, isn't it? Where she's working?'

Brenda says, 'Yes, Brussels.'

Maggie turns around and carefully looks at Brenda.

'Is she putting on any weight over there? I hear the food can be fattening.'

'No. I mean, I don't know.'

'Didn't send a photograph or anything?'

Brenda shakes her head.

'Whereabouts in Brussels is she, anyway? I know Brussels actually; competed there once a few years ago.'

'I . . . I don't know.'

'The address, you must have seen the address, when you write to her and that?'

'I . . . I can't remember.'

'Are you sure it's Brussels at all? It's not somewhere else?'

Brenda gives a slow blink and cocks a cheeky lip at Maggie.

'I think I know where my own sister is, thank you. Anyway, I better go now, I told my mother—'

'Sure now – it's not the home for unmarried mothers, you know, out there near the old airport road? The home where they lock you up and make you scrub floors for your sins and then when your baby is born the nuns drag it out of your arms and give it to some couple who pretend it's theirs. And then you come on home with the spirit kicked out of you, and everyone thinks you're just a bit thick because you don't appear to have learnt much French in Brussels or wherever the fuck it was you were pretending to be.'

Brenda's face is white; her mouth begins to wobble. Maggie throws the envelope on the ground at her feet. 'You tell your mother from me, keep her money. Keep it for her grandchild. And if I ever see your snide little face here again, I'll punch it.'

Then Brenda runs off, and Maggie goes back into her house.

They come out of the yard without looking at each other; without saying a word. Agatha linking Karl, Elaine walking behind Rachel and Paul. Brenda is waiting on the corner by the Townsends' bushes.

'Is it true?' Paul asks her and hands her the envelope that Maggie threw on the ground.

'Yes,' Brenda says. 'Yes. Yes. Yes.'

'Bitch, to say it like that, though, in front of everyone,' Karl says. 'Fucking old cow.'

'Poor June,' Rachel says, 'what will happen to her now?'

'I don't understand how she found out,' Brenda says. 'How the hell did she . . . we were so careful. I'll have to tell my parents. Will I? Will I have to tell them? My father will go mad. He tore the place asunder when June told him she was pregnant. Kicked the washing machine, the fridge. The whole kitchen got it. Oh, fuck June anyway, she's ruined all of our lives now.'

They sit in a row on the Townsends' wall and for a few moments nothing is said until Karl stands up – 'Jesus, Agatha,' he says, 'are you all right? What's wrong?'

Elaine looks down the line and sees that Agatha is crying.

'Agatha?' she says and gets up. 'Agatha – what's happened? What's the matter with you?'

'I'm in trouble,' she says simply, 'I need your help,' and then she puts her arms out to Elaine.

13
Winter Present
January

BY THE TIME I get into town and wander around and get home again, hours have gone by and the light is already fading. I come into the house and there is no Lynette. My father is not in the sitting-room. The kitchen door is ajar and I see through the crack the side of his wheelchair. I imagine all sorts: his colostomy bag has burst and he's frantically searching for paper towels to clean up the mess; someone has broken into the house and has dragged him into the kitchen . . .

I rush into the kitchen and find him calmly positioned by the counter. It's the first time I've seen him in this room since I was a child and it throws me a little.

'I'm so sorry,' I say, 'I forgot about the time. Isn't Lynette here? She's supposed to be here, she told me she would be, she *swore* she'd only be an hour late.'

'I told her to take the day off. Car trouble. She'd to go the bank for an overdraft.'

I note he is dressed and shaved and that there is no smell from his bag.

'Did Mrs Larkin help you to—?' I begin.

'I looked after myself.'

Even so, I see Mrs Larkin's paw marks all over the kitchen. Everything has been tidied away; damp teacloths folded at the edge of the sink and her rubber gloves pegged from an overhead utensil rack, so that they hang like cows' udders – a habit that really annoys me.

I wonder if he called her or if she just appeared out of nowhere, as she sometimes likes to do.

The kettle is on, beginning to boil. 'Is that for tea?' I ask and move towards it. 'You want tea?'

'I can manage,' he says, giving the wheelchair a deft little turn and reaching out for the kettle. He makes old-fashioned tea, scoops of leaves from a caddy, a scalded pot, a strainer, milk, sugar. Everything laid out and prepared in advance.

'Oh God, I forgot your newspaper. I'm sorry, I can go back down now and–'

'It's all right,' he says. 'Mrs Larkin brought it.'

'Of course.'

'Would you like a cup?' he asks and I can't resist the novelty of having my father make old fashioned tea for me, in the kitchen. *In the kitchen.*

There is a silence in the room although it's not as jagged as I might have expected. Still we could do with a buffer. I look for the dog and there he is, standing at the glass panel of the back door, looking in at me. He lifts a limp paw and makes three effete scratches on the wooden frame.

'He's much better now,' my father says, and then niftily whizzes past me to the door and lets the dog in. 'Mrs Larkin gave him bread and soup. I think the plainer diet may suit him better.'

The dog comes to me and I try not to fuss too much over him.

'Hello, Boy,' I say and give his head a couple of cool-handed pats. The dog licks my wrist and then goes to my father, who surprises me by the affection he shows, outdoing me by quite a few degrees – ruffling the dog's head, stroking his back, playing tenderly with his ears.

He turns away, lifts the teapot and pours two mugs of tea. He hands me one and says: 'Yes, there's another couple of years left in the old dog yet.'

Our eyes catch and I wonder, just for a second, if he may be making some sort of a joke.

'I bought turbot for dinner,' I say and then look away, because if he has just made a joke, I don't know how to deal with it.

'Ah,' he says, 'actually, I've already eaten.'

'Mrs . . ..?'

'Yes. Stew. A rather big plate of it, I'm afraid.'

He deals with his tea, and I notice he takes only one spoonful of sugar – a spoonful less than I have been giving him for the past few months. Then he lifts the mug with one hand while the other begins reversing his wheelchair towards the door. Once there, he holds the door open himself then, in a three-point turn, leaves the kitchen for the sitting-room.

I put the turbot in the fridge and take my mug of tea upstairs. The dog follows.

On my dressing table is yet another page torn from my mother's telephone message pad, the pad so old by now it could almost be a collector's item. My mother would have bought this pad when I was very small and she was acting as a sort of secretary for my father – before he could afford an office in town and the salary for a real one. There is something almost childish about the pad, as if it's come from a 'Let's Play Office' set. I can't bring myself to throw it out but, at the same time, wish Mrs Larkin would stop using it.

On each page there are three lines to be filled in – *Telephone call from: Taken by: Received on:* – and there is a space at the bottom for the message itself.

The message is from Michael. That's all it says: Michael called 2 p.m.

I open the drawer and place it along with the other messages I have received through Mrs Larkin. One from the vet's secretary, three from the bank. One from Lynette. And two from Brenda Caudwell. Brendie's messages are scrunched up into two angry little balls.

I lie on the bed and the dog lies on the rug and cocks an eye at me now and then. I am crying – but so what? Lately I am often crying or on the verge of doing so anyway. It's just something that comes on me and without warning, a bit like the lewd thoughts I can find myself entertaining about some unsuspecting man, often young enough to be my son. It's the hormones, I suppose. The hormones in reverse. The last splurge before they go tumbling down the hill.

The dog lifts his head and looks me as if to say – what this time?

He is used to my poor-little-me tears by now. They are never too tragic; no choking sobs or sense that my heart is bursting at the seams. Just a resigned sort of loneliness that, this time, happens to be for Michael. We both know this will pass soon enough.

'I can't believe he remembered the number. I can't believe he bothered to find me. Again.'

The dog is unmoved; he settles his head back down on his front paws, gives a small contented whine and begins to snooze.

*

The last time Michael Shillman found me was in New York. He found me before the age of the Internet when, to find someone in New York – someone who didn't want to be found anyhow – you would almost need to be a trained detective.

It was shortly before I went into business with Serena – I would have been about thirty-six, Michael thirty.

I was working in a small, upmarket French restaurant at the time where, one rung from the top, I was only answerable to the owner.

I had got there by working longer and harder than anyone else and the fact that I was one of the few in the business who wasn't using drugs probably helped too. Now I was holding that position by being something of an uptight bitch who tolerated slackness in neither work nor behaviour.

One morning the receptionist came into my office and told me there was somebody in the bar area waiting to see me. We'd been recruiting new staff – and the notice had made it clear that the hours for the interview were between four and six in the afternoon. 'Obviously thinks he can cut ahead of the rest,' I said. 'Let him come back, or let him wait.'

He waited.

The Michael Shillman I remembered was a toothy boy who seemed to be soldered onto his racing bike; his shoulders forever pushing into the distance, his head craning side to side. He passed messages between myself, Agatha and Rachel. He kept watch while we raided his parents' cocktail cabinet or while Rachel stole money and cigarettes from her mother's purse. He was quick witted, had an innocent face which kept the adults at bay and was a boy who didn't mind breaking the rules for the sake of adventure.

I came out of the office and thought, there's a good-looking waiter looking for work – let's hope his resumé looks as good as he does. But it was little Michael Shillman, my friend's younger brother, maybe five or six years younger than me. Except he was now big Michael Shillman, and handsome and dark and tall like his father, and funny like his sister and clever like his mother, and I had always liked him in a big sisterly sort of way – until I saw him standing there beside the bar grinning at me, and the big sister part took a jump out the window.

I ended up taking the afternoon off, we went drinking and then we went to bed. The next day, he said, 'How do you feel?'

'Hungover,' I said.

'I know. But do you feel – you know, awkward . . .?'

'Awkward?'

'Embarrassed in any way?'

I thought for a moment and said, 'No, actually. Do you?'

And he said, 'Not in the least.'

And then we nearly fell out of the bed laughing.

I called in sick – my first sick day ever – even though
everyone had seen us go off together and knew exactly what
Miss Tightass had been up to. I just didn't care. We stayed in
bed all day. We stayed in bed the following day, and I would
have stayed for many days more, only he had to go back to work
on a construction site in Queens and, for that reason, I went
back to the restaurant.

We were together for almost six months. During that time, we
often talked about Agatha and everything that had happened.
We talked about it a lot. It became a sort of project, each of
us bringing a little something to it every time we met. But we
moved slowly. I only knew so much, Michael even less. And of
course, there was that one thing I could never tell him. Even so,
neither of us knew the full story. Nobody did – except maybe
Agatha.

We asked each other questions. I asked how his parents
found out and about their reaction. He told me that his mother
took the call in the middle of the night. The call came from my
father. A short while later, Mr Caudwell knocked on the door
with news from the hospital.

'Then there was that meeting in your house,' Michael said.

'There were three meetings. One with all the parents and us.
Another one with just the fathers – and me.'

'What was that like?'

'Oh, Jesus! A mini court case with all these questions over
and over. Then I was sent to my room. They were afraid, though.
I could see that. Afraid of the scandal, the newspapers. The legal
implications – as Caudwell and my father kept saying. The last
meeting was between Serena and my father.'

'You ran away,' Michael said. 'I remember, everyone out
with flashlights, looking for you all over the valley.'

'Jonathan told them where to find me.'

'Then you were gone.'

'Then I was gone, off in a taxi with Serena and Patty.'

One night we were walking home from a restaurant and Michael asked me if it was true that Karl Donegan was the father of Agatha's child.

I said, 'Well, she was always in his house.'

'But does that mean he's the father?'

I shrugged. 'Everyone thought so, anyhow.'

'Did you?'

'Yes,' I said, 'I suppose . . .'

I was glad we were out of the restaurant, that I was walking beside him when he asked me instead of facing him across a table. It was the only deliberate lie I ever told him.

One afternoon in bed – almost always in bed – he told me about the Shillmans. A few days after I left with Serena and Patty, they left. First they left the neighbourhood, and then about a week afterwards they were at the airport and heading for a new life in London, where his father had managed to find another job. The week in between was spent in a country hotel about an hour's drive away from their own house. They took two rooms. Rachel and Mrs Shillman slept in one. Danny, Mr Shillman and Michael took the other. Rachel never stopped crying the whole time they were there. He never knew if his parents went back to the house – it wasn't discussed. But his father did go out a lot during that time. The car was sold; he spent a lot of time on the phone. Eventually, he found a job.

'It's not a patch on my old job,' he heard his father tell his mother, 'but it's a fresh start.'

'Is it?' his mother said. 'Oh, is it, really?'

He remembered this because it was one of the few conversations his parents had during that time. One way or another, the whole thing was a big strain on their marriage. About a year after they moved to London, they split up.

In the end, it was an argument over Mrs Shillman, of all people, that would break us up. Marvellous Martha, and I sticking up for her. Michael was telling me about the split. She was the one to leave the house. Rachel was left to take care of the family. His father really hit the bottle then, ran out of money, eventually gave up working altogether, died a few years later.

He had already told me how Rachel was an overweight nurse living in Australia and how Danny was working in an all-night bar in Barcelona.

'And your mother?' I asked.

'She still lives in London.'

'Do you see her?'

'When I have to. I find it too much having to listen to her rewrite history. She joined AA, you know. They tell them they need to look after themselves before they can look after anyone else. They allow them complete exoneration. It's okay that you fucked everyone up while you were drinking. But you can also swan off and let everyone else clean up all your shit. I sometimes think it gave her the excuse she'd always been waiting for – to leave us.'

'I don't think you should blame your mother for everything,' I said.

'She fucked off. Danny was only a little boy. My father was a good man up till then.'

'I just don't think it's fair to say she's completely to blame.'

'Oh, what the fuck do you know about it?' he said.

And that was pretty much that.

Michael is still my friend. I can call him if I want – as long as I call him in work and not at home: his wife doesn't care for me. I can meet him for an occasional coffee. He is someone who understands me. We haven't gone to bed in years – we never did after we broke up – and there have been many men between my sheets since then. But yet in a way we have remained intimate. In many ways we are more intimate now than we were when we used to lie naked sniffing each other and screwing around the clock. Michael knows me as much as anyone could. He knows the bits I keep hidden, even from myself. Maybe that's what bothers his wife.

I wipe my little tears for Michael, flap the side of the quilt over my legs and stare up at my little section of the sky. I wonder what time it is in New York and if it's still snowing. And then, like the dog at my feet, I'm asleep.

*

When I come back downstairs, I'm not sure how much later, I discover my list is missing. The kitchen is so tidy, there is no point in looking but I do anyway: in the drawers, then the cupboards, then between the pages of my mother's old cookery books, which have been neatly inserted back into their box. I try the kitchen bin – empty: the pouch of a new black plastic bag neatly puckered inside.

On the table, the large brown envelope sits alone, surrounded by shiny laminated wood; the crest of the American lawyers stamped on the top right hand corner. There is no way my father could have missed it.

Cursing Mrs Larkin, I go out to the yard and begin rummaging through the recycling bin that's supposed to be exclusively for waste paper. I know my father can see me through the French doors, but I don't care. I want my list. Eventually, I do find it, soiled and stinking in a plastic bag in the other bin along with the everyday garbage.

I pinch the corner of it and shake it out. It's my list. My list. I take it back inside, smooth it out, brush off a few tealeaves, mop a damp stain with a paper towel.

I take the rest of the groceries out of the bag and put them away for tomorrow's recipes: lemons, unsalted butter, a lobe of foie gras. Then I unwrap the two new ramekin dishes I've bought for the soufflé. I remove the fish from the fridge: a soft, cold, futile pile on my hand. I open it out on the kitchen table and Mr Turbot, in his brown speckled coat, shows me a sulky profile. I could throw him out. Or I could cook him anyway. It's a large fish, too big for one – but if I don't cook it tonight, it stays on the list.

Shallots, white wine vinegar. Knife. I lift the enamel pot out of the cupboard.

Piano notes strike into the house and I hear his brisk fingers trot up and down the flights of scales. I fetch the ice bucket and pile in the cubes. By the time I open the sitting-room door, I'm walking through the first fragile rays of Debussy's moonlight.

I place the glass down beside him and he stops playing.

'You're not having one yourself tonight?' he asks and I shake my head.

'Keeping a clear head then?'

And I nod my head.

He takes a sip from his drink. 'That turbot,' he says, 'if you're still making it, I might try a bit – that is if you don't mind.'

'Not in the least,' I say.

As I leave the room, I casually say, 'I have some papers from my lawyers in New York. I wonder if you'd mind taking a look at them later on?'

'Not in the least,' he says, echoing my own reply.

I open the fish along the spine and begin to ease the fillets from the bone. It's been a long time since I've performed such a task and I need to hold my nerve. Behind me, the piano music is steady and measured.

When I was a child, I believed no one could play the piano like my father. I used to think that, instead of prancing around courtrooms in silly wigs and gowns, he should be playing on a concert stage or at least have his own television programme. I know now that he is a competent pianist: he plays safe but he plays without distinction.

I stop working the knife for a moment while I listen to him enter and then scramble though that tricky batch of notes at that last bend in the piece, and I find myself worrying for him. It's unlikely he'll falter or make a mistake – he has practised this piece so many times in his life, even more in recent days. But he plays it as if he is searching for something and I think, now, that is what makes me uneasy.

I want to go into him and tell him what Simon Fischer said to me a long time ago – 'It's not the moonlight that makes the music, honey, but the sea that moves beneath it.'

But then, there are many things I would like to be able to tell him. Many things I wish he would tell me. We are leaving so much unsaid between us, and it feels mutually disrespectful somehow. As if I'm handing him a bag of my dirty underwear and he is handing me a bag of his.

I stand back and look down at my own little piece of work laid out on the slab. I lift a roll of green flecked butter in my hand, insert it under the turbot's dank skin, pleased and more than a little proud that I have managed to keep it intact.

After dinner, I take away the clean plate on the tray and bring him the envelope. By the time I come back in, maybe ten minutes later with his evening mug of tea, he is sitting at his desk, specs down on nose, pen angled in one hand, thumb pressing down on the top of it, click after urgent click.

I go out to the car, bring in the final bag from today's shopping expedition and take it up to my room. There, I remove a new hard-backed journal from the bag, followed by a new ballpoint pen. It feels nicely weighted between my fingers. The journal smells reassuringly clean. I sit at the dressing-table and open it.

The dog wanders off; the dog wanders back. He lies down and sighs out a fart that appals the air. I open the bedroom window and send him downstairs in disgrace. He rambles through the house, comes back up the stairs, manoeuvres himself stiffly down on the rug and sleeps. And still I have nothing.

Through the ceiling I hear the first self-important notes announce the arrival of the nine o'clock news. Some time later these notes strike out again, this time in farewell. And still I am here, and could be here till morning, cowering over this open journal, my pen poised and, at the same time, paralysed.

As I sit here, I begin to feel a – by now familiar – prickly sensation heating up under my skin. I look into the dressing-table mirror, ready to catch it in the act. There's my fading skin, the tweaks of grey at my temple, the prickles starting to crawl across my chest and in short, narrow patches up along my neck. I remember another occasion when I looked in a mirror in this room after Agatha had said something to embarrass me. An adolescent blush then, so forceful I thought it would blow my whole head open. It seems like such a short time: the first flush of youth to the first flush of age.

I catch a glint of my mother's expression in my eyes: a sort of gloating. And now I am looking at her, looking at me, through a small window in a darkened room.

I go back to the bed, arrange my pillows around me, draw up my knees and begin.

My name is Elaine.

*

My name is Elaine Nichols and I am sixteen years old. My friend is a year older. My friend is pregnant. My friend is pregnant and blind and asks for help. My friend says: 'I don't want to end up like June Caudwell, left in the hands of angry nuns, not even able to see the child when they pull it out of my arms.'

My friend is afraid. She begs for help. She sobs.

A plan is made. A stupid, adolescent plan that seems complete-ly feasible so long as everyone sticks to it and nobody blabs to anyone outside the circle. Everyone is in this circle. Except Jonathan.

I am never quite sure why Jonathan is left out; at first I think it's because he is an outsider, but then Patty is an outsider too, and she practically runs the whole show until she suddenly decides to back out of it.

Paul makes the decision to leave Jonathan out. After Patty, Paul is the one in charge; without his help there would be no plan. He says Jonathan is a stoner now and going away soon anyhow; away to Germany and France and Holland. Jonathan is not to be trusted to take the secret away with him and hitchhike it all over Europe.

In the years to come, I will sometimes wonder how Jonathan felt when he discovered all that had happened – relieved, of course, to be free from blame, but maybe hurt too, not to have been trusted. Because that had been such a big part of it: trusting each other, while Agatha in turn trusted us.

There are meetings. The meetings are held in different places: in Serena's kitchen when she is out. A few times, in Agatha's glass room when the Hanleys are out. Once Agatha suggests it might be more comfortable to meet in the shed in the Hanleys' back garden and I hear myself shout, 'No!'

I don't want to go back to that place and remember all that I saw there: his trousers, his keys, his underpants. And Agatha's naked body, her blank eyes not able to see the ugly, twisted face he was making while he pushed himself up and into her.

The later meetings take place in Agatha's absence and always in the gap between the Shillmans' house and the Caudwells' – the safest place in the neighbourhood. These are the meetings where the main decisions are reached. Agatha finds the wall too difficult to climb and the discussions too upsetting to listen to. She says she only wants to know what she needs to know and that I can be the messenger.

We are like Indians in a teepee, knee to knee, shoulder to shoulder, pow-wowing away. We are like children playing a game
    Everyone talks over each other, firing suggestions around,

arguing, shouting. The simplest solution seems to be the gin-and-hot-bath treatment. But the slightest whiff of alcohol has Agatha vomiting her guts up for hours and Brenda tells us that's how Junie was found out – drunk and sobbing in her friend's bathroom (and still bloody pregnant), so we decide to disregard it.

Then I remember the medical books in Dr Townsend's surgery. And so I say it – out loud. 'What about those medical books, Paul? Wasn't there something in one of them about women who . . . well, you know . . .?'

Karl and Paul sneak into the surgery. They find a book and put it into Karl's haversack. 'It's never off his back anyway,' Paul says. 'My parents won't think twice if he happens to have it on him when he calls in to see me.'

The book will be the first thing they steal from his father's surgery.

We have four days to prepare. Four days before Serena's art exhibition party. An ideal opportunity: every adult in the neighbourhood will be distracted; every adult that matters, anyhow.

And so the book is studied and passed around between Patty, Paul, Karl and even Brenda, who has somehow become part of the circle. As Patty explains it, she was present when Agatha first broke the news and so knows as much as there is to know. 'The more involved she is, anyhow, the less likely she is to squeal.'

In the medical book, there are several case histories which are intended as warnings but which we take as instructions. There are diagrams and even some photographs that I pretend to look at whenever the book is put into my hands.

The case histories are considered – Mrs X from Ohio, mother of eight. Mrs Y from Bhopal, mother of fifteen. Miss A from Kentucky, thirteen years old, raped by her father – something that shocks everyone into silence, even Patty and Paul.

The Mrs X from Ohio case involves a bar of soap and a bottle of Dettol. I can hardly understand the logistics, but at least it lacks the violence of other methods such as wire clothes hangers and knitting needles or even punches in the stomach.

The soap and Dettol method is discussed at length but the timing needs to be right. I find these discussions highly embarrassing and wish they didn't have to happen in front of the boys. Even the word 'period' makes me go red. I know Rachel, Brenda and Karl feel the same – their hot, awkward faces and darting, evasive eyes. Patty and Paul have no such trouble; they bandy the word around while lightly frowning, as if they are some sort of doctors. I run around to Agatha and ask when she last had a period but she can't remember because she was never regular. The only thing she knows for certain is that she is pregnant. And so, after all that, the Dettol and soap plan is dismissed.

For the next two days the haversack stays in the gap wrapped in plastic. In my head it becomes a sacred animal that is waiting to be fed. Everyone has to bring something to it. Paul and Karl bring an instrument they find in Dr Townsend's surgery that most resembles the picture in the medical book. They wrap it in a pink flannel pillow case. The flannel, Paul says, will be useful later, when she starts to bleed. They steal pills. 'Tranquillizers,' Paul explains, rattling the box, 'two to be taken an hour before the event. One every few hours after that.'

The instrument in its pillowcase, the pills in their little box are put into the haversack.

I take a big cotton sheet from my mother's hot press – the whitest one I can find because I think it will be the most sterile. And then I worry myself sick all day that it's so white because it's never been used and that my fussy house-proud mother is bound to miss it. The sheet, of course, will be the least of my worries.

Rachel brings four packets of sanitary towels and a few of Danny's old terry-cloth nappies. Brenda Caudwell also brings a sheet, an old sheet. 'Flannel!' she proudly announces and looks shyly over at Paul, who gives her a restrained nod of approval. She has cut her sheet into careful strips and folded them into a plastic bag. Patty brings her army sleeping bag. Except she doesn't actually bring it. She tells Karl she will leave it on the back lawn and he can jump over Paul's wall and take it. I will remember this fact later on, when I hear my father say, 'And what about you, Patty? What did you bring to this sorry business?'

'Oh, I brought nothing, sir,' Patty will say without lying.

Just as Paul, when asked, 'And who came up with the idea, Paul? Who first suggested it?', will truthfully be able to say, 'Elaine. It was her idea to look in the medical books.'

The plan is this: on Thursday evening, when everything is ready and packed into the haversack, it will be hauled over the wall into my back garden where I will hide it behind the bushes. On Thursday night, when I see my chance, I will carry it over to Agatha's and put it under her bed.

On Friday night, the night of Serena's art exhibition party, we will 'stop Agatha from being pregnant' – as Brenda Caudwell likes to put it. Karl and Paul will sit on the Hanleys' front wall, pretending to be just hanging around and having a smoke, but really they will be keeping watch. They will also be on standby should anything go wrong. Later they will move in, take away all the evidence and help the girls make the room right again, so that on Saturday morning when Mrs Hanley looks in on her niece, it will seem as if Agatha has been innocently sleeping all night long. The Hanleys have recently been spending Saturdays at Ted's mother's house so Agatha will be able to stay in bed all day. Rachel and I can spend the day with her and make sure that she's all right.

At the party, Patty, Rachel and I will wait till everyone starts to get drunk then we will slip out and say we are going to keep Agatha company – Agatha will already have said she doesn't want to go to the party.

Brenda will remain at the party, pretending to help Serena out, but really keeping an eye on the Hanleys and ready to raise the alarm if needs be. 'It will also,' Patty says, 'keep her out of the picture and stop her blundering around with her two big left feet.'

Agatha has already said that she only wants the girls to be present – unless something goes wrong, in which case, she will agree to allow Paul Townsend in, because he seems to know more about it than anyone else – or because he is the doctor's son, I can't help thinking.

We go over it, and over it.

At eight o'clock, Agatha will take the tranquilisers. The girls will arrive an hour later and make the necessary preparations. We will take everything out of the haversack, lay the army sleeping bag on the bed, put the clean sheet over it then make a sort of nest out of the torn pieces of sheet where Agatha will sit.

'Elaine, you will scald the instruments and then – look, I've drawn you a diagram,' Paul says, 'you need to hold it like this, and only to go this far and then you just – look – are you looking?'

When he shows me the diagram and begins gesturing with the instrument, I start to cry. Up to that point, somewhere in the back of my mind, I had thought that it was all a game, a game that could be stopped at any moment, or that, in any case, circumstances would somehow intervene and save us from actually having to go through with it.

I cover my face with my hands. 'I can't do it,' I say. 'I can't do it, I just can't.'

Patty says, 'Okay, I'll do it then.'

Paul says, 'Look, if it comes to it, I can do it. She'll be zonked out anyway and won't care.'

Rachel says, 'No, no, she would hate that – if Patty can't bring herself to do it, then I will.'

But on Thursday morning Patty backs out. They are all there when she breaks it to them, standing at Arlows' orchard wall. She says, 'Listen, I've been thinking things over: I'm the oldest one here and the only one over eighteen – this goes wrong and well, basically, I'm fucked. I'm sorry but count me out. And I think we should tell them, Agatha, I really do.'

When she says this, Agatha's face turns white. She says, 'Do you not think my life is handicapped enough?'

'I think we could at least tell my mom,' Patty says.

'And what, Patty? You think she's going to help *me*, that's she's not going to tell *them*? Is that what you think?'

'I don't know. I don't fucking know. For Christ sake, you won't even tell us who the father is! It's his responsibility – not ours.'

'What does it matter who it is?' Agatha says. 'It's not going to make any difference.'

'We need to tell *someone*,' Patty says.

Then Agatha goes hysterical. She has a sort of breakdown; she dunts her head off the wall and begins to pull at her stomach. 'I don't want it in here,' she sobs. 'I hate it, I want it out of me, out of me. Do you hear me? *Out.*'

In the end, Patty promises she won't say a word to anyone. 'But, I want to make it clear, now, that I am no longer any part of this.'

Patty turns and walks away. I watch her face as she passes me by. Our eyes catch and I think, 'She is going to tell.'

I half-expect Paul to back out too. But he chews his lip and says nothing.

On Thursday evening I am helping Serena get everything ready
for tomorrow night's party. Ted Hanley is also in the house,
advising Serena on how best to arrange her paintings for the
exhibition. Serena standing in the door – of what she now calls
her studio – biting her thumbnail. Ted Hanley trying to respond
to her request for his 'Complete honesty now, Ted, I mean it. I
really do.'

'Ahhha, I see what you've done there. Yes, interesting, hmm.
Ah, I see. Of course, yes. That's the . . .? The moon – is it? Ah,
yes, I see that now. Very good, yes.'

A knock at the door and then Mrs Hanley is standing there,
looking for Ted. 'Your mother, Ted, I'm afraid there's been a call
– she's been taken to hospital.'

Mrs Hanley now looking at me.

'I can stay with Agatha,' I say, 'until bed time anyhow.'

'Thank you, Elaine. If you're sure you won't mind.'

'I just need to get something from my house first. You go
ahead, I won't be long.'

My mother in her sitting-room, watching her television. My
father in his dining-room, working. I wait until Ted Hanley's
car leaves the estate. I sneak down to the end of the garden, lift
the haversack up in my arms and take it over to Agatha's house
and shove it under her bed. And so I carry out my first part in
the plan.

That night, I am asleep when I hear the sound of stones on my
window. I look down and there is Michael Shillman on his bike,
scooping his hand over his head and then pointing over to the
Hanley house. I look across at the driveway and see Ted Hanley's
car is still absent. My bedside clock says half-one in the morning.
When I left, a couple of hours before, Agatha was already in bed.
I throw on some clothes and go out to Michael.

'Rachel told me to get you,' he says. 'I think something
awful must have happened.'

I go round to the side of Hanleys' house and find Rachel coming out, chalk-faced and shaking all over.

Half-shouting, half-whispering, she says: 'She's done it herself, she's only gone and done it herself. She's fucking gone and done it herself.'

I push past Rachel and find Agatha lying on the bed, a large spread of blood beneath her, the shape of a tree. Her legs are smeared, her arms, even her face and her hair. There are handprints of blood everywhere, on the floor, on the wall, on the bedside locker.

Rachel behind me: 'I don't know what made me call round. I couldn't sleep thinking about tomorrow and thought she might be nervous and so I– Jesus, what are we going to do? Oh God, what are we going to do? Why did she do it, Elaine? Why would she have to go and do it on her own?'

'To stop us from getting into trouble,' I say. 'And maybe she thought Patty was going to tell.'

'But why would she think that? Patty promised, she wouldn't say a–'

'Because I told her. Because I thought Patty might. I told her, I told her.'

Oh, Agatha.

I stay calm. For years to come, I will wake in the night and wonder how I did that. I go to Agatha and see that she is alive.

'An ambulance,' I say.

Agatha grabs my hand and says, 'Don't. Don't leave me.'

I can see through the window, Michael and his bicycle at the side of the pillar.

'I'll get Michael to do it.'

Rachel is screaming now. 'Well, I'm getting Karl at least; he should be here. He's the bloody father – it's all his fault. Oh God, oh God, what will we do?'

Agatha won't let go of my hand. 'No,' she says. 'No, Elaine, please. No.'

'I have to call an ambulance, Agatha,' I say. 'I *have* to.'

'Karl isn't the father,' Agatha says and then, slowly and precisely, presses a name into my hand.

'I know,' I say out loud.

Agatha presses another few words into my hand – a question.

'For the past few weeks,' I reply.

Then once again, she shapes words on my palm – a request this time.

'Never. I promise – not a soul, not a word.'

Paul Townsend and Karl are in the room now and I see Michael is gone from the pillar.

'The haversack, get the fucking haversack out of here,' Paul is saying.

He doesn't go near Agatha, he doesn't say a word about an ambulance, he just begins to gather things off the floor: the instrument, the pill box, his drawing. He is shouting at Karl to help him. Karl is standing there, hands by his sides, staring at Agatha with his mouth wide open, crying.

I prise my hand free from Agatha's grip and run out of the room. No longer calm. I am running now into the cul-de-sac. I know I am heading for the Shillmans' house, running, running, running. But just as I get there, I see Michael standing at the gate. Michael's feet firm on the ground, the shape of the bike beside him in the dark.

'What's happened?' he says. 'Is it Agatha?'

I nod.

'Why are you here?'

'What?'

'Why are you *here*?'

I see the light on next door in Mr Slater's garage, and now I am running up his driveway then pulling the door of his garage open with both hands. The sound of all his little trains whirring around. Mr Slater's shocked face looking at me. He lifts both his hands as if to say, 'No – whatever it is – *no.*'

I come out of Slaters' and stand for a moment on the arch of the cul-de-sac, turning, turning, turning. And now I am running again, back round the corner, and then I am howling outside Mrs Ryan's door, banging on it.

*

My father is studying the racing page when I finally come back into his room. Tomorrow's racing: life goes on, it always goes on.

I ask him if he wants anything before I go to bed and he says I'm looking a little pale and I tell him that it's nothing.

He nods and wheels himself back to his desk then lifts the big brown envelope. 'I marked a few things,' he says, 'nothing to worry about, but in case you want to double check . . .'

He looks at me. We both know the lawyers in New York are not only thorough, but they are also on my side: his marks are unnecessary and I think of my mother's little message pad upstairs and can't help thinking – who's playing office now?

He says, 'Have you done whatever it was you needed that clear head for?'

'I have.'

'Maybe you should have that drink now.'

As I begin towards the drinks cabinet, he adds: 'Do you know – I might join you. No ice, though, it's too late for ice.'

We sit companionably enough for a few moments as I flick through the documents and pretend to take an interest in the few pencil marks he has made.

'So . . .' he says then,' I take it you'll be going back?'

'Yes, I say, 'there are things I need to . . .'

'Of course. And when are you going?'

'Tuesday. I booked the flight today.'

'Tuesday,' he repeats.

There is a moment. One small, solid moment – I could almost hold it on the palm of my hand. A moment when I think he may ask me to stay, or to return anyhow, after I've done whatever I need to do in New York. And I know if he takes the moment, that I will say yes. He looks into his drink and then looks up at me.

'Well, we'll see each other anyhow, before you go.'

When he says this, I am heartbroken and at the same time entirely relieved.

*

I drag Karl's haversack out from under my mother's bed, remove it from the black plastic sack and spread it out on the floor. My eye hops from badge to badge. The white eagle of Poland. The red kiwi of New Zealand. A London bus. A few different versions of the American Flag. A map of Africa. I see the elk of Norway. The gates of Dublin. The twin lions of Holland, the single lion of Venice. I see Turkey and Hong Kong and Cairo; I see the whole world collected in small faded badges.

I hold up the haversack, grope around the edges. Then I lift it up and shake it. There appears to be nothing inside. I unpick the cord at the top, stretch it open and stare down into the mouth of it. It smells like a bold boy's schoolbag. I put my hand down into it and feel around. Nothing. I go through the pockets on the side and on the front – all empty. No instrument, no sheet, no pillow case, no scraps of flannel.

I haven't a clue what happened to these things, whether they were found by a parent and destroyed in our interest, or if Paul managed to get rid of everything. I don't know. And I don't need to know.

I turn the haversack in my hands and examine the exterior more closely. There are stains on it, a variety of stains, but none too large or noticeable. These stains could be anything: beer spills or cider stains, a leak of oil from a bike or motorbike, the grass from the lawn that no longer belongs to the Shillmans. Anything.

I sit back on my heels and wonder what I should do with this haversack. I know it can't stay in this house. Somehow, I will have to get rid of it. I could dedicate my last day to it: maybe take it to the beach where Serena used to bring us on drives, follow the tide as it peels away from the strand. The sea roaring dully ahead in the dark. I could go in as far as I could before flinging the haversack into the waves. Agatha would have got a kick out of that.

Or I could bring it somewhere and burn it. Down into Arlows' valley, where it would hardly be noticed – just another charred heap on the dog-walkers' route. One last night walk, myself and the dog. I could say goodbye to Agatha there. I could call Brendie next day from the departure lounge, tell her she can stop worrying now.

I wrap the haversack up again and leave it by the door, then go back into my own room and take the journal from my bed. I put it in a drawer where Mrs Larkin is bound to find it. She may or may not show it to my father. He may or may not choose to read it. Who knows, he may even want to write down his version of events in it some day.

I find my suitcase and take it back to my mother's room where I lay it on her bed. It is way too large for purpose. I don't have much to bring back to New York, or at least I don't intend taking much with me.

I feel light and ready to start again. Not a clean slate though – never that. I know it will always be something of a struggle. There will still be those nights of waking suddenly to the sound of something scuttling: inside the wall, under the bed, on the far side of the ceiling. Bleats of shadow will inhabit my days. There but not there, caught but not caught, always one scurry beyond my line of vision.

THE END

CHRISTINE DWYER HICKEY is a multi-award-winning novelist and short story writer, teacher, and member of the Irish Arts Academy and Aosdána. Her novel *The Cold Eye of Heaven* won the Irish Novel of the Year award in 2012, and *Tatty* (2005) was named one of the Fifty Irish Books of the Decade. She divides her time between Ireland and Italy.

MICHAL AJVAZ, *The Golden Age.*
The Other City.

PIERRE ALBERT-BIROT, *Grabinoulor.*

YUZ ALESHKOVSKY, *Kangaroo.*

SVETLANA ALEXIEVICH, *Voices from Chernobyl.*

FELIPE ALFAU, *Chromos.*
Locos.

JOAO ALMINO, *Enigmas of Spring.*

IVAN ÂNGELO, *The Celebration.*
The Tower of Glass.

ANTÓNIO LOBO ANTUNES, *Knowledge of Hell.*
The Splendor of Portugal.

ALAIN ARIAS-MISSON, *Theatre of Incest.*

JOHN ASHBERY & JAMES SCHUYLER, *A Nest of Ninnies.*

GABRIELA AVIGUR-ROTEM, *Heatwave and Crazy Birds.*

DJUNA BARNES, *Ladies Almanack.*
Ryder.

JOHN BARTH, *Letters.*
Sabbatical.
Collected Stories.

DONALD BARTHELME, *The King.*
Paradise.

SVETISLAV BASARA, *Chinese Letter.*
Fata Morgana.
In Search of the Grail.

MIQUEL BAUÇÀ, *The Siege in the Room.*

RENÉ BELLETTO, *Dying.*

MAREK BIENCZYK, *Transparency.*

ANDREI BITOV, *Pushkin House.*

ANDREJ BLATNIK, *You Do Understand.*
Law of Desire.

LOUIS PAUL BOON, *Chapel Road.*
My Little War.
Summer in Termuren.

ROGER BOYLAN, *Killoyle.*

IGNÁCIO DE LOYOLA BRANDÃO, *Anonymous Celebrity.*
Zero.

BRIGID BROPHY, *In Transit.*
The Prancing Novelist.

GABRIELLE BURTON, *Heartbreak Hotel.*

MICHEL BUTOR, *Degrees.*
Mobile.

G. CABRERA INFANTE, *Infante's Inferno.*
Three Trapped Tigers.

JULIETA CAMPOS, *The Fear of Losing Eurydice.*

ANNE CARSON, *Eros the Bittersweet.*

ORLY CASTEL-BLOOM, *Dolly City.*

LOUIS-FERDINAND CÉLINE, *North.*
Conversations with Professor Y.
London Bridge.

HUGO CHARTERIS, *The Tide Is Right.*

ERIC CHEVILLARD, *Demolishing Nisard.*
The Author and Me.

MARC CHOLODENKO, *Mordechai Schamz.*

EMILY HOLMES COLEMAN, *The Shutter of Snow.*

ERIC CHEVILLARD, *The Author and Me.*

LUIS CHITARRONI, *The No Variations.*

CH'OE YUN, *Mannequin.*

ROBERT COOVER, *A Night at the Movies.*

STANLEY CRAWFORD, *Log of the S.S. The Mrs Unguentine.*
Some Instructions to My Wife.

RALPH CUSACK, *Cadenza.*

NICHOLAS DELBANCO, *Sherbrookes.*
The Count of Concord.

NIGEL DENNIS, *Cards of Identity.*

PETER DIMOCK, *A Short Rhetoric for Leaving the Family.*

ARIEL DORFMAN, *Konfidenz.*

COLEMAN DOWELL, *Island People.*
Too Much Flesh and Jabez.

RIKKI DUCORNET, *Phosphor in Dreamland.*
The Complete Butcher's Tales.

RIKKI DUCORNET (cont.), *The Jade Cabinet.*
The Fountains of Neptune.

WILLIAM EASTLAKE, *Castle Keep.*
Lyric of the Circle Heart.

JEAN ECHENOZ, *Chopin's Move.*

STANLEY ELKIN, *A Bad Man.*
The Dick Gibson Show.
The Franchiser.

FRANÇOIS EMMANUEL, *Invitation to a Voyage.*

SALVADOR ESPRIU, *Ariadne in the Grotesque Labyrinth.*

LESLIE A. FIEDLER, *Love and Death in the American Novel.*

JUAN FILLOY, *Op Oloop.*

GUSTAVE FLAUBERT, *Bouvard and Pécuchet.*

JON FOSSE, *Aliss at the Fire.*
Melancholy.
Trilogy.

FORD MADOX FORD, *The March of Literature.*

MAX FRISCH, *I'm Not Stiller.*
Man in the Holocene.

CARLOS FUENTES, *Christopher Unborn.*
Distant Relations.
Terra Nostra.
Where the Air Is Clear.
Nietzsche on His Balcony.

WILLIAM GADDIS, JR., *The Recognitions.*
JR.

JANICE GALLOWAY, *Foreign Parts.*
The Trick Is to Keep Breathing.

WILLIAM H. GASS, *Life Sentences.*
The Tunnel.
The World Within the Word.
Willie Masters' Lonesome Wife.

GÉRARD GAVARRY, *Hoppla! 1 2 3.*

ETIENNE GILSON, *The Arts of the Beautiful.*
Forms and Substances in the Arts.

C. S. GISCOMBE, *Giscome Road.*
Here.

DOUGLAS GLOVER, *Bad News of the Heart.*

WITOLD GOMBROWICZ, *A Kind of Testament.*

PAULO EMÍLIO SALES GOMES, *P's Three Women.*

GEORGI GOSPODINOV, *Natural Novel.*

JUAN GOYTISOLO, *Juan the Landless.*
Makbara.
Marks of Identity.

JACK GREEN, *Fire the Bastards!*

JIŘÍ GRUŠA, *The Questionnaire.*

MELA HARTWIG, *Am I a Redundant Human Being?*

JOHN HAWKES, *The Passion Artist.*
Whistlejacket.

ELIZABETH HEIGHWAY, ED., *Contemporary Georgian Fiction.*

AIDAN HIGGINS, *Balcony of Europe.*
Blind Man's Bluff.
Bornholm Night-Ferry.
Langrishe, Go Down.
Scenes from a Receding Past.

ALDOUS HUXLEY, *Antic Hay.*
Point Counter Point.
Those Barren Leaves.
Time Must Have a Stop.

JANG JUNG-IL, *When Adam Opens His Eyes*

DRAGO JANČAR, *The Tree with No Name.*
I Saw Her That Night.
Galley Slave.

MIKHEIL JAVAKHISHVILI, *Kvachi.*

GERT JONKE, *The Distant Sound.*
Homage to Czerny.
The System of Vienna.

JACQUES JOUET, *Mountain R.*
Savage.
Upstaged.

JUNG YOUNG-MOON, *A Contrived World.*

MIEKO KANAI, *The Word Book.*

YORAM KANIUK, *Life on Sandpaper.*

ZURAB KARUMIDZE, *Dagny.*

PABLO KATCHADJIAN, *What to Do.*

JOHN KELLY, *From Out of the City.*

HUGH KENNER, *Flaubert, Joyce and Beckett: The Stoic Comedians.*
Joyce's Voices.

DANILO KIŠ, *The Attic.*
The Lute and the Scars.
Psalm 44.
A Tomb for Boris Davidovich.

ANITA KONKKA, *A Fool's Paradise.*

GEORGE KONRÁD, *The City Builder.*

TADEUSZ KONWICKI, *A Minor Apocalypse.*
The Polish Complex.

ELAINE KRAF, *The Princess of 72nd Street.*

JIM KRUSOE, *Iceland.*

AYSE KULIN, *Farewell: A Mansion in Occupied Istanbul.*

EMILIO LASCANO TEGUI, *On Elegance While Sleeping.*

ERIC LAURRENT, *Do Not Touch.*

VIOLETTE LEDUC, *La Bâtarde.*

LEE KI-HO, *At Least We Can Apologize.*

EDOUARD LEVÉ, *Autoportrait.*
Suicide.

MARIO LEVI, *Istanbul Was a Fairy Tale.*

DEBORAH LEVY, *Billy and Girl.*

JOSÉ LEZAMA LIMA, *Paradiso.*

OSMAN LINS, *Avalovara.*
The Queen of the Prisons of Greece.

ALF MACLOCHLAINN, *Out of Focus.*
Past Habitual.

RON LOEWINSOHN, *Magnetic Field(s).*

YURI LOTMAN, *Non-Memoirs.*

D. KEITH MANO, *Take Five.*

MINA LOY, *Stories and Essays of Mina Loy.*

MICHELINE AHARONIAN MARCOM, *The Mirror in the Well.*

BEN MARCUS, *The Age of Wire and String.*

WALLACE MARKFIELD, *Teitlebaum's Window.*
To an Early Grave.

DAVID MARKSON, *Reader's Block.*
Wittgenstein's Mistress.

CAROLE MASO, *AVA.*

HISAKI MATSUURA, *Triangle.*

LADISLAV MATEJKA & KRYSTYNA POMORSKA, EDS., *Readings in Russian Poetics: Formalist & Structuralist Views.*

HARRY MATHEWS, *Cigarettes.*
The Conversions.
The Human Country.
The Journalist.
My Life in CIA.

Singular Pleasures.
The Sinking of the Odradek.
Stadium.
Tlooth.

JOSEPH MCELROY, *Night Soul and Other Stories.*

ABDELWAHAB MEDDEB, *Talismano.*

GERHARD MEIER, *Isle of the Dead.*

HERMAN MELVILLE, *The Confidence-Man.*

AMANDA MICHALOPOULOU, *I'd Like.*

STEVEN MILLHAUSER, *The Barnum Museum.*
In the Penny Arcade.

RALPH J. MILLS, JR., *Essays on Poetry.*

CHRISTINE MONTALBETTI, *The Origin of Man.*
Western.

NICHOLAS MOSLEY, *Accident.*
Assassins.
Catastrophe Practice.
Hopeful Monsters.
Imago Bird.
Natalie Natalia.
Serpent.

WARREN MOTTE, *Fiction Now: The French Novel in the 21st Century.*
Oulipo: A Primer of Potential Literature.

GERALD MURNANE, *Barley Patch.*
Inland.

YVES NAVARRE, *Our Share of Time.*
Sweet Tooth.

DOROTHY NELSON, *In Night's City.*
Tar and Feathers.

WILFRIDO D. NOLLEDO, *But for the Lovers.*

BORIS A. NOVAK, *The Master of Insomnia.*

FLANN O'BRIEN, *At Swim-Two-Birds.*
The Best of Myles.
The Dalkey Archive.
The Hard Life.
The Poor Mouth.
The Third Policeman.

CLAUDE OLLIER, *The Mise-en-Scène.*
Wert and the Life Without End.

FOR A FULL LIST OF PUBLICATIONS, VISIT: www.dalkeyarchive.com

PATRIK OUŘEDNÍK, *Europeana.*
The Opportune Moment, 1855.

BORIS PAHOR, *Necropolis.*

FERNANDO DEL PASO, *News from
the Empire.*
Palinuro of Mexico.

ROBERT PINGET, *The Inquisitory.*
Mahu or The Material.
Trio.

MANUEL PUIG, *Betrayed by Rita Hayworth.*
The Buenos Aires Affair.
Heartbreak Tango.

RAYMOND QUENEAU, *The Last Days.*
Odile.
Pierrot Mon Ami.
Saint Glinglin.

ANN QUIN, *Berg.*
Passages.
Three.
Tripticks.

ISHMAEL REED, *The Free-Lance
Pallbearers.*
The Last Days of Louisiana Red.
Ishmael Reed: The Plays.
Juice!
The Terrible Threes.
The Terrible Twos.
Yellow Back Radio Broke-Down.

RAINER MARIA RILKE,
The Notebooks of Malte Laurids Brigge.

JULIÁN RÍOS, *The House of Ulysses.*
Larva: A Midsummer Night's Babel.
Poundemonium.

ALAIN ROBBE-GRILLET, *Project for a
Revolution in New York.*
A Sentimental Novel.

AUGUSTO ROA BASTOS, *I the Supreme.*

DANIËL ROBBERECHTS, *Arriving in
Avignon.*

JEAN ROLIN, *The Explosion of the
Radiator Hose.*

OLIVIER ROLIN, *Hotel Crystal.*

ALIX CLEO ROUBAUD, *Alix's Journal.*

JACQUES ROUBAUD, *The Form of
a City Changes Faster, Alas, Than the
Human Heart.*

The Great Fire of London.
Hortense in Exile.
Hortense Is Abducted.
*Mathematics: The Plurality of Worlds of
Lewis.*
Some Thing Black.

RAYMOND ROUSSEL, *Impressions of
Africa.*

VEDRANA RUDAN, *Night.*

GERMAN SADULAEV, *The Maya Pill.*

TOMAŽ ŠALAMUN, *Soy Realidad.*

LYDIE SALVAYRE, *The Company of Ghosts.*

LUIS RAFAEL SÁNCHEZ, *Macho
Camacho's Beat.*

SEVERO SARDUY, *Cobra & Maitreya.*

NATHALIE SARRAUTE, *Do You Hear
Them?*
Martereau.
The Planetarium.

STIG SÆTERBAKKEN, *Siamese.*
Self-Control.
Through the Night.

ARNO SCHMIDT, *Collected Novellas.*
Collected Stories.
Nobodaddy's Children.
Two Novels.

ASAF SCHURR, *Motti.*

GAIL SCOTT, *My Paris.*

JUNE AKERS SEESE,
Is This What Other Women Feel Too?

BERNARD SHARE, *Inish.*
Transit.

VIKTOR SHKLOVSKY, *Bowstring.*
Literature and Cinematography.
Theory of Prose.
Third Factory.
Zoo, or Letters Not about Love.

PIERRE SINIAC, *The Collaborators.*

KJERSTI A. SKOMSVOLD,
The Faster I Walk, the Smaller I Am.

JOSEF ŠKVORECKÝ, *The Engineer of
Human Souls.*

GILBERT SORRENTINO, *Aberration of
Starlight.*
Blue Pastoral.
Crystal Vision.

Imaginative Qualities of Actual Things.
Mulligan Stew.
Red the Fiend.
Steelwork.
Under the Shadow.

ANDRZEJ STASIUK, *Dukla.*
Fado.

GERTRUDE STEIN, *The Making of Americans.*
A Novel of Thank You.

PIOTR SZEWC, *Annihilation.*

GONÇALO M. TAVARES, *A Man: Klaus Klump.*
Jerusalem.
Learning to Pray in the Age of Technique.

LUCIAN DAN TEODOROVICI,
Our Circus Presents...

NIKANOR TERATOLOGEN, *Assisted Living.*

STEFAN THEMERSON, *Hobson's Island.*
The Mystery of the Sardine.
Tom Harris.

JOHN TOOMEY, *Sleepwalker.*
Huddleston Road.
Slipping.

DUMITRU TSEPENEAG, *Hotel Europa.*
The Necessary Marriage.
Pigeon Post.
Vain Art of the Fugue.
La Belle Roumaine.
Waiting: Stories.

ESTHER TUSQUETS, *Stranded.*

DUBRAVKA UGRESIC, *Lend Me Your Character.*
Thank You for Not Reading.

TOR ULVEN, *Replacement.*

MATI UNT, *Brecht at Night.*
Diary of a Blood Donor.
Things in the Night.

ÁLVARO URIBE & OLIVIA SEARS, EDS.,
Best of Contemporary Mexican Fiction.

ELOY URROZ, *Friction.*
The Obstacles.

LUISA VALENZUELA, *Dark Desires and the Others.*
He Who Searches.

PAUL VERHAEGHEN, *Omega Minor.*

BORIS VIAN, *Heartsnatcher.*

TOOMAS VINT, *An Unending Landscape.*

ORNELA VORPSI, *The Country Where No One Ever Dies.*

AUSTRYN WAINHOUSE, *Hedyphagetica.*

MARKUS WERNER, *Cold Shoulder.*
Zundel's Exit.

CURTIS WHITE, *The Idea of Home.*
Memories of My Father Watching TV.
Requiem.

DIANE WILLIAMS,
Excitability: Selected Stories.

DOUGLAS WOOLF, *Wall to Wall.*
Ya! & John-Juan.

JAY WRIGHT, *Polynomials and Pollen.*
The Presentable Art of Reading Absence.

PHILIP WYLIE, *Generation of Vipers.*

MARGUERITE YOUNG, *Angel in the Forest.*
Miss MacIntosh, My Darling.

REYOUNG, *Unbabbling.*

ZORAN ŽIVKOVIĆ , *Hidden Camera.*

LOUIS ZUKOFSKY, *Collected Fiction.*

VITOMIL ZUPAN, *Minuet for Guitar.*

SCOTT ZWIREN, *God Head.*

AND MORE . . .